Critical acclaim fo

BLACK TIDE

'Caroline Carver's books keep getting better ... an exciting adventure with a memorable heroine' *Sunday Telegraph*

'This mystery's a Black Beauty ... make sure you've slipped on the lifejacket for this adventure on the high seas, as it moves at such a rate of knots it'll leave you reeling'
Peterborough Evening Telegraph

'The most entertaining romp I have read in a long time ... the romance straightforward and rather touching. It is good to be reminded that in the hands of a writer like Caroline Carver crime – even the most despicable – can be enormous fun' *Sherlock*

'An exciting and well-written tale ... a good "page-turner" in an unusual setting' *Tangled Web*

'This is a roller coaster of a book, great escapism ... one shares the tension of India's escapades right to the very last page. An exciting read' *New Books magazine*

DEAD HEAT

'An exciting book and I hardly stopped to take a breath as I raced through it. Carver completely engaged me' *Mystery News*

'If you want a read to consume you, this is the one to pick, but don't be surprised if you have no nails left by the final pages'
Peterborough Evening Telegraph

'Carver follows her award-winning debut with a riveting sophomore effort . . . delivers a fast-paced, tightly written thriller that bursts at the seams with action and surprises' *Mystery Scene*

'It would be an understatement, not to mention a gross injustice, to classify *Dead Heat* as just a good book. This is an extraordinary work of fiction any author would aspire to achieve. Caroline Carver succeeds on all fronts in composing a tale worth a reader's full attenion' *Round Table Reviews*

'I know – you don't read Australian thrillers. Well, bury that prejudice. This is probably the most consistently exciting thriller I've read this year – and by "consistently" I mean start-to-finish, chapter-by-chapter, don't-let-up thrills and excitement. I loved every minute' *Crime Time*

'A fast-paced, exciting murder mystery . . . An excellent writer who grabs your attention right away and never lets go until the very last page. I literally couldn't put the book down until the final chapter was finished' *Who Dunnit*

BLOOD JUNCTION

'Carver's first novel garnered for its author the Crime Writer's Association Debut Dagger Award. It's easy to see why! A plot that moves with the speed of a wild dingo . . . believable and emotionally rounded characters, and an overwhelming sense of locale, this is one of those "don't miss" titles that comes around all too infrequently' *Mystery News*

'One of the most riveting thrillers of recent years'
New Zealand Sunday Times Book of the Week

'Exciting, frightening, plenty of suspense ... a nightmarish adventure of close calls and surprising escapes ... an exceptional first mystery' *Publishers Weekly (starred review)*

'An intriguing premise allows *Blood Junction* to take off at a whirl, capturing the reader's imagination ... you won't put this down until the whole truth is uncovered' *Romantic Times*

'Powerful writing, a gripping plot and a unique setting ... an outstanding debut' The Mystery and Thriller Club

Caroline Carver was born in the UK. She has successfully completed the London to Saigon Motoring Challenge. She blames her love of adventure on her parents: her mother set the land speed record in Australia and her father was a jet fighter pilot. Her first novel, *Blood Junction*, won the CWA Debut Dagger. *Black Tide*, her third novel, follows *Dead Heat*. She lives near Bath. Visit her website at *www.carolinecarver.com.*

By Caroline Carver

Black Tide
Dead Heat
Blood Junction

BLACK TIDE

Caroline Carver

An Orion paperback

First published in Great Britain in 2004
by Orion
This paperback edition published in 2005
by Orion Books Ltd,
Orion House, 5 Upper St Martin's Lane
London WC2H 9EA

1 3 5 7 9 10 8 6 4 2

A CIP catalogue record for this book is available
from the British Library.

ISBN 0 75286 488 2

Typeset by Deltatype Ltd, Birkenhead, Merseyside

Printed and bound in Great Britain by
Clays Ltd, St Ives plc

www.orionbooks.co.uk

For my brother, who first introduced me
to the high seas on the farm pond.

Acknowledgements

Special thanks to Eric Atkinson, harbour master at Fremantle Port, for his extensive knowledge and help. You've been brilliant.

Thanks also to my Western Australian researchers, Carmen Miranda and Tania Harper. Boy, did we have fun.

A debt of gratitude goes to Sara O'Keeffe for all her hard work and for supporting me so enthusiastically, and last but not least thanks to Susan Lamb, Ian Hearsey, Ginny Walker, Tony Williams and my fantastically patient and hardworking back-up crew: Jane Wood, Angela McMahon, Alison Tulett, Elizabeth Wright and Lucie Whitehouse.

Prologue

He couldn't believe his eyes. Right in front of the building site, leaning his broad back against the JCB's excavator, sat Albert Jimbuku. His face was smeared with clay, his bare torso covered with dots and messy swirls of yellow and white paint. He had opened up a dead rabbit and taken out the guts and was making a weird wailing sound. He seemed oblivious to the watching crowd. Men wearing hard hats, men in overalls, Maisie Wilson and her daughter, the on-site caterers. Some twenty people, all agog.

Albert threw the intestines on the ground. A breeze suddenly picked up, stirring dust around the Aborigine's big dirty feet, and the next instant the stench of burst entrails hit Bobby's nostrils like a blow.

'Jesus, Albert!' He raced across to the man and his bloody carcass. 'What the hell are you doing?'

Albert didn't look up. He was poking at the rabbit with a forefinger and chanting in a discordant tone.

'Don't you know Jack's due any minute?'

The Aborigine abruptly stopped his chant and sat there in silence. His shoulders were bowed, his woolly head slumped.

It was a freezing day in August, Australia's winter, and although the sun was bright, the sky a vivid blue all the way to the ocean's edge, Bobby felt as though he had an icicle laid directly on his face. His eyes were watering, his nose running, and he wished he could leg it for Maisie's van and warm up with a cup of coffee but he knew he couldn't. Not until he'd shifted Albert first.

'Come on, Albert,' Bobby urged. 'If Jack sees you here, he'll go nuts. He's already months behind thanks to you.'

'This is my camp,' Albert said. His baritone carried easily to the crowd. 'You can't build your bloody houses here.'

'Yes we bloody can,' called out Laurie Harris, Jack's foreman. A couple of people started to laugh, but stopped when Albert got to his feet.

Despite the blubber hanging over the waistband of his jeans, he was an imposing sight. Standing at six feet four, he didn't have the wiry frame of many Aborigines and his thighs were the size of railway sleepers, the hands hanging at his sides large as steel couplings. The ghostly clay on his broad face took away any thoughts of a gentle giant and gave him a peculiarly menacing air.

'This is our sacred place. The springs here are holy—'

'Bollocks!' shouted Laurie. 'You're no more the traditional owner of this area than Kylie Minogue. This isn't your camp, Albert, and you know it. Whole town bloody knows it.'

Oh my God, Bobby thought. What in the hell possessed me to come over this morning? All I wanted was to see how the building was coming along and here I am standing between a crowd of people who want to work so they get paid at the end of the week, and a giant, paint-splattered Aborigine with a bunch of cockatoo feathers stuck in his hair. He considered making a bolt for it, but if Jack heard he'd turned his back . . .

'Albert,' he pleaded, 'think about it. You've got no chance. What about the cops? The council and the local government?'

'You paid 'em off.' Albert's lips tightened. 'Whole place knows what your family get up to. You buy yourselves into anything or out of anything any time, no caring what mess you leave behind. You shouldn't be here, mate. No way.'

'And nor should you.' He tried to be reasonable. 'Or have you conveniently forgotten about the restraining order?'

'It is my ancestral right to be here.'

Bobby looked at Albert in disbelief. 'It's your ancestral right to wreck our machinery? Pour sugar into the fuel tanks and spray red paint all over our site?'

There was a small pause, then Albert turned and addressed the crowd.

'The springs are part of our Dreaming. We are linked to them by our spirit. Our very being . . .'

As Albert started the same old spiel he'd been dishing out over the past six months Bobby felt panic begin to nip the pit of his stomach. He'd have more luck moving the excavator with his bare hands than moving Albert when he was in full flow. In desperation he rang one of his cousins, a cop at Perth's police H.Q., and asked him to send someone over quick fast and remove Albert before Jack arrived. His cousin said, no worries, Kuteli's in the area, give him twenty, and hung up.

'You see, long time ago,' Albert was saying, 'a great hero lost his son hunting here, and in his grief, his tears fell to the ground. When the tears struck the ground, a spring of fresh water rose, giving me and my people a supply of water for many generations.'

'Just turn on a tap, why don't you, Albert?' a man called out and someone sniggered.

'You white fellers don't know nothing.' The Aborigine looked into the chill blue sky and the handful of seagulls wheeling there, then back at the crowd. 'These coastal springs are holy. And you are breaking this thing of mine. This is my home—'

'Bullshit,' said Maisie stoutly. 'You've a house in town like the rest of us. You're just making trouble, you are.'

'Like all of them,' Laurie Harris agreed. 'He just wants a whacking great payout for agreeing not to bugger us around.'

'I want what is mine,' insisted Albert. 'If my lot came to

one of your churches and said it was theirs, knocked it down and put a camp there, how would you feel?'

'Who bloody cares?' someone muttered, and Bobby saw Albert flinch at the murmurs of agreement.

'Before Neville came and buggered us about, my lot used to visit this place for important ceremonies,' Albert pleaded. 'Sacred, secret rituals, at many times of the year. I need to protect my heritage.'

'Crap,' said Maisie, and spat on the ground.

'Why don't you piss off, Albert, and let us get on with our work?' a man yelled from the back.

Bobby made a gargantuan effort not to run for his car and lock all the doors. 'Look, Albert,' he said in an undertone, sweating, urgent, 'why don't you go home and wash that stuff off and I'll meet you down the pub later? I'll sort something out with you, no worries.' He patted his back pocket, which held his wallet.

'You can't buy me off like you did the others,' Albert said loudly, and Bobby flushed. 'This is not about money. It is about my ancestors. I am telling you white people if you stop this building, things will be all right.'

Bobby felt a moment of utter disbelief.

'Are you *threatening* us?'

The Aborigine turned and looked at him straight. His eyes were deep brown and rimmed with red, as though he had been weeping. 'Stop breaking my place,' he said gently.

'Or you'll do what?'

Albert gestured at the sad bundle of eviscerated fur now crawling with flies. It may have been winter, but the Aussie blowfly could smell dead meat a mile off, whatever the weather.

'I didn't want it to come to this.'

Bobby's mouth turned dry as a billabong in drought when he saw Jack's Land Cruiser pull up behind the crowd. 'Shit, Albert. Jack's here.'

Albert gave no indication he'd heard.

'I talked with a sorcerer, a knowledgeable medicine man who knows the greatest secrets. He told me to do this. He says this land will turn against any white people who come to live here on our sacred ground.'

The small cold breeze suddenly increased, making the hairs on the nape of Bobby's neck stand bolt upright. A plastic cup rattled across the ground and he could see a miniature dust devil spiralling across the site's entrance. The crowd had, amazingly, fallen absolutely still.

Bobby tried again. 'Please, Albert. Just go home, would you?'

A plastic tarpaulin started to flap in the stiffening wind as Albert gazed at him with an expression he couldn't quite define.

'You feel the way the wind has heard me?' the Aborigine asked quietly. 'It has begun. Jambuwal, the Thunder Man, is coming.'

The crowd stirred uneasily, looking around and over their shoulders at the horizon, where a streak of dark clouds had appeared.

'For God's sake, Albert,' Bobby was almost gasping with the effort not to scream at the stubborn Aborigine, 'you know what Jack's like. *Go home.*'

To his horror, he saw the man's eyes fill with tears.

'It is too late. Jambuwal is already angry.'

With great dignity, Albert stepped over the rabbit's corpse and started to walk away. His final words were spoken under his breath, a whisper against the increasing rush of wind, but Bobby heard them.

'Jambuwal will wreak his vengeance.'

One

It was the first time in a week India had been on deck. The howling southerly had finally dropped and the sun had come out, blazing off the green ocean. Scrubbing *Sundancer*'s deck aft to fore alongside the crew, she was humming to herself, glad to be outside at last.

She paused to watch an inquisitive sooty albatross following *Sundancer*'s wake. Five hundred Ks from Antarctica, the air was so raw it felt as though it could strip layers of flesh from her face. In spite of the moisturising sunscreen she kept re-applying to prevent her skin cracking, she knew her lips were already chapped and the veins in her cheeks red and broken. Strange to think of everyone at home boiling in the midst of the Australian summer. It was January now, the only sensible time to head into the Arctic wastes of the Southern Ocean and avoid colliding with too many icebergs. She'd expected the weather to have been better, but the trip so far had been rough. Good job she wasn't seasick or the last four weeks would have been unbearable.

The albatross swooped starboard, and that was when she saw it: a speck on the horizon. Eyes watering from the cold she blinked hard, expecting it to disappear, but it didn't. Her binoculars confirmed it was another ship, and her nerves gave a little hop of excitement. It couldn't be a commercial vessel, because the shipping lanes from Perth to Cape Town crossed way north of the turbulent Arctic seas. Was it one of the supply ships that serviced the research and scientific stations in the area? There was only one way to find out.

India headed for the bridge, taking care to keep 'one hand on ship' in case *Sundancer* gave a sudden roll and mashed a limb against one of the ladders or steel walls. Several crew members were already there along with Cuan, the expedition leader, Ned, and *Sundancer*'s captain. They were all studying the speck in silence, expressions intent. She crossed her fingers for luck. She'd been reporting daily to her editor at the *Sydney Morning Herald* about life on board the Greenpeace boat, the continual maintenance, the fire drills, tightening shackles, splicing ropes, and she was sick of trying to be inventive to keep her readers' interest. She wanted evidence of the Japanese fleet hunting illegally in the Southern Ocean Whale Sanctuary and she wanted to make it public. Only last night she had suddenly realised she might return home empty handed. Boy, did she hate to fail. And boy, had she been naïve. She'd taken one look at the bubble helicopter strapped on board and assumed it would do a couple of recces and lead them directly to the whalers.

Wrong.

The chopper did a regular scout, but only when the weather was clear. And since Antarctica had the strongest winds on the planet and the most hostile waters of the world's oceans, it had only been up three times. Nor had she realised that the whaling area was around two and a half times the length of Australia. It was mind-bogglingly *huge*, and they were just one boat searching for a fleet of five. The Greenpeace team had made an educated guess based on the whalers' past behaviour and had been hoping they stuck to form, but they may as well have been looking for a single four-leafed clover in a thousand acres of the stuff.

Knees bent to absorb the rock and slide of the boat, she carefully panned her binoculars around the horizon. The sea was relatively calm, for Antarctica that was, the breeze light. Five minutes later, India spotted another speck off their starboard beam sailing steadily behind the first.

'There!' she said.

'Yes!' shouted Ned in delight. 'We'll get the buggers yet!'

She was laughing. His enthusiasm was as catching today as when she'd first met him eight years ago. Which was probably why she hadn't gone completely mad being imprisoned on a ship in the middle of nowhere. Ned was her tonic, her confidant, and without him she'd have lasted about twenty seconds before picking a fight with one of the crew. He gave her a happy grin as the captain spun the wheel and pushed *Sundancer* for the Japanese boat.

'Oh dear,' said Ned a little later, binos pressed hard against his face. 'I've some really bad news.'

'What? *What?*' pressed India, itchy with excitement.

'It's the *Kagoshima Maru.* The factory ship. And she's got an addition to her stern since we last met – some socking great water cannons.' He put down the binos and sighed. 'I wonder who they're for.'

They realised the factory ship had spotted *Sundancer* when she suddenly picked up speed and started sailing fast in the opposite direction. With Ned's permission, India called them over the VHF.

'Hey, if we didn't know better, we might think you're running away from us. Have you something to hide? We know you're doing some scientific whaling, we're just curious to know what your quota is. And to make sure you're keeping warm because it's very cold out there. We're cold too, you know.'

The radio was silent as the factory ship steamed away with *Sundancer* in pursuit. That was the normal response, Ned said. Catchers, factory ships and scouts fled the second Greenpeace showed up, and did their utmost to try and hide behind an iceberg.

'Can you slow down a bit?' India laughingly asked the factory ship a little later. 'We can't keep up!'

To their astonishment, the ship responded.

'Get bigger engine for your boat,' a man said in a thick accent.

'Okay, we'll put an order in,' India replied without a beat. 'Which particular engine do you have in mind?'

'More easy to get bigger boat.'

'Next time we'll bring the *QE2*.' She chuckled. 'How does that sound?'

'Ah, this is good. You can have hot bath while you chase us.'

'Now there's a thought.'

'You keep warm also,' said the whaler, and disconnected.

At seven p.m. the *Kagoshima Maru* reached 60 degrees south, the northernmost edge of the fleet's whaling area, and kept going. To their surprise, it was joined by two catchers.

'I don't believe it,' said Ned. 'It's like they're headed home.'

'We've chased them out?'

'I'm not sure.' He frowned. 'I'm wondering if they're trying to lure us north to get us out of the way so they can race back here.'

Ned, Cuan and *Sundancer*'s captain started an intense debate about what to do next, and India left them when she smelled the rich, greasy aroma of toasted cheese and chorizo. Fantastic, she thought, scrambling for the mess room. I may be thousands of miles from my nearest takeaway, but I've Joe and Emma on board, and they make great pizza.

After supper, huddled in her Polartec fleece, hands shoved into gloves, India prowled the deck. The ship gave a sudden roll and she grabbed a railing, cursing the fact that *Sundancer* didn't have a keel. Sure, it meant that if the ship hit some ice she'd be lifted out of it rather than being crushed, but it didn't make life any easier. She was covered in bruises from the past weeks' storm and two crew members had broken bones.

Leaning over the side she saw mist drifting across the tops of the waves. Waves from the ice edge, where minke whales were hanging around, feeding on krill and fish. And where there were minkes, there were whalers. Goddam it, they'd better catch up with them soon or she may as well resign.

'Hi, India.'

India looked around. It was Katy. India took the proffered cigarette and they both lit up with sighs of satisfaction. They did not need to speak to fill the silence, they were completely at ease in each other's company now. After a while India gave a snort of laughter.

'What's funny?'

'You and me.'

Katy grinned. 'You uptight cow.'

'Barbie doll.'

They finished their cigarettes in mutual satisfaction and pocketed the stubs. Said good night, and headed inside.

India reported to the bridge at five minutes before midnight to find Cuan had abandoned the northerly chase and set *Sundancer* due south once more.

'Cat and mouse, that's what this is about,' he told her with a yawn. 'We never saw the spotter, and I'll bet the *Kagoshima* and the boys are speeding back to join her.'

India pulled out the chart and had a look. They were further north than she'd realised. At 53 degrees south, the nearest land was the bleak coast of Heard Island 900 Ks away, populated by nothing but seals, sea birds and millions of macaroni penguins. Talk about being in an icy, watery wilderness, she thought.

Ned had settled himself on the padded chair at the helm and was peering outside. Although it was the middle of the night, the sky still held a little light. Not that India could see much. She could barely make out the bow of the boat thanks to a thick fog. At least it was calm, she thought, and everyone would sleep well tonight.

With another yawn and a wave of his hand Cuan left the bridge, and India poured herself a cup of strong, black coffee from Ned's thermos before sitting beside him. Since a mate and a deck hand had to be on watch at all times, and India had undergone a heap of training to enable her to be of use on board, they were on from twelve till four. Sipping coffee, they talked over the minutiae of their days. How she'd had her fingers curled around a door jamb and nearly got them severed when *Sundancer* gave a sudden lurch. How Ned had got the time completely wrong when ringing friends in London and woken them before dawn. Despite his cheerful demeanour, Ned wasn't looking so hot, and she wondered if he was coming down with another cold, maybe even the flu. India didn't like the sweaty sheen on his face, nor the slightly yellow hue to his skin. His breathing was loud and raspy and sounded as though his lungs were full of fluid. She asked him if he was sure he shouldn't hand over his watch to someone else.

'I'm not *sick*, sick,' he said, shocked. 'It's just the start of a cold or something, that's all. Besides, I want to keep an eye on this . . .'

He indicated an echo on the radar about eight nautical miles to the south and heading directly their way.

India frowned. 'The spotter?'

'Could be, but I'm thinking it's another catcher wanting us to think they've given up. It's just a trick.'

Using channel 16, the emergency channel that all ships monitor, he called them up. No response. 'Must be part of the fleet,' he said with a shrug, 'or they'd have answered.'

Their talk soon turned to home. India talked a little about Mikey and Polly, and Ned talked a lot about Ellie. How much he missed her. His plans for a second honeymoon some day. Fraser Island, maybe the Solomon's. What he'd like to name the baby.

'Albert?' India said, horrified. You can't call the poor kid Albert!'

Ned looked disgruntled. 'That's what Ellie says.'

'Why Albert, for God's sake?'

'He's the guy who protested about Jimbuku Bay being built. His ancestors used the springs there for generations, you know. He tried to save it.' His expression grew distant. 'I thought if we named our baby after Albert . . . well, that they'd be safe.'

'What do you mean, safe?' Ned remained silent while she studied the sickly glow on his face. Then he glanced at his watch.

'Time for your rounds.'

He was fobbing her off but she didn't mind. She had another four weeks to find out what was going on. Ah well, she thought, better get on with it. Before she left the bridge, she glanced at the radar and saw the echo was closing in.

'Yes, I'm changing course.' Ned gave her a quick grin. 'They won't come within cooee of us, okay? Now, off you go. You've thirty shipmates, all fast asleep and in your care, remember?'

First, India scouted the galley, touching each stove to make sure they were cold. Then the laundry followed by the engine room, ear protectors in place, looking for oil leaks, constantly checking for fire hazards, and sniffing the air for smoke. If the ship caught fire they'd have nowhere to go except into the life rafts.

Finally India went out on deck. Made sure the helicopter, the Zodiac and the Avons – rigid inflatables – were strapped tight and unmoving. Everything looked fine. She would, she thought, have a quick nicotine hit before she rustled up some soup for her and Ned. Resting a hip against a railing she lit a cigarette and looked into the peculiarly green half-lit mist, her face already damp with droplets of fog.

Out of nowhere she thought she heard a faint throbbing sound and pushed her head to one side, listening hard. It couldn't be the ship they'd seen on the radar, surely, not if Ned had changed course.

Taking another puff, she looked at her watch. Two-thirty a.m. Which made it five-thirty in Sydney. Mikey and Polly would be fast asleep. Mentally she blew them both a kiss and glanced around the ship, wanting to imprint the moment on her mind so she could tell Polly about it later. Not that there was a lot to see. *Sundancer*'s lights were smudged by fog and visibility had to be down to less than fifty metres.

She had just finished her cigarette when she became aware the throbbing sound was louder. A ship. It was a goddamn ship. Scanning the rolling waves, the fine curling mist all around, she couldn't see another vessel, but the throb-throbbing was increasing. To her horror, she realised the ship was closing in.

Two

India raced for the bridge. She told herself she was overreacting, that Ned had already taken evasive action, but her adrenalin was in full flow and she catapulted on to the bridge calling urgently, 'There's a ship out there, Ned ... Oh, Jesus ...'

Ned was sprawled unconscious on the floor.

India sprang for the radar. There were two echoes, but where one was around half a mile away and chugging steadily south, the other had nearly merged with their own and was terrifyingly close, heading straight for them from starboard.

Fuck, fuck, fuck.

She glanced through the windows. Nothing but fog. But the radar told her the ship was on a collision course with them ... She hit the fire button. Alarms hollered.

Oh, please get Cuan here quickly, he'll know what to do ... Jesus, the air horn, you idiot, use the bloody horn ...

Fire alarms ringing, air horn blaring, she fumbled for the radio. Called up the ship on channel 16. Voice panicky, she said, 'This is *Sundancer*, we're on a collision course, please go to starboard immediately ... GO STARBOARD!'

No response.

Since *Sundancer* was the give-way vessel India immediately altered to starboard, frantic to try and pass round the stern of the ship, praying they'd do the same. She could hear voices yelling as the crew raced to their emergency posts. Suddenly Cuan and Katy were beside her, barefoot, slickers over their nightwear.

'India,' gasped Katy. 'Oh, God. Ned. What's happened?'

'Christ,' said Cuan, and at the same time India saw a dark shape to starboard. A huge ship, looming out of the mist and steaming straight for them. Her breathing stopped.

No lights, she thought.

'Deploy the Zodiac, the Avons!' yelled Cuan into the ship's tannoy. He spun round. 'You two, *out*.'

India belted after Katy down the metal staircase. Hit the bottom and tore down the corridor, grabbing a couple of life vests. She yanked one on, buckled it up as she ran across the mess room and past the galley. Burst on to the port deck to see the Zodiac was already being lowered into the water along with one of the Avons. A distant part of her mind registered that *Sundancer*'s engines had stopped. The crew were shouting, the air horn still blaring. Katy was staring at something behind India, her face white. India glanced round to see the great white prow of a container ship streaked with rust filled the sea, the sky. They had a handful of seconds before it hit.

India shoved the second life vest at Katy, yelling, 'Put it on!'

Katy caught the vest, got one arm through, then she grabbed India's hand, and they were yelling, tiny sounds lost in the giant bang as the ship smashed straight into *Sundancer*'s starboard flank.

India's hand was wrenched from Katy's as she crashed to the deck. There was a deafening howl of metal tearing, groaning and screeching. *Sundancer* rolled violently and India wrapped her arms around a railing. The next second, she was under water. For a moment she thought the cold might kill her. It made her lungs squeeze and her heart contract. But she wasn't dead, she was just submerged in freezing water, so all she had to do was hang on tight and hold her breath and wait for *Sundancer* to right herself, heave herself out of the ocean, but then the boat tilted further.

Oh my God. She's going to flip.

The water was filled with a dull grinding sound that went on and on. Clinging desperately to her railing she prayed that *Sundancer* wouldn't roll.

I don't want to get buried at sea.

The grinding sound stopped and at the same time, the sea rushed away. *Sundancer* slowly recovered herself. India crouched on deck, choking and gasping, and watched what appeared to be half an ocean pouring out through the scuppers. Gradually she made it to her feet. She looked round. Saw the huge form of the container ship easing past *Sundancer*, just metres of sea between them, rust streaking its sides like bloody claw marks. It didn't appear to be slowing. It was continuing its steady path as though nothing had happened.

Then she took in the black tide of oil leaking from *Sundancer*'s bowels. The way the ship sat low in the water. How she was taking more prolonged rolls against the swell. She was flooding fast. They had maybe five minutes, no more, before she sank. She could hear panicked shouting, Cuan's voice on the tannoy, but she couldn't make out what they were saying.

Another split-second glance at the container ship as it chugged away, seemingly oblivious. A snapshot image of a dent on its transom, like a footprint, and traces of red-painted lettering. *The Pride of Tang*-something, from . . . only two letters of the ship's home port were clear. AA. She couldn't see a registration number.

She could hear the steady throb-throb of *The Pride*'s engines and looked round, dizzy, shivering violently, frantically searching for Katy. People were in the water. She saw one of the crew on deck fling a life jacket at a man, shouting for him to GRAB IT! Others were lighting flares and aiming searchlights. One man was clinging to a rope and was being slowly hauled from the water up the hull. More yelling as waves washed two men toward the ship's stern. A woman was shouting HELP! as she drifted further and further away. The Zodiac was powering after her. People were trying to swim for the life rafts. She could hear them choking and sobbing. A shout made her look around. Joe was screaming at the still form of his wife in the freezing ocean, screaming at Emma to SWIM, dammit, SWIM!

And then Joe was leaping overboard. A tiny splash as he hit the water but India didn't stop to watch any further.

'Katy!' she yelled. She could see lots of deckhands, but not Katy. Katy had been with her, she'd been *holding her hand.* Leaning over the railings she scanned the mist curling over the greeny-grey waves. Please God, let Katy be all right. To her horror, she caught a glimpse of something shiny and humped floating away from *Sundancer*'s flank. Katy's slicker. No life vest. She was face down. Motionless.

India shouted so hard her voice cracked. 'Katy!'

Sundancer's stern was listing sickeningly, her bow rearing up. Sweet Jesus. She was down flooding. The boat was in her death throes, alarms sounding, air-horn horn still blaring, and she could hear Cuan's voice, instructing everyone to get into the inflatables, the life rafts, the ship was going down . . .

'Someone get Katy!' she yelled at the Zodiac, but it was on the port side of the bow, pulling two people aboard and couldn't hear her.

India was trembling. Katy would die unless she went in for her, hauled her to one of the inflatables. Grabbing a horseshoe life buoy from a railing, she flung it into the water just next to Katy's motionless form.

Joe did it.

The instant she hit the water her muscles cramped with cold. *Jesus!* a voice in her mind yelled, and she yelled the name over and over as she determinedly kicked out for Katy. Her clothes were dragging her down but she didn't remove anything. She would need every ounce of fibre to hold warm water against her skin and keep her body temperature from freezing once she got to the life buoy. She swam as hard as she could, forcing her sluggish muscles to keep working, icy salt in her mouth and eyes, panting and gasping, the cold air tearing at her lungs like broken glass. She clawed her way to the glistening shroud of Katy's slicker just ahead. Katy was close. Nearly there . . .

A wave broke over her head, flooding her mouth and windpipe with salt water. She coughed and choked, gasping for air, her mind shrieking with panic.

Treading water, she cleared her lungs, steadied herself for a second before punching her feet though the water, lunging for Katy. She got swept past the life buoy, struggled back within reach of it again, and finally hooked her elbow over it. Her muscles were turning rigid but she managed to catch the back of Katy's slicker, find the collar. Giving a terrific heave, she hauled Katy's head on to her shoulder. Tried to shake her, but Katy was too heavy.

'Katy!' Her voice was a low croak. 'For God's sake, Katy!'

Exhausted and desperate, she gripped the woman's hair and put all her energy into shaking her head as hard as she could. *If she doesn't come round, I'll have to leave her. I'll never make it to a life raft otherwise.*

'Katy!'

Another couple of shakes, then a sudden gasp, a spluttering cough. She was breathing.

'Katy . . .' She could barely make herself heard through her shuddering. 'Hold on to the life buoy!' With a monumental effort she took Katy's left arm and hooked it over the plastic rim. '*Hold on to it!*'

A wave slapped near her face and India wanted to duck away from the spray but found she couldn't. Her body was refusing to respond. It was beginning to shut down. Hypothermia was creeping through her veins. *Must get help*, she thought.

Straining her eyes over the waves she saw *Sundancer*'s lights go out. Blue sparks arced into the water. The only light cutting through the gloom came from the sweeping dots of searchlights. She and Katy would be invisible to them. They'd drifted too far away to be seen. She felt a moment's overwhelming sense of disbelief.

I can't die, she thought. *I promised to take Polly to the zoo next week.*

A wink of light appeared and disappeared behind the swell. It looked as though it was coming their way. Please God, let it be the Zodiac.

Then she realised Katy's grip had slipped. She was drifting away. India grabbed her oilskin and hauled her back, pulling her into her shoulder so her face was free of the water. But the weight of her was dragging her down . . .

'Katy! Help me, dammit!'

No response.

India clung on to Katy's unconscious form with one arm, the other around the life buoy, and dragged her knees up to her waist, trying to reduce any more heat loss. She couldn't feel her hands any more, nor her arms, her legs or feet.

'Katy!'

She couldn't feel her heartbeat, or her lungs working. Her vision started to blur. There was a noise tapping at the edge of her consciousness, she didn't know what, couldn't think. Her shivering lessened as she started the final slide into hypothermia.

Katy. The word wasn't even a whisper, just a thought.

Red light strobed her eyelids. The noise grew louder. Red was replaced by glaring white. With a final desperate effort, she opened her eyes and was nearly blinded by the searchlight fixed on her and Katy.

A man was shouting but she didn't understand what he said. She stared, transfixed, at the hands reaching for her. Then she was being hauled out of the sea, and she wanted to help but she couldn't move. Her body was like a block of frozen cement, and just as heavy, given the grunts of effort from her rescuers. She wanted to tell them to save Katy too, but her mouth wouldn't work.

The next instant men were landing her on to a slippery deck like a big fish. Her nostrils were filled with the putrid reek of blood and fishy entrails and she retched and heaved, bringing up what felt like a gallon of salt water. Incredibly, her mind formed a thought: *I can't be dead, I've just thrown up!*

A man was barking orders and she tried to work out what he was saying, but it was unintelligible. A moment later she was being carried along corridors and down companionways, then into a saloon with a TV blaring, the atmosphere thick with cigarette smoke. The heat felt incredible. Then someone was cutting off her socks and jeans and sodden fleece. G-string. She hadn't been wearing a bra.

She could hear men laughing and she wanted to cover herself but she couldn't move. She felt a weight on her left breast. She couldn't see what it was but she knew it was a man's hand. More laughter.

Another man spoke, his voice deep and commanding. The laughter stopped abruptly.

'So sorry,' the voice said. 'I take you somewhere private.'

The man didn't seem to care that she was naked, and nor, it seemed, did she. With his cloying smell of fish, sweat, and stale cigarettes at the back of her throat, she let him carry her down a corridor as effortlessly as he would a carton of beer.

Inside someone's quarters now, another TV set on full-blast, an unmade bed, piles of oiled sweaters and socks tossed in one corner. Carefully, the man laid her on the bunk. 'No need for shyness,' he said briskly. 'Emergency.'

She could feel him patting her dry. 'No rub,' he said. 'Very bad to rub skin now.' He wrapped her limbs in a variety of towels and blankets separately, then covered her with more blankets. Helped her sip a cup of hot, bitter tea.

She started to shiver. Gently he raised her thick mane of hair in one hand and wound another towel around her neck.

He said, 'We must be slow. Sometimes the limbs contain blood that is very cold. It is dangerous for you if it gets to the heart.'

India couldn't even manage a nod. She simply lay there for what seemed like an age. Eventually she heard him leave, and some time later return. She felt him touching her as though checking whether she had defrosted and was ready for cooking. He murmured something. His voice was calm and soothing. She didn't say anything back, she was absorbed in trying not to cry out with the pain of her limbs returning to life. White-hot flames were shooting through each vein like bullets fired from a gun. After a long time, she opened her eyes. A pair of dark, expressionless eyes looked back. Ruler-straight eyebrows. Wide mouth, square jaw. Skewed, flattened nose that looked as though it might have been punched a few times. Black hair, flecked with white above the ears. If the man hadn't been dressed in filthy oilskins and reeking to high heaven, she might have thought him distinguished.

'You stay, keep warm. I will come back.'

She managed to say, 'Katy. My friend . . .'

Immediately the eyes brightened. 'Your friend is okay. She asks for you too.'

'Ned. What about Ned?'

'He is your captain?'

'No. The first . . . mate.'

Immediately he ducked his head. 'So sorry.'

'Ned's dead?'

'So sorry.'

Her vision began to waver. 'Who . . . are you?'

'I captain of this ship.' He looked uncertain whether to say anything else, then added quietly, '*The Kagoshima Maru.*'

If she hadn't been so weak, so feeble and aching so much, her jaw would have dropped in astonishment.

They'd been rescued by the whaling fleet's factory ship.

Three

The *Kagoshima Maru*'s paramedic checked India several times during the night. When dawn broke he drew back the blind covering the porthole hatch. She looked out at the grey sky and white-crested sea that she knew was as cold as the hand of death and said, 'Could you close it, please?'

She didn't want to see the ocean right now. Pulling the blankets up around her shoulders, she wriggled her toes in the captain's too-large socks, and wondered if she'd ever feel warm again. The next trip I take, she told herself, will be to the Sahara. Lots of heat and sun where the only water around is in bottles.

Her mind suddenly switched to Ned's unconscious form sprawled on the bridge. Had he regained consciousness after the collision? Had he drowned under a landslide of water as the boat sank? However her friend had died, she hoped it had been fast and that he'd known nothing of it.

She lay there thinking about Ned for a long time, and finally rustled up the strength to go and check on Katy. Because her clothes had been surgically removed after she'd been landed on deck, India followed a crew member down mile-long corridors dressed like a whaler: baggy blue trousers held up with string, rubber boots and an oily sweater that smelled of fish.

'Hey, nice outfit,' Katy greeted her.

'Nice outfit, yourself.'

Katy wore a pink robe dotted with yellow pansies. She had black rings around her eyes. India took her hand, glad to feel it was warm.

'How are you?'

'They told me you saved my life.'

India looked away. 'I'm not sure about that.'

'So who was holding my head out of the water while I was unconscious, a seal?'

India smiled and gave Katy's hand a little shake. 'I was hoping you'd come round and offer me a cigarette.'

The faintest smile brushed Katy's face, then her expression sobered. 'Thanks, India.'

'No worries.'

Katy slumped back on her bunk, closed her eyes. 'Sorry, I'm so tired.'

'I'll come back later.'

Hoping to find the rest of the crew, India began walking down a lengthy corridor that smelled strongly of unwashed ashtrays. She thought about the first time she'd met Katy, how she'd felt like an unkempt and malnourished carthorse next to Katy's thoroughbred good looks. Talk about opposites. Katy was outgoing and physically expressive, India was neither. Katy had curves, India had angles. Katy had a shiny blond bob, India a black mane that was always tangled into a mass of corkscrews. They would never have bonded so quickly if it hadn't been for the fact they were the only smokers among the crew. Marlboro buddies from their first training session six months before.

She was on her third lengthy corridor when she bumped into Cuan, also dressed like a whaler, and when he opened his arms she didn't balk as she normally would. She walked straight into his embrace and hugged him back.

'Good on you,' he said, and she felt him press a kiss on her head as he held her close. 'You're a bloody star, jumping into that water for a mate.'

Tears leaked down her cheeks.

'Look, love, you ought to know . . . We lost Emma. And Keith, Matt, Vince and Marie . . .' He leaned back and looked at her straight. 'We lost Ned too.'

'Yes.' She buried her face into his shoulder.

His embrace tightened. 'I'm sorry, India. I know how close you were.'

'How did he die? Did he drown?'

'After the collision . . . well, the bridge was a mess. He'd hit his head . . .' Cuan cleared his throat. 'He never came round.'

Her fingers spasmed on the rough wool of his whaler's sweater. 'What about *Sundancer*?'

'She stayed afloat long enough to get us all off. But when she went, she sure went. She reared bow-up and went down so fast it was like she was yanked under by a giant squid or something.' He kissed her hair again. 'You'll feel better if you get something to eat, preferably high-calorie. They're serving brekky at the moment, and I think you should give it a go.'

She'd never felt less like eating in her life, but she said obediently, 'Okay. But you'd better direct me or I'll never find it.'

'I show you,' a voice said behind them. They turned to see the *Kagoshima Maru*'s captain standing there looking determined. Cuan gave the captain a nod and walked away. She watched him head down the corridor, his normally straight back bowed, his shoulders low, and she didn't move until he'd turned the corner.

Breakfast was a bowl of hot, savoury noodles and a huge mug of green tea accompanied by clouds of cigarette smoke. She didn't think she'd ever seen so many smokers. Out of the one hundred-strong-crew she saw two women and one man who didn't have a lit cigarette dangling from their lips and for the first time in her life, the thought of lighting up herself made her feel distinctly sick.

The captain, 'you may call me Shinzo', had given her Ned's watch after Cuan had left. She hadn't cried or shown any emotion. She'd taken it gingerly, feeling peculiarly numb and disbelieving, and knew the tears would come later, when the full force of what had happened sank in. Ned's watch was now on her left wrist and above her own, which had stopped working. Mikey had given it to her last Christmas as a reminder she was always late home for supper. Mikey would hit the roof when he heard about the collision, he was always banging on at her to try and keep herself out of trouble, but she was more concerned with having to face Ellie.

Ned, killed by an unregistered container ship. Why hadn't the ship answered Ned's radio call? Why hadn't it stopped to help? No lights. They hadn't wanted to be seen. Why? If they'd been hit by a fishing trawler it would make sense, but a *container ship*? The shipping routes were over 2000 Ks north of where they'd collided. And they'd been coming from the *south*. Where there was nothing until you hit the desolate snowbound coastline of Wilkes Land. India couldn't work it out.

Gulping down another mouthful of noodles – her appetite had kicked in as soon as her tastebuds informed her they were remarkably good – she looked at Shinzo sipping his bitter green tea. He'd rescued the entire Greenpeace crew. He'd pulled nine people from the freezing ocean and recovered the bodies of those that hadn't made it. Four people dead from hypothermia, two from injuries suffered when the ship hit them. Shinzo told her that he'd radioed the Canberra authorities and prepared the port of Fremantle for their arrival. He was obviously not looking forward to facing the officials and their questions: what had he been doing hunting in the Southern Ocean Sanctuary, a critically protected area for whales? And why did his ship have the meat and blubber of over a hundred minkes in its hold?

Before he'd shown her to breakfast, she'd asked for a tour, and to her surprise, he'd agreed. Most of his crew were taking it easy; playing cards, reading in their bunks or watching videos in one of the lounges. There wasn't much else for them to do when they weren't actually processing whales or resupplying the other ships.

'Deck crew can process a whale in under fifteen minutes,' Shinzo had told India. 'Any longer, the meat will not taste so good.'

Fifteen minutes, she had thought glumly. And to think it takes a minke a full eight years before it is sexually mature.

He'd allowed her a glimpse into the ship's freezer: row upon row of flensed flesh the colour of salmon stretched as far as her eye could see.

'What on earth do you do with it all?' she'd asked innocently.

'Scientific purpose,' he'd replied.

'Yeah, right,' India's tone could have stripped an engine. 'I gather your scientific whale samples retail for over a hundred million bucks a year as a luxury food.'

He had grinned, showing a gold incisor. 'Good business for me, heya?'

'But they're *endangered*. What happens when you've killed the last whale? What about your future business?'

'Plenty of whales for me.'

'Shinzo, you're *wiping them out*. They don't breed like rabbits! They have a single calf every two years or so and it takes that calf *years* before it can reproduce! Don't you understand? They can't keep up with your killing sprees!' She had realised she was shouting, but couldn't seem to stop herself. 'Thanks to you they'll be extinct in the next few years, you selfish son of a bitch!'

Shinzo had calmly dug in his overalls and passed her a greasy-looking square of cotton. When he pointed to her face she'd suddenly realised she had tears on her cheeks and, ignoring his gesture, stalked off. They hadn't spoken since.

Looking at Shinzo now, she felt swamped with guilt. Not only had the man saved her life and shown remarkable tenderness and respect for her as he thawed her frozen body, but he'd offered her his handkerchief for her tears. At that moment he looked up and caught her eye but she ducked her head, pushing away her noodles. Shinzo was like all whalers. He only cared about the money.

The *Kagoshima Maru* was twice as fast as *Sundancer*, but it still took them four days before they neared the coast. Four days of numbed disbelief, hushed voices, passive smoking and endless cups of green tea. India was glad she was with people who were physically affectionate; she needed every hug that came her way. She knew it was stupid, but she kept looking for Ned's head of fair hair among the crew members, and when she didn't see him, she'd crumple inside.

Not long after dawn on Sunday, Shinzo dropped anchor. The sea was calm, the sky filled with high grey clouds. India scanned the horizon over the slop of steel-coloured water, but couldn't see any land. Just a fishing trawler speeding their way.

'Friends of yours?' she asked him.

Shinzo didn't answer.

They were on the bridge, Shinzo squinting against the smoke drifting from his cigarette. Ned's body was already on deck along with the other dead crew members, each shrouded in fine muslin-like netting the same pale grey-pink colour of intestines.

She watched the fishing trawler make fast against the factory ship, then a bulky man in overalls climbed on board and headed their way.

'This man,' said Shinzo, 'will take everybody ashore.'

India eyed Overalls carefully. He looked unwashed, overweight and very Japanese.

'Let me guess,' she sighed, 'he's a cousin of yours.'

Overalls came to Shinzo and they shook hands. India saw Shinzo slip the man a fat oil-skinned package and realised he'd lied. Shinzo hadn't alerted the authorities in Canberra and Fremantle at all.

She waited until Overalls was back on his trawler before she confronted Shinzo. 'You bribed him, didn't you?'

'You are alive.' His mouth set in a stern line that indicated she owed him. Remorse washed over her. He could have ignored *Sundancer*'s pleas for assistance at sea, but he hadn't. He'd then risked the possibility of his ship being spotted as it neared the Australian coast and reported to the police and Customs, the Japanese Consul and everyone in between, in order to bring them safely to shore. She couldn't blame him for the bribe.

'Shinzo, I'm sorry.'

He gave a formal bow and India held out her hand. His grip was strong and hard as a monkey wrench.

'If you hear of the container ship, or see it at all, could you ring me? It'll have a whacking great dent in its bow from hitting us, but as well as that, her name—'

'*The Pride.*' He gave a curt nod.

'Yes. Would you call me at the *Sydney Morning Herald*? Would you do that for me?'

He blinked. 'You are a reporter?'

'Yup.'

He made a grunting sound at the back of his throat that could have meant anything from gratification to disapproval.

'I know I've been rude.' She softened her tone. 'After all you've done ... Don't think I don't appreciate it. It's just that my friend died.'

He rested a hand lightly on her shoulder. His voice was gentle. 'May the best of your friend's past follow him to his future.'

Touched, she put her hand over his, feeling the heat of him against her palm, the roughness of his skin, the calluses ridging his knuckles, and was surprised when he didn't pull away.

'Thank you,' she said solemnly.

A glint of humour crossed his face.

'Next time you chase me, bring your *QE2*. We have drink on board your ship. I beat you at poker.'

She grinned. 'It's a deal.'

Four

'It was an accident,' Detective Inspector Zhuganov repeated, and glanced at the door as though he wished he could walk though it and never return.

'Yes,' India said, 'but there's no way they couldn't see we were in trouble, that we had people overboard. They left us to *die*.'

She was in Fremantle's police station with Cuan and two federal cops. Because the collision had taken place on the high seas and outside Australian waters, the feds had turned up on behalf of AMSA, the Australian Maritime Safety Authority in Canberra. The rest of the crew were making their statements in the squad room, leaving the five of them crammed into a room the size of a walnut that smelled of stale coffee and fly spray. Three chairs, but nobody was sitting.

'Why would they do that?' one of the feds asked.

'Because they had something to hide.'

'Any ideas?'

'Not yet.'

'No ship's come in with a damaged bow,' the other fed reiterated, 'but we'll keep looking. We've put up a couple of planes to see if they can spot her along with the *Kagoshima Maru*.'

India wasn't holding out much hope. Shinzo had dropped them a good four hours from the coast, which meant he'd had heaps of time to make a getaway. She wondered if he'd headed back to the whaling grounds and thought probably not. His holds had been pretty full. He'd be sailing home.

Detective Inspector Zhuganov began briskly to round off the meeting. They had been there for over two hours making their statements and, as they left, everyone agreed to keep the disaster under wraps for as long as possible while the next of kin were informed. India would only phone her editor and grab the headlines once she'd been given the go-ahead from Cuan. She didn't want any unsuspecting relatives to learn of the death of their loved ones from her newspaper.

In the squad room, the cops were trying to sort out how to get everyone back home. One constable was handing out ten-dollar notes so the crew could buy themselves sandwiches and coffee; others were making phone calls. The atmosphere was frenetic and tearful and India felt a combination of claustrophobia and panic rush through her. She turned and hastily started for the door.

'India, wait!' Katy scurried after her.

'Got to go.' Her voice was clipped. 'Sorry.'

'Can't we give you a lift? William's on his way.'

India didn't want to be with anyone from *Sundancer*. She had to be alone, to gather her thoughts before she saw Ellie.

'Thanks, but I'll be fine.'

A light rain was falling outside. Dismal weather for a dismal day. Cars splashed past but there were few people on the street. India gulped several lungfuls of damp air, pretending she could taste the endless wheat fields from across the flat expanse of the city, and the deep red desert stretching behind them. Gradually, a sense of distance and space trickled through her, and she felt herself calm.

She wanted to ring Mikey but didn't dare just yet. He'd hear the tears in her voice and then he'd be on the next flight to Perth and she didn't want that. She wanted to be in the snug haven of their home tonight with Polly when she told him what had happened, not in some bland hotel room.

She was wondering what she should do next, when she heard someone exit the station behind her. Before they put an arm around her shoulders, she already knew who it was. She'd only been at sea with the crew for a month but she felt as though she was linked to them by tensile steel.

'You're going to Ellie?' Cuan asked.

She nodded.

'May as well drive Ned's ute home for her.'

She didn't have Ned's car keys but it didn't dissuade Cuan. They caught a cab to Victoria Quay where, to her astonishment, he hot-wired the thing, and showed her how.

'You think because I'm expedition leader I'm squeaky clean?' he said, trying to lighten his tone, but it was tight from stress and India quickly said, no, she didn't think he was squeaky clean at all, and that she'd always thought of him as a car thief, and was proud of his speciality.

'Love you too, babe,' he said and kissed her cheek before waving her off. 'Speak soon.'

It was late afternoon before India finally arrived at Jimbuku Bay, and she parked Ned's car by the beach and lit a cigarette. Her hands were shaking and she knew she had to calm herself before she faced Ellie. An easterly punched the side of the car from time to time, making it shudder and India flinch. What she needed was a stiff drink, but she wouldn't get that until she'd broken the news.

She eyed the thundering surf and the plumes spraying off the tops of dunes, then turned her gaze to the artful jumble of designer homes hugging the furthest reaches of the wind-blasted beach. Not for the first time she felt a sense of disbelief as she gazed at the place. Jimbuku Bay, with its little turrets and rounded nautical windows, would sit nicely on the banks of Perth's Swan River, but here, in the middle of the flat, dusty wilderness of the mid-west coast, it looked seriously out of place.

Back home in New South Wales there were pretty anchorages and little towns nestled into green hills, but here it was wild and lonely, with sea fans and cuttlebones on the beach and coral on the road. The air smelled of brine and snakebush and the sky seemed to go on for ever, the horizons stretching like elastic at the corners of your eyes. And right in the middle of this salty wasteland, sat a bunch of houses the colour of smarties. It wasn't that the place hadn't been well designed, she thought, it *didn't fit in.*

Ned had asked her what she'd thought of their new home, and she'd said without thinking, 'It's sweet.' He'd immediately taken offence, and she'd wisely said nothing more because she knew she'd only compound the insult.

Stubbing out her cigarette, India started up the car and headed for Ellie's. Dread squirmed in her gut, making her feel queasy. How to tell Ellie that the man she'd fallen in love with at The Tate wouldn't be around any more? She could remember the day Ellie had met Ned like it was yesterday. Ellie blasting into the flat yelling at the top of her voice, 'We had coffee! And he loves Kitaj as much as I do and I can't believe it! He's perfect!' and then Ned saying to India in the kitchen as he opened a bottle of wine the following week, 'I can't believe she likes Kitaj. She's perfect.'

They'd been married for four years when they decided to return to Australia and have children. They'd set up home near Ellie's parents who lived in Geraldton, and everything had been perfect. But now Ned was dead.

India halted outside Ellie's cherry-red front door, and concentrated on clamping her emotions. She had to be strong. Her own grief could wait until later. She wished she didn't have to do this, but she knew she had to. Cold comfort to think of other crew members doing the same. With an unsteady hand, she pressed the bell.

When Ellie opened the fly-screen door, her expression

immediately turned into alarm. 'What's happened? Why are you back . . . ?' Her gaze swept over India's too-short baggy trousers clinched at the waist with a length of string, her rubber boots, and the blood drained from her face.

'Where's Ned?'

'Let's go inside.'

Stock still, Ellie stared at India.

'Where is he?'

India crushed the wave of grief threatening to rise and hurriedly shoved it into a small black box inside her, locked the lid. 'Let's go inside,' she repeated, voice steady. Calm.

'No.' Ellie's stare grew unfocused. 'Oh, God. No . . . He's in hospital, isn't he? Is he all right?'

'I'm sorry, Ellie. There was an accident—'

'No, no. *No.*' Ellie's voice started to rise. 'No, don't tell me he's dead, please, no, not that, please, *please* . . .'

'We collided with a container ship. We lost six crew . . .' Her voice started to crack but she forced herself to finish. 'Including Ned.'

India held out Ned's watch. 'Ellie, I'm so sorry . . .'

'NO!'

Ellie's shout came from deep within her heart, and wrenched India so hard that the box she'd locked flew open and she was crying and trying not to, she wanted to be *strong*, and Ellie was falling to her knees, her face contorted as she screamed, her hands balled into fists and smashing the ground. India dropped beside her and tried to hold her but Ellie fought her off, hitting and punching, her terrible wail piercing India like a knife.

'I'm sorry,' India kept saying over and over. 'I'm so sorry.'

Ellie raised her face to India and for a second India thought she was going to punch her but then she had her arms around her and was sobbing against her neck, great gusting howls that came from her core, and India knew her friend's heart had broken.

A long time later, when Ellie's sobs quietened, she managed to get her inside. Pushing aside a stack of baby magazines, she sat her on the sofa and took her in her arms again. She tried not to think of how Ellie would get through her pregnancy without Ned. She had another seven months to go. India rocked Ellie and stroked her hair, wishing she'd had the foresight to arrange for a doctor to be on hand. She reckoned Ellie could do with an elephant-sized tranquilliser to get her through the next few days.

Suddenly Ellie slumped so hard against her that for an instant India thought Ellie had lost consciousness, but then she realised Ellie was still crying.

'H-how did it happen?' Ellie asked. 'Tell me. Everything.'

'Maybe later,' India said gently. 'When I've called a doctor.'

Ellie twisted upright, her expression suddenly fierce. 'No, India. Now. I want you to tell me everything that happened. His last day. I have to *know*.'

So India told her. When she got to the part when she and Ned had been on watch, talking about naming the baby Albert, Ellie stiffened. 'He mentioned the curse?'

India frowned. 'What curse?'

Ellie stared past her. 'The one on this place.' Her voice was a whisper.

'What do you mean?'

'I never believed it. Ned did. He wanted to sell up.'

'Why?'

'He was scared. People have been falling ill, some of them even died . . . Oh, God, and now Ned's gone . . .' A fresh storm of weeping overtook her and India held her until it eased.

'I'll ring for a doctor,' India said.

'No,' Ellie managed. 'M-mum and Dad.'

After India had called Ellie's parents, who said they were on their way, hold tight, India stood by the kitchen window.

Her eyes were sore and her face felt swollen. She gazed for a long time at the carefully planted bottle brushes and yellow banksias, the feathery bracken ferns lining each front pathway. Aside from a dusting of sand on the pavements, the street was endlessly neat. Even the tin boat in number 20's driveway looked as though it had received a polish.

Going to the fridge, she brought out some orange juice, and paused at a memory of Ned giving her an avid tour of his Ocean Green appliances; the fridge-freezer, the ice-machine and air-conditioning units. 'They came with the house,' Ned had said gleefully and she could understand why he was so smug. When CFCs had been banned, the efficiency of refrigeration had immediately plummeted but Ocean Green had found a new way of chilling air effectively without damaging the environment. India wanted an Ocean Green fridge too, but since you had to take a mortgage out to own one, India was waiting for the price to eventually drop. Her throat tightened. Ned had been so proud of his goddamn fridge.

India took thc juicc to Ellic, wishing she could have given her a shot of something stronger, but she knew Ellie wouldn't touch it while she was pregnant. India drank black coffee and sat with Ellie until her parents arrived. Faces set with anxiety, Ron and Jill didn't seem to take in the fact that India was dressed like a Japanese whaler. They saw nothing but their daughter's distress.

'Ron, did you know this place was cursed?' India asked Ellie's dad a little later. Ron was making tea in the kitchen and looking miserable.

'Yeah. Ned mentioned it a while back.'

'Not Ellie?'

He gave a sigh. 'You know my gal. She doesn't believe in all that mumbo-jumbo.'

'But Ned did?'

'He was up for moving, but Ellie . . . Well, she loves the place.'

'She said people had been ill.' She swallowed the ball in her throat. 'And that some died.'

'Too right. Sick as parrots a lot of them. They've lost five in the past year.' He put a liver-spotted hand briefly over his eyes. 'And now Ned.'

She let him compose himself before pressing further. 'How did they die?'

'To start with they reckoned it was a virus. But when Bob Jarrett keeled over last October they got real worried. Fit as anything, that bloke. So they started checking stuff out. You know, water, the electrics, radiation. You name it, they've been over it, okayed it all, but even so, Jilly and I . . . Well, we wanted 'em to move too, but no, not Ellie.'

'Isn't she worried about the baby?'

Ron dropped a teabag on the floor, but didn't seem to notice. 'Actually, she has been a bit bothered. But she said not to tell Ned or he'd sell the house for nothing he was so wired up over it.'

She recalled Ned's unconscious form sprawled on *Sundancer*'s deck.

'You'll make sure she stays with you?' India asked anxiously. 'I don't know what's going on here, but it sounds pretty weird.'

'She'll come home with us, no worries.' He looked down at the teabag on the floor as though unsure where it had come from. 'She wants to see him, you know. Any chance of giving us a hand with it?'

India immediately rang the Fremantle cop shop who told her that Ned and the five other deceased crew members were at the Royal Perth Hospital. She rang the mortuary to be told that yes, they could come down any time after nine a.m. the following morning. Hanging up, her mind turned to the rest of the crew. How were they getting on? What was

Cuan doing? Where was the container ship now, and why hadn't it stopped?

She checked her watch, forgetting it wasn't working. It was stuck at forty-two minutes past twelve. Had it stopped when she'd been rolled underwater and clinging on to *Sundancer*'s railing, or when she'd jumped in after Katy? Her mind slowed to a crawl and she had an urge to fall to the floor and curl up and go to sleep.

'India?'

She turned to see Ron looking worried.

'Ellie wants you to come to the mortuary tomorrow. I don't want to be a bother, but—'

'Of course I'll come.'

His relief was palpable. 'Thanks, love.'

If she was going to stay overnight she had to ring Mikey. No way could she risk him or Polly hearing about the collision before she told them she was okay. She found a bottle of cooking brandy in one of the cupboards and poured herself a slug. She hated brandy, but she forced it down. It felt as though it was sandpapering her throat, but the hot glow it lit beneath her diaphragm seemed to help.

Taking a deep breath, she dialled Mikey's number at the North Sydney cop shop.

'Hey, gorgeous,' he said. 'Caught the bad guys yet?'

'Er . . .' She cleared her throat. 'Actually, they rescued me.'

Silence.

'How's Polly?' she asked.

'Polly can wait, I want to know—'

'I'm absolutely fine. Never better. I just need some new clothes, that's all.' She thought she was getting it just about right. A light tone, inconsequential chatter. 'My whaler's outfit stinks.'

'Whaler's *what*?' he said in a strangled tone.

'We had a little accident and a whaling ship kindly brought us to shore. I'm going to stay overnight with Ellie, then I'll jump on a flight and be home in time for supper tomorrow. How about some steak? I love the way you do it with that pepper cream sauce.'

Another silence, then, 'You're okay?' Anxious but trying not to sound it.

'Yup. Cross my heart and hope to die. I'm fine.'

'You don't sound it.'

'Thanks. Next time I'll let you read about it in the papers.'

He made a groaning sound. 'That bad?'

Her lungs contracted and she knew she was going to lose it any second, but she wanted him to stay there, be *at home* for her when she got back.

'See you at supper,' she said brightly and hung up.

The next morning India drove Ellie's car to Perth. Ellie sat up front, glassy-eyed and pale, her parents buckled up in the back. Nobody spoke. The sea had lost its colour, a dull slate against a concrete sky. It was as though the sun was hiding behind the blanket of clouds in sympathetic grief.

The autopsy report stated Ned had died from a blood clot after a massive knock on the head.

'He would have been unconscious at the time,' the woman pathologist said kindly. 'He wouldn't have known a thing.'

While Ellie's parents walked their daughter outside, India stayed behind, saying she'd catch them up in a minute. Turning to the pathologist, she said, 'Would you mind if I ask a couple of quick questions about Ned?'

The pathologist frowned. 'It depends.'

India told her how ill Ned had looked on the bridge of *Sundancer*, describing his rasping breath and sweats, and that he'd lost consciousness while he was on watch and just before the collision.

'I didn't realise,' the pathologist said, running a hand over her eyes. She looked suddenly exhausted.

'No.' India knew the woman probably wouldn't release any sensitive information to her, especially if she knew she was a reporter, but she asked anyway. 'Did you find anything that would explain him passing out like that?'

'Well, he suffered from asthma,' she said, as if that explained everything.

Startled, India said, 'He did?' It was the first she knew about it.

'His lungs were constricted and filled with inflammatory cells.'

'You're saying he died of asthma?'

'No. He died from a blood clot after something hit him very hard on the head. But an asthma attack would explain him losing consciousness.' The pathologist studied her carefully. 'I think it's best if you go now.' Her voice was gentle. 'I'm very sorry for your loss.'

Out on the street, Ellie white as chalk and propped between her parents, India kissed her friend goodbye. Both cheeks. Proper kisses where she planted her lips against her friend's skin, chilled with shock. She wanted to pull Ellie into a hug and hold her close, to instill her with some of her warmth and strength, but she looked so fragile, as though she might shatter at the slightest touch, that India held back. She said again how sorry she was, and no, she didn't need a lift, thank you. She was happy to walk.

The Royal Perth was a stone's throw from the city, and India headed briskly for a bank and a handful of change for a couple of phone calls. She thought she was coping pretty well until she paused at a set of pedestrian lights and glanced around to see a man about twenty metres behind her suddenly dive into a sandwich shop. Her breathing stopped. He'd worn a blue fleece, jeans and deck shoes, and had a blond pony tail. For a second she'd thought he was Ned.

Still staring at the door where the man had vanished,

India felt a surge of anger ignite beneath her breastbone. If it's the last thing I do, she swore, I'm going to hunt that container ship down.

Five

The ANZ Bank personnel were kindness personified. India was barely halfway through her story when she was swept to the manager's office and sat down with a cup of coffee, a plateful of sandwiches and assorted pastries. She was being treated as though she'd been shipwrecked and deprived of food for days, but she wasn't complaining. After a diet of noodles, rice and raw fish, she was desperate for some decent carbohydrates.

Eventually she was issued a visa card along with seven hundred bucks, and she headed for the shops. Swapping her whaler's outfit for her usual uniform of jeans and boots, stretchy shirt and broad silver-buckled belt, she then went and bought some supplies: cigarettes and a lighter, a cheap watch and a notepad and pen. Coming out of the stationers, she swung right, searching for a taxi, and that was when she saw him again.

Blue fleece, jeans and deck shoes. Blond pony tail.

He was looking in the window of a store opposite, hands in his pockets, and as she stared at him, he turned and she could have sworn he looked straight at her, but then he was walking down the street, and she realised he wasn't anything like Ned. He was shorter, for a start, and stocky, nothing like Ned's lean frame. It must have been the pony tail that had caught her out, along with the man's clothes.

Two taxis cruised down her side of the street and she forgot about the man as she waved at the first and climbed inside, asked it to take her to Fremantle Port.

The sky was still leaden and her senses felt as dull as her

surroundings when she arrived. It had to be in the mid-twenties at least, but she felt chilled and shivery. She walked to Corkhill Landing, her steps sluggish, the smell of the ocean like a salt-lick on her tongue. She could see a bunch of tourists outside one of the broad weatherboard sheds, queuing to catch a ferry to Rottnest Island or hire a whale-watching boat. Standing next to one of the No Fishing signs, India looked across the harbour at the main port, North Quay, bristling with piles of containers, cranes and cargo ships. A couple of ships' air conditioners roared dully across the water.

Sundancer had been moored here before she set sail for Antarctica. She could picture the swarms of crew loading boxes of kit on board, hear their cheerful shouts. She could see Emma ticking off lists and packing away groceries; Keith, the chief engineer, double-checking the main engine and the two auxiliaries; Vince helping load a spare helicopter blade on board; Matt and Marie taking blood samples so they'd know who matched who; Ned overseeing, always everywhere.

All six of them dead.

She closed her eyes, remembering when she'd first met the crew. The way she'd groaned inside when she'd seen the dreadlocks, piercings and leather necklaces. Lots of strong, white teeth and happy faces. She hadn't known any of them, aside from Ned, but gradually she'd felt her natural prickliness ease under their wholesome friendliness, and after a few days she'd felt as though she was travelling with an oddly diverse, highly enthusiastic, and multi-cultural family.

Swallowing hard to ease the ache in her throat, India opened her eyes, took a breath, turned around and headed for the eleven-storey blue and white building right behind her, topped with a navigation control tower. The Port Authority offices.

Reception had high ceilings, lots of natural light, and a

sixteen-foot model of an Orient liner, *Orford*, inside a glass case. It felt overly cold with air-conditioning and goose bumps rose on her arms. She wished she hadn't lost the Greenpeace fleece she'd been given at the start of the expedition.

'Can I help you?' a woman asked. She was one of three behind a wrap-around desk that looked as though it could have flown the *Enterprise* without any trouble.

'Is the harbour master around?'

The woman looked dubious until India told her what it was about, and then her demeanour turned brisk. Picking up the phone, she dialled. 'Chief? Are you under the pump? No more than usual, huh . . .' She gave a muffled laugh. 'Stop whinging, will you? I've someone here about the Greenpeace incident . . . sure, I'll bring her up.'

The offices were airy with teal-blue carpet and large windows that let in yet more natural light. Everyone used security swipe cards to get around and greeted each other cheerfully.

Hank Gregory, known by everyone as the chief, was a giant of a man with wildly curly, dark brown hair and bright blue eyes etched with laughter lines. His shirt sleeves were pushed back to reveal a tattoo on his right forearm of a dove carrying a banner in its beak. He took one look at her and grinned. His teeth were big too, she saw, big and white and as strong as the rest of him appeared.

'Not every day we get a nice surprise like this,' he said, unashamedly raking his eyes up and down her body. 'You a model or something?'

'A reporter.'

His face grew guarded. 'Jenny didn't say anything about that. What do you want?'

He hadn't asked her to sit down, so she stood in his office overlooking the dull slate harbour and ranks of cargo ships and forklift trucks beetling back and forth like insects in the distance, and told him.

'Holy shit,' he said. 'You're the journo who went into the water after your mate, aren't you? Talk about gutsy.'

India looked away.

'You've talked to the federal police?' he asked. 'They're working with The Australian Maritime Safety Authority.'

'Yes.'

He looked puzzled. 'How can I help?'

'I just wanted to know if you'd seen the container ship docked here. She'd have a dent on her bow from—'

'The collision, sure.' The chief was nodding. 'My brief says she's around ninety metres long, fifteen metres wide, four derricks.'

'You haven't seen her?'

The chief shook his head. 'Sorry. She's not in our records. We checked the classification society, our movement schedules, ships in port, that sort of stuff. The feds reckon she never called into Australia.'

'Do you have any idea what a container ship could have been doing in the middle of the Southern Ocean?'

He scratched his chin. 'Can't see any skipper wanting to sail half a million bucks' worth of ship in that place.'

'How would you suggest I track it down?'

'The feds are doing that.'

'Me too.'

He held her eyes a moment. 'I see.'

'She's called *The Pride of Tang*-something,' she prompted.

'Yeah, I know.' He flashed her a grin as he finally waved her to a chair. 'And she's from a port which has two As in its name.'

'Two As that were quite well spread apart,' she told him. 'With maybe three or four letters between them, like Manila.'

The chief took a seat and picked up the phone. 'You fancy a coffee?'

Two minutes later coffee arrived in a pair of china mugs.

His had a naked woman with a feather boa on it, hers a kangaroo wearing a pair of boxing gloves emblazoned with the Australian flag. The contradiction of smart and efficient offices against Aussie tat made her smile, and while the chief tapped on his computer, taking great glugs of his coffee, India sipped.

'Only ship coming up on the Lloyd's Register is *The Pride*. No suffix, just *The Pride*. She runs out of Hong Kong. Want me to give the port a call?'

'But Hong Kong doesn't share the same port letters, AA.'

'Don't you want to eliminate her from your inquiries, at least?' The chief was grinning at her, obviously enjoying himself.

'I guess so.' India hesitated. 'Shouldn't the feds be checking out the ship in case she is the right boat?' She didn't want to alert the ship's owner they might be sued, and for them to bolt into hiding.

'Look, I won't put the wind up them.' The chief leaned forward. 'I'll just make a house call, find out where she's at. If she could have been anywhere near your accident.'

Reassured, India sat back. 'That would be brilliant.'

Twenty minutes later, the chief hung up. He looked disappointed. 'She's on her way back from the North Pacific. Been delivering stuff to Anchorage. No way could it be her. Sorry.'

India said more to herself than the chief, 'How on earth will I find her?'

He ran a hand through the wild curls. 'Well, the feds are checking the registers world-wide, so not much point you covering the same stuff. I'd get the word out through the docks. Melbourne, Sydney. Get everyone talking. Offer a nice big reward. A seaman might have seen her in another port somewhere. But are you sure you should be messing with this kind of stuff? Could be dangerous.'

Choosing to ignore that India said, 'Should you hear of a boat with a dent on its bow . . .'

'Sure, I'll let you know.'

Reception kindly called India a taxi to take her to the airport, and while she waited, she went outside for a cigarette. The second she stepped outside she saw him. Blue fleece and pony tail.

He was drinking from a can of Coke and leaning against a dark blue Ford in the car park but the instant she appeared he hopped inside. India let her eyes wash over him and his car and fixed her gaze on a long, ash-coloured ship moored across the harbour, air-conditioning units going full blast.

What the hell was going on? Was he following her? If so, he wasn't doing a great job of it. But then if he hadn't reminded her of Ned, she probably wouldn't have noticed him. Nerves tight, she smoked two cigarettes, waiting for him to drive away, but he didn't.

When her taxi turned up, she heard him start his car, watched him as surreptitiously as she could as he pulled his blue Ford behind them as they exited the car park. He followed her all the way to the airport, hanging well back as she checked in, drifting behind her through the departure lounge, and she wondered whether to confront him or not.

Better the devil you know.

He hung around while she used the restroom, bought a car magazine after she'd purchased a newspaper, and it was only at the security check at the bottom of the escalators when he let her go. The last she saw he was on a mobile phone and walking briskly outside.

At Kingsford Smith airport, India did her best to see if she had another tail, but it was difficult with so many people around. Besides, if they were serious about it this end, and were using a team of guys with walkie-talkies, she knew she'd never spot them. Even so, when the taxi dropped her outside her block she studied the street. A woman in her twenties with a boy in tow, a fat kid of about ten. Several suited men and women walking from the path that led from the city ferry. A window cleaner and a guy walking his retriever. She filed them all as best she could in her memory, along with the two cars that drove past; one white Lexus and a rusting mini-moke.

In the lift, rattling up to the fifteenth floor, she tried to stop her mind from gnawing at the man she'd spotted in Perth. How long had he been following her? Just from the mortuary, or had he watched her at Ellie's? And *why*? Who was he reporting to?

No point in worrying about it now, she told herself firmly. You're home, and have more important things to do. Like explain to Mikey what has happened and hope he doesn't hit the roof.

To her relief Mikey was halfway through trimming a pile of sugar snap peas when she arrived, steaks marinating to one side, two bottles of Merlot already decanted. If he was angry with her, he never cooked, let alone cracked open a bottle of wine.

'Polly in bed?' she asked.

'She's waiting for you.'

She'd bought Polly a present at the airport, but as soon as she saw the little girl was fast asleep, she put it aside. It could wait.

Polly's sheet was twisted around her skinny waist, ribs like sticks no matter how much she ate. A tiny teddy bear the size of a pack of cigarettes lay on the pillow beside her, its tartan bow tie askew. India pulled up the sheet and tucked it around the girl's shoulders despite the fact it was warm. Maternal instinct maybe, but she liked to see Polly snug in her bed.

India brushed a strand of dark curly hair from Polly's forehead before pressing a kiss there. She'd first met the young Aboriginal girl in a baking outback town slap bang in the middle of nowhere, and when she and Mikey had discovered Polly had recently been orphaned, they had formally adopted her. India smiled and gave Polly another kiss before heading back to the kitchen.

Mikey poured her a glass of wine and watched while she sipped. His eyebrows lifted. 'Still given up?'

'Yes,' she said. He didn't have to know about her puffing away on deck with Katy, or the pack of ten she'd chain smoked outside the airport.

With a nod he turned back to the sugar snaps. Then he said calmly, 'Tell me what happened.'

India went to the window and glanced outside. No Lexus or mini-moke. No people sitting in parked cars staring at her window. Sipping her wine she told Mikey about *Sundancer*'s collision, checking the street from time to time, but seeing nothing to alarm her.

Gradually she felt herself relax and when she finished he looked at her a long time, expression unreadable. Then he put down the knife and came to her and wrapped her in his arms. Kissed her at length. Led her to their bedroom and slowly undressed her, kissing each bruise, every little cut, before making love to her with an intense concentration that made her clutch his shoulders and cry out his name.

'I should have near-death experiences more often,' she said in his arms a little later.

'It was a toss up between putting you over my knee and spanking the hell out of you for terrifying me so much or—'

'Glad it was the Or,' she said, laughing.

'So.' He shifted a little to peer into her face. 'How do you fancy getting hitched?'

Oh God, she thought. *Not again.*

'What, right now?' India tried to keep the mood light.

He grinned. 'Right now would be perfect.'

'I have no intention of getting married naked,' she protested.

'At least I'd see exactly what I'd be getting.'

She gave him an arch look. 'And what you're getting right now is a cup of nice, hot cocoa.' Climbing out of bed she reached for his towelling robe, paused to look down at him. 'Or would you prefer a glass of red?'

'What I'd prefer . . .'

Mikey reached up and put his hand around her wrist and pulled her back on to the bed.

The next morning India studied the street to see commuters walking for the ferry, others driving. Nothing unusual struck her about the scene, and she wondered if her mind had been playing tricks on her. After all, she'd been stressed to the max as well as upset while she'd been in Perth, and she couldn't think of any reason why anyone would follow her. She would, she thought, still keep an eye out, just in case.

After she'd downed her coffee and Polly and Mikey had finished their usual breakfast of scrambled eggs and toast, India gave Polly her present.

'A prezzie?' said Polly, agog. 'But it's not my birthday or anything.'

'It's a missing-you present,' India told her. 'Because the second I saw it I wished you were with me to see it too, and I missed you like mad.'

'Go on, Poll',' urged Mikey. 'Open it.'

Tongue between her lips in intense concentration, Polly unfolded the tissue paper. Went absolutely still as she stared at the aboriginal bracelet. Then she made a sound at the back of her throat, a half click, half grunt, and picked it up, carefully inspecting the polished black wood decorated with tiny white and yellow dots, the shadows of brown that could be roos, could be dogs or porcupines, India couldn't tell, but Polly obviously could.

'I can see a camp,' she said breathlessly. 'And a waterhole. A flock of cockatoos.' Thrusting it up her skinny arm she appraised it against her skin, and then the little girl's smile burst like the sun from behind a thundercloud. 'It's got a whole story!' She flung her arms around India's neck. 'It's the best prezzie *ever.*'

Later that day, after an intense debriefing from Scotto, her editor, and her office colleagues, which culminated in an extremely long and alcoholic lunch, India was back at her desk and trying not to think about Mikey's light-hearted reference to getting hitched. It was the fifth time in as many months. But why get married? After all, they were living together, and with Polly they were a family already. She didn't think a piece of paper would make any difference, but Mikey obviously thought otherwise. India rubbed the bridge of her nose. What had Mikey said the last time?

It's the commitment, India. It's saying you love me that much you want me for life too.

She'd thought the life part sounded like a jail sentence but hadn't said anything, just given him a bright smile to cover her dismay and said she'd think about it. She was hoping something would point her in the right direction at some point, like a sign crashing on top of her, lit with flashing lights either saying STOP or GO.

Sighing, she picked up her office phone and started making calls to the major Australian ports. Then she began to work her way through the ports that had two As in their name: Dar es Salaam, Auckland, Jakarta, Punta Arenas, Mar del Plata. A lot of a reporter's life was drudge work like this, and India hoped if she was thorough enough, she'd eventually strike lucky.

With Cuan's go-ahead, the *Sydney Morning Herald* carried her story the following day, with an artist's sketch of the what the bow of *The Pride* probably looked like after the ramming, and offering a reward for anyone who had information about the ship. They received a handful of crank calls after the reward money, but nothing else. The feds kept up their search but had no luck in finding the container ship or the *Kagoshima Maru.*

'Without a distress beacon, it's like searching for a needle in a haystack,' one of the feds told her, sounding frustrated. So India kept ringing round the ports, reminding people she was still looking, trying to keep the dented container ship at the forefront of their minds.

It wasn't until the end of the week when she spotted her tail.

A woman in her twenties, with a fat kid in tow.

Six

The woman didn't always have the boy with her, which was why India reckoned she hadn't spotted her earlier. The woman wasn't always around either, and India guessed she took her tailing duty in turns with someone else. Who, she couldn't tell. They were obviously much better at the job than the woman because she never saw anyone remotely suspicious.

Her awareness heightened, India began to notice other things. Like when she came into her office on Friday morning her computer keyboard was on the right of her screen when she always pushed it to the left after she'd finished typing. And the papers on her desk weren't quite as she remembered leaving them.

She checked with the cleaning crew, but they only cleaned the news team's offices on Sundays, when the place was pretty much empty. India asked them to give her office a miss this weekend, and before she left, made a mental note of how her desk looked, exactly where her pens and notebooks were, her dictionary and Thesaurus, how the insides of her desk drawers were arranged.

On Monday, it all looked exactly the same. At first glance, that was, because everything, she realised, was just a little out of kilter, but what clinched her concern was when she checked her computer. Under *file* were four documents that had been opened in her absence.

All were to do with *Sundancer*'s sinking.

'But we've security.' Scotto pulled off his little gold-rimmed glasses and rubbed the space between his eyes. 'Nobody can just walk in off the street and go through your stuff.'

'Quite.'

'What about the cleaners?'

'They swear they never came near it, and I believe them.'

'What do you think they're after?'

India told him about the files which had been opened, adding, 'My guess is they want to see how far I'm getting with finding the container ship.' She gave a long sigh. 'Which is pretty much nowhere.'

'You talked to Mikey about this?'

'Not yet. I don't want to worry him.'

Scotto made a humming sound. 'You want locks installed for your office?'

India thought it over. 'No. I don't want to alert them. I'll keep anything sensitive with me. But if you see anyone in my office—'

'I'll arrest them myself,' Scotto said.

The next few days were spent going to funerals, and no matter how hard India looked she couldn't see any sign of anyone keeping tabs on her. Mind you, they'd have to have huge resources and be incredibly well organised considering she'd flown to Melbourne on Tuesday morning, Brisbane that afternoon, and then to Western Australia on Wednesday. No man with a pony tail was waiting for her in Perth's domestic terminal, and nobody appeared to follow her hire car out of the airport, nor up the highway. As she approached Geraldton there were no vehicles behind her at all, and India finally felt herself relax.

Her mood lasted until after Ned's funeral and she discovered that Ellie wasn't staying with her parents.

'Aren't you worried about the curse?'

Ellie looked away.

'But what about the baby?' India insisted, and went on to

tell Ellie what the pathologist had said about the constriction in Ned's lungs. 'You can't stay there.'

'He's all around me at home.' Ellie gestured helplessly. 'I don't want to be anywhere else. Maybe in a few weeks I'll feel differently, but not now, India.'

The next service was for Marie, back in Brisbane, but India didn't see anyone following her there, or at Emma's, held up in drought-torn Northern Australia. Standing ankle-deep in red dust, sweat pouring in the forty-degree heat, India watched Katy park next to her hire car and hop out, looking as cool as only the air-conditioned driver of a brand-new top-of-the-range Land Cruiser could.

'What's with the stickers?' India gestured at the GET ACTIVE! logos plastered all over the Land Cruiser. 'I thought you were up here saving the Bilby from extinction, not advertising a fitness regime.'

'It's William's new name for his company. He chose it to mean *get active* and support his products and therefore support the environment. He's hoping it'll increase sales.'

India raised her eyebrows. She'd have thought William's sales were doing fine considering he'd been listed as one of the wealthiest men in Australia last year. The biggest producer of green household products in the country, William's ads were on every TV station telling the public that his washing-up liquid and floor polish did the same job as any competitor but with far less harm to the environment. His logo was a leaping dolphin with a man streamlined alongside, one hand on the big fish's dorsal fin, and not only had *Sundancer*'s cupboards been filled with William's eco-friendly cleaning materials, but hers and Mikey's were too. William's company, India seemed to recall, had also recently invented an apparently ecologically perfect, self-disposing package.

'Is he involved with Ecopac?'

Katy beamed. 'Isn't he brilliant?'

Brilliant wasn't the half of it, India thought, Ecopac was

going to change the world. All those plastic orange juice and milk cartons would no longer clutter landfill spaces but would be turning brittle beneath the Australian sunshine and disintegrating into sand.

'Well done him,' India said, impressed. 'When's it being launched?'

Katy glanced at a dusty airstrip running alongside the road, then at the sky, frowning. 'He'll tell you himself, when he gets here, that is. He's panting to meet you.'

The faint sound of organ music reached them, and they took one dismayed look at each other before bolting through the simmering heat for the little whitewashed church.

After the service, feeling seriously dehydrated, India was walking to her hire car and a litre of mineral water when she heard her name being called. She turned to see a dark-haired man in his early forties striding towards her. Nice suit, she thought appreciatively, and bet it was hand tailored. He had that look about him even if he was sweating hard in the heat. Smooth and sophisticated.

'India Kane?'

'Yup.'

He held out a hand. 'I'm Katy's husband. William Hughes.'

She covered her surprise that he wasn't nearer Katy's age by shaking his hand enthusiastically and saying, 'Hey! Great to meet you!'

He grinned. 'It's my pleasure, believe me. She told me you saved her life.'

'Well, if I hadn't, I'm sure someone else would have.'

'I doubt it,' he said.

Always uncomfortable with praise, India shrugged.

'I'd like you to join Katy and me for lunch, if you're free. And thank you profusely and at great length—'

'I'd love to have lunch,' she interrupted, 'but only if you promise not to thank me any more.'

He gave a small smile and inclined his head in graceful acceptance. 'Can't I do it once?'

She gave another shrug. Brushed sweat from her eyes.

He nodded solemnly. 'We'd best get it over with, then.'

He was teasing her, she realised, and she smiled.

'Okay,' he said, and taking both her hands in his, he studied her gravely, then bent his head and kissed her on each cheek. No airbrushing, but firm kisses where she felt his lips imprinted on her skin. Flushing and feeling awkward, she willed herself not to move and respect whatever Katy's husband felt he had to do.

Still holding her hands he said solemnly, 'Thank you, India Rose Kane, for saving the life of the woman I love. I owe you a debt that should you ever need to call on me, I swear I will honour.'

Deftly he shifted so that they stood side by side, her arm through his. His grin was back. 'I've brought a picnic.' He pointed at a light aircraft parked at the end of the airstrip. 'Fresh seafood and Chablis okay by you?'

Back in Sydney, India continued watching out to see if she was being followed, but she didn't see anyone, and her office appeared untouched. Finally she allowed herself to think they'd given up. Which was a big relief, aside from the fact she didn't know who they were or what, precisely, had been their intention. One of life's weirder mysteries, she thought, and wondered if she'd ever discover what it had all been about.

The media coverage over *Sundancer*'s sinking continued steadily through the following months. TV shows interviewed Greenpeace survivors, and the Government was calling for international co-operation in finding *The Pride*, but absolutely nothing turned up. It was as though the ship had vaporised. Had it sunk after the collision? Or had the owners scrapped it before it could be found?

Refusing to be disheartened at the lack of progress, India kept plugging away, faxing and phoning ports and reminding harbour masters from Mexico to Madagascar that she was still searching for the container ship that had left thirty crew to die in the Southern Ocean, but it wasn't until winter blew in that she got her first lead.

Late July, she was shaking out her umbrella after dashing out for some lunch. Soaked from the knees down thanks to a rain storm, she kicked off her shoes and dumped her burger on her desk before checking her messages. Excitement rushed through her when she heard a boyish voice asking if there was still a reward out for information on the container ship. India immediately rang him back.

'I've someone who knows your ship,' he told her. 'How much will he get?'

God, she thought, he sounds about twelve years old. It has to be another wind up.

'What ship?' she snapped at him, hoping he'd get scared and hang up.

'How much?' he insisted.

'Look,' India said, sighing, 'the reward is for real, hard information about the Greenpeace disaster. Unless you have—'

'What will I get?' His voice turned whiny, but her antenna twitched when she noticed he'd changed the 'he' to 'I'.

'That depends.'

'On what?'

'Whether it's the right ship.'

'How about *The Pride of Tangkuban*, then? It's a dry cargo ship operating in the Indian Ocean. Ninety-one metres of rust bucket with a socking great dent in its bow.'

India nearly crashed from her chair.

'Four winches and derricks,' the boy was saying, 'one big hatch. Indian master, Philippino crew.'

'Okay, okay,' she gasped, amazed she was still sitting down. 'It sounds like her.'

'So how much?'

'Where is she? Are you with the ship now? Is she in Australia?' India had to make a huge effort to rein herself in when she realised she was giving him no chance to respond. 'Hello?' she asked after a few seconds, heart thudding. Oh God, had she scared him off? 'Are you still there?'

She heard a hissing sound and after a few seconds realised he was sucking air through his teeth.

'I'm not answering any questions until I've got the money.'

India did some rapid thinking. 'Where are you?'

'Perth.'

Perth was over 4,000 Ks away but she didn't hesitate.

'I'll be there tomorrow. Six-ish any good for you?'

'How much will I be getting?' he persisted.

'It depends, but maybe up to say . . . two grand.'

'Is that all?' He tried to sound casual and offhand, but she could hear the excitement in his voice and knew she didn't need to negotiate any further.

'That's all,' she confirmed. 'Where shall we meet?'

'The Dolphin. It's a pub in Fremantle.' His words came out in a rush. 'And come alone. I don't want no cops or AMSA guys. Just you.'

'How will I recognise you?'

'You won't.'

'But—'

'I know what you look like from the papers.'

When he hung up, India considered whether to call the feds or not and decided against it. They'd only have the pub surrounded and tip the boy off and she had no intention of losing the only lead she had. She got the go-ahead from Scotto and was booking her ticket when she realised she hadn't consulted Mikey. Or thought of Polly, for that matter. God, living with people made life so *complicated*.

That evening, over a late meal of Thai coconut chicken and sticky rice, Polly tucked up in bed with her little teddy bear, India filled Mikey in.

'Scotto's up for it. My flight leaves first thing tomorrow.'

He put down his china spoon and wiped his chin of coconut juice. 'And Polly?'

'Can't your mum have her after school?'

His dumper truck of a jaw tightened. 'Not indefinitely, India. God, you are so single-minded sometimes, you're utterly unaware of anyone's existence aside from yours.'

Refusing to look away and acknowledge the shame spearing her, she said, 'Polly could always come with me.'

His look of horror said it all. 'No way.'

'Your mum it is then.'

'No.' The word was said very flat.

'But where else will Polly—'

'I don't want you to go.'

India stared at him. 'I'm sorry?'

Slowly, Mikey got to his feet. He faced her across the table. 'You're a magnet for trouble. I know you like to see the whites of their eyes, but this time get someone else to do your leg work. Last trip you took, you nearly didn't come back. Or have you forgotten that?'

'Jesus, Mikey, the Greenpeace thing was an *accident*.' She pushed her chair back with a screech on linoleum. 'Are you saying I shouldn't investigate what happened? Stay home with all the doors locked?'

'No, I'm just saying you shouldn't put yourself in danger.'

'I didn't board *Sundancer* thinking she was going to get sunk!'

He crossed his arms, looking satisfied. 'Exactly.'

'I want to know what happened,' she said tightly. 'You of all people must understand that.'

'No, India.' His voice started to rise. 'I don't want this again. It's like a drug to you, it takes over your life. Polly and I cease to exist . . .' He glanced away as though he couldn't bear to look at her. 'You look more alive than I've seen you in ages.'

'Thank you.'

He uncrossed his arms and stood there, fists clenched.

'Shit,' he said suddenly, and strode outside.

She heard Mikey turn on the TV. Oh God, she thought, I should have warned him first, asked him if he'd be okay with it, given him a chance to talk it over. How could I have been so *stupid*?

Peering into the living room she saw Mikey was firmly glued to the TV and she could tell by the way his arms were folded along with the set of his mouth that she'd have better luck making peace with a salt water crocodile, so she washed up – always her way of apologising since she hated any sort of housework – and went to bed.

She'd turned out the light and was already in the thick of sleep when she felt the bed dip. Mikey climbed in and lay with his back turned towards her. India shuffled her backside fractionally towards him, wanting his heat against the cold winter air he'd introduced, but the infinitesimal movement he made told her she wasn't welcome.

Feeling small and shamed, she curled into a ball. She didn't think she'd sleep she felt so miserable, but when she woke it was after dawn, and she felt strong and refreshed. Mikey's breath was on her neck and his right arm hooked around her ribs, the same as usual, as though they were a couple of shrimps glued together.

Seven

Early evening, India collected Ned's ute from the airport, amazed as always at the average Aussie's incredible ability to do favours at the drop of a hat. When she'd called Ellie to tell her she was flying out, and could she stay, her friend hadn't asked her about her transport arrangements, just said, 'My neighbour's due in Perth then, I'll ask her to drop Ned's ute off for you. She'll get a lift back, no worries.'

India hadn't argued. A free car was always welcome, and she promised herself to buy a gift for Ellie's neighbour as thanks.

Driving out of the airport gates, India checked her rear-view mirror. She hadn't seen the man with the pony tail at the airport, but it was worth keeping her eyes open. Especially now she had a lead. But nobody was behind her, no car, no motorbike, not even a bicycle. Driving straight to Fremantle, known affectionately by the locals as Freo, she killed some time wandering the art galleries and shops before her meeting, checking people out of the corners of her eyes, over her shoulder. She was surprised at the feeling of disappointment each time she saw no one was there.

It was dark when she finally headed for the Dolphin. Sticking her head around the door she saw a crowded bar, filled with smoke and noise and the smell of sweat and beer. ACDC were belting out 'Highway to Hell' on the jukebox and two thickset men in overalls were arm-wrestling in the corner, surrounded by a cheering mob. Through a room on the right she could see men playing darts and pool, and five scantily clad and sweating female bar staff were working flat out behind the counter, serving schooners of beer to a queue three deep. Although the atmosphere was buoyant, India hesitated. She didn't think she'd seen so many hard-drinking blokes in such a small space before and wasn't too sure of her welcome. India was dithering in the doorway when she heard her name being yelled.

'Yo! India!'

A shot of relief catapulted her through the door. 'Chief!'

Fremantle's harbour master was wading through the crowd, face red and shining and split with a grin.

'Well if it ain't my favourite reporter.' He beamed. 'Can I buy you a drink?'

'A beer would be great.'

The chief did a queue jump that nobody seemed to mind, least of all a pretty girl with breasts the size of footballs who started pouring a schooner of Emu Export for him without being asked.

'You came to see me?' the chief asked India, eyes bright.

'I'm actually here to meet someone who says they've got my ship.' She bit her lip then added, 'I didn't tell the feds. I didn't want him scared off.'

The chief didn't seem to be fazed at her confession and passed over her beer. 'I won't tell if you don't.'

She raised her eyebrows.

'Harbour masters are meant to be pillars of society.' He glanced at the barmaids and then back at India, expression abashed. 'The management would have a fit if they knew I was here.'

India crossed her heart. 'Your secret is safe with me.'

He chinked his glass against hers before taking a long draught. 'Who's this bloke you're meeting then?'

India ran through her telephone conversation with the kid, and he straightened up, scanning the room. 'Why don't you stay here where I can keep an eye on you? When he turns up, I'll check him out. Make sure you'll be okay.'

Another shot of relief. 'Chief, that would be brilliant.'

'I'll be over there.' He gestured across the room to the far corner where a dozen or so men were squeezed around several circular tables. 'The guys will be well pissed off I didn't bring you over. They're always partial to a pretty face.' He gave her a cheerful leer and she laughed.

She watched his broad bulk weave effortlessly through the boisterous crowd before he settled with his mates, back to the wall. He raised his glass to her and sent her a wink. She did the same back. All the guys at his table turned their heads to her and did the same, which made her laugh again.

Barely five minutes had passed when she felt a hand on her arm. She flinched. The young guy who'd touched her flinched too.

'Shit, sorry,' he said.

'No worries.'

'Sorry,' he said again, eyes jumping around the room like rubber balls. 'You're the reporter, right?'

'India.' She held out her hand and they shook. He had a surprisingly strong grip, even if it was slick with sweat.

'Danny.'

Danny was barely twenty and could have been the archetypal surfer, aside from his hair. Tanned and skinny, long hazel eyes. Black curly hair the same texture as a water spaniel's. Eyes belonging to the same spaniel. She didn't think he'd be any trouble but she still glanced across the room. The chief was nowhere to be seen.

'Where's the money?' Danny demanded.

'Somewhere safe.'

'Fuck.' The spaniel eyes watered in dismay. 'Are you telling me you didn't bring it?'

She was about to respond when a man in a pair of overalls lurched into her, making her spill her beer over her hand and up her arm. Putting her beer down she said, 'It's too crowded here. Let's go—'

'Next door's quieter. Hi, I'm Hank.' The chief pushed a paw out to Danny. 'Hank Gregory. Friend of India's.'

Danny looked taken aback, but he shook.

'Couldn't have a pretty woman unchaperoned in a place like this,' the chief told Danny smoothly. 'I'm sure you understand.'

'But I thought—'

'I won't say a word. Pretend I'm not there.'

With a hand on her elbow, another on Danny's shoulder, the chief ushered them into the room next door, which was fractionally quieter, and took a table in the corner. India shrugged off her coat and draped it over the back of her chair. She sat opposite Danny with the chief between them, broad shoulders propped against the wall.

'Off you go, then,' the chief prompted them.

Danny ran a tongue over his lips. 'Where's the money?'

Reaching into her coat pocket India withdrew the envelope and put it on the table. 'Two grand.'

Two emotions crossed his face in quick succession: greed, then fear.

'So, Danny, how come you know *The Pride of Tangkuban*?'

'I crewed for her.'

Bingo!

'When was this?'

Danny pushed a beer mat away from him with two fingers, then back, away and back. 'January.' He glued his eyes on the table then muttered, 'Sorry.'

What felt like a cold drop of water splashed down India's back. *He'd been on board* The Pride *when they'd collided.*

Keeping her voice calm, she said, 'Tell me who owns the ship.'

'Dunno.'

'What about the master or ship's agent? Its rep? Where can I find them?'

'Dunno.'

'Okay. What port does *The Pride* come from?'

He chewed his lip for a while, then said, 'Jakarta.'

At last, she thought, something concrete. 'That's great, Danny. Now, what were you doing in the Southern Ocean?'

'I never said we were there!' He looked horrified.

She was going to say he'd practically admitted it by saying sorry, but took a breath instead and rearranged her thoughts. 'Okay. Tell me how long you crewed for *The Pride*.'

'Just the once. The master was four crew short in Sydney. They did a bunk just before they were due to sail.'

India frowned. 'Did a bunk?'

'Vanished. They were from the Philippines,' he said, as though it explained everything.

'I take it you're suggesting they're now illegal immigrants in Australia.'

'Damn right I am.'

'And the master was forced to take you and another four crew on from Sydney.'

'Two. We're a bit more expensive than your average Philippino.'

Danny jumped when a man gave a yell behind him, but it was a triumphant bellow from the winner of the pool game, nothing to worry about.

'I see. So what was the master's name?'

He shook his head.

She tried again. 'Where's *The Pride* now?'

'Dunno.' He took in the look on her face and hastily added, 'She dropped me at Chennai and I got work on to Port Elizabeth. Worked the South Atlantic a bit before coming home.'

Chennai, India knew, used to be known as Madras. On the east coast of India, it was an enormous, teeming city with a huge port to match.

'What cargo were you carrying on *The Pride*?'

'Cargo?' The horrified look was back. 'What's that got to do with anything?'

'Just tell me, Danny.'

'No, no. Nothing.' He was shaking his head. 'Dunno nothing about any cargo.'

'Surely you must have some idea,' she insisted, and spun the envelope on the table but this time he didn't react. Two beads of sweat worked their way from his hairline and down his forehead but he seemed oblivious and didn't wipe them away. 'You get the lot if you tell me.'

'Honest, I don't know.' Danny's tone turned desperate, spaniel eyes on hers, pleading. 'I swear it. I was just employed for a couple of weeks. Help out, fill in for those blokes who let their master down. That's *all*. I don't know nothing about any cargo, okay?'

'So what's the problem?'

'Nothing!'

Like hell, she thought. The second she'd mentioned the word cargo he'd acted as though he'd sat on a firecracker.

'Danny, give me a name. A broker, a company shipping with you, anything you saw on a lading bill, *any name*.'

He made to stand but the chief put a hand on the boy's shoulder and pushed him back down.

'Let me go,' he begged.

'No,' said the chief quietly.

Danny was practically quivering with anxiety and she doubted she'd get any more out of him, not even a weather report. She was about to give him two hundred bucks and let him go, when he said, 'Harris and . . . I can't remember the second part.'

'It's a company?' She leaned close, tone urgent. 'Where did you see it?'

There was a long silence while she looked at him and he tried desperately not to look at her.

'Shit,' he said, dragging a hand down his face. 'Look, we took some stuff of theirs on here in Freo. Will that do?'

He made to grab the envelope but India was faster.

'Sorry, Danny,' she said, 'but what you've given me is hardly two grand's worth of information.'

She gave him 600 bucks and watched him stuff it into his back pocket. The chief raised his eyebrows at her and she shook her head and let Danny leave. Shoulders hunched and without looking right or left, he scurried between two strapping blokes holding pool cues and shot outside like a terrified rabbit.

'Thanks, Chief,' she said and, grabbing her coat, pelted after him.

Eight

The wind was bitingly cold and she pulled her coat collar close around her throat as she followed Danny's hurrying figure down the street.

An unshaven man in a ragged woollen overcoat strode past her for the Dolphin; otherwise the street was empty. Just rows of parked cars discoloured by street lights and shops with their shutters down, litter and dead leaves skittering in the gutters. In summer the place would be heaving, but in midwinter when the wind was up, people stayed inside.

Her footsteps sounded loud as machine-gun fire on the pavement but Danny didn't seem to hear. He was walking fast, almost trotting, head down, oblivious to everything but his urge to get away. At the newsagent on the corner he turned right and then left at a crossroads. A car drove past, music booming, and disappeared.

India reckoned Danny was going home. Home would be digs of some sort, a temporary shelter until he got another job on another ship, and all she wanted was to see where he was staying so she could let the feds know. After all, Danny hadn't told her not to tell anyone about their meeting, just that she should come alone, and she had no doubt the feds would lean hard on Danny and squeeze a lot more information out of him than she had.

Another couple of turns, and then she saw a sign that told her exactly where Danny was headed. The Flying Angel Club. Every major port around the world had one. Owned by the Church of England, it was a Mission to Seamen, nicknamed because of its symbol of an angel. She should have known that's where he'd be staying. It was the perfect place for a crew member to rest up, where they'd be among people who knew which ships were in port, and where to find work.

A car drove past and as it approached Danny it showed its brakes and slowed almost alongside him. Her first thought was that it was an unmarked cop car checking him out, but then it accelerated past him and she didn't think anything of it until it stopped and two guys got out and started walking Danny's way. Nothing wrong with that, but the car's engine was still running, the rear door open, and the driver's head was turned, watching his companions. He expected them back any minute.

India saw the guys walk towards Danny, one on either side, almost as though they were readying themselves to block him if he made a run for it. She felt a surge of apprehension. Were they muggers? Or was she overreacting? Maybe they were friends of his ... But their body language was all wrong. They were walking purposefully, arms swinging loosely at their sides . . . She thought she saw a metallic glint in one of the men's hands. Oh, God. Was it a gun? Apprehension abruptly turned to alarm.

'Danny!' she yelled.

His body jerked around at her shout and the two men paused.

'Look out!'

He was still looking at her when one guy lunged at him, bringing him to the ground. Danny was struggling, but the guy was punching, hitting him, and she was backing away, fingers fumbling for her mobile in her pocket, when the other guy peeled away and sprinted straight for her.

Oh shit. No time to phone . . .

India turned and tore back the way she'd come, racing for the safety of the pub and the chief. Head down, she charged to the end of the street and swung left, and then left again. She could hear the man's footsteps pounding behind her as she belted right, tearing down the next road, her eyes fixed on the crossroads ahead and praying she could keep the distance between them constant, hoping beyond wild hope she might even extend it.

She hit the crossroads and as she pelted right her boots skidded on a handful of wet leaves and the next instant she was falling. Slamming on to her hip she felt the breath rush out of her body but her hands were pushing her upright, her feet scrambling, and she was trying to take a lungful of air when she saw the man rushing at her, saw the glint of metal in his hand.

The man had a knife.

Fear rocketed a rush of oxygen into her lungs and propelled her down the street. Legs and arms going full pelt, her breathing uneven and ragged from her fall, her right side aching fiercely, she pushed her body hard, forcing it to keep running. His footsteps were closing in now. She spun left at the next junction and could see the pub brightly lit at the end of the street but nobody was around. Nobody walking their dog, not even a car driving along, and she was running as hard as she could, cold air like stripped foil in her throat and she wanted to scream for help but she had no breath.

She heard the man behind her grunt. Say something that sounded like, 'You . . .' And felt him slam into her from behind. His hands went around her thighs, her knees. The bulk of him bringing her down.

She crashed on to the pavement. All her breath was gone. Not even a whimper in her throat. Just a screaming need to inflate her lungs, but there was a huge weight on top of her, crushing her on to bitumen and she was struggling, wriggling beneath him, and she could smell his breath as his head aligned with hers. Bitter and antiseptic, like crushed herbs.

She could see light spilling from the pub door. A handful

of people fell outside and her gaze was fixed on them, the way they moved unsteadily, full of beer, clapping each other on the back. They were her saviours but she couldn't speak, couldn't shout. She had no breath against the bitter herbs in her senses, and she could feel the man's arm drawing back and she thought, He's going to stab me! Jesus, no!

She grabbed a lungful of air but his hand pressed against her mouth, stifling her shouts, his body on top of her, heavy as a bear, and she was trying to fight him, get to the guys outside the pub, when she realised the man on top of her was speaking.

'Shut the fuck up.'

His words barely permeated her panic and she continued to fight, yelling against his hand and bucking against his weight and he was gasping into her ear, into her hair, '*Shut up.*'

She lessened her struggle a fraction and felt the man's grip across her mouth ease and she looked at the light pouring from the pub, the men dispersing and she took another lungful of air to shout for them, but the man on top of her clamped his hand back over her mouth.

'Shut it, or I'll fucking suffocate you.'

She tried to bite his hand but he simply pressed his palm harder against her face, so she could barely move her head, let alone make a sound.

'Chill out, bitch,' he murmured.

The men from the pub were walking away. Two heading north together, three south, a single man tottering unsteadily towards them.

'You chilled yet?'

She stopped struggling and concentrated on the man stumbling their way. She gave a nod.

'I'm going to let you up, okay?'

She gave another nod.

'You try and bite me again, and I'll hit you so hard your ears will ring for a week. Get it?'

Another nod and the weight of him rose off her and as his hands pulled her upright she stumbled slightly, then they slid over her stomach and came to rest beneath her ribs, his chin nestled on her shoulder as though they were lovers.

The man from the pub was nearing. Maybe twenty metres away, muttering, half-singing to himself.

'You shout at that bloke for help,' he murmured, 'and I'll slip this knife beneath your ribs quicker than a snake slips under ground.'

The man weaved his way along the pavement, footsteps careless and loose with alcohol.

As he approached, India bunched her muscles and felt her captor do the same, easing his body close to hers, so close she could feel the strength of his thighs against hers, his belly against the small of her spine, and she could feel something pressing into her and for an instant she thought it was a cosh or a gun, but with a shock she realised it was neither.

The man had an erection.

A rocket of anger and fear shot through her but he'd been ready for her and his right arm came up and she felt the cold press of steel against the side of her neck. His knife. Held just below her ear and hidden by handfuls of hair.

'Don't,' he hissed.

He was breathing hard and she could feel his breath against her cheek. The smell of rosemary and thyme crushed underfoot.

The man from the pub shambled past them with barely a glance, mumbling incoherently.

India turned her head to try and follow where he went but the man said, 'Don't even think about it,' and held her even more tightly against him. She couldn't feel his erection any more. She hoped he'd lost it for ever, that he'd never get it up again . . .

Concentrate, she told herself. He's relaxed, just a tiny bit now the drunk has passed and his hand isn't pressed as hard against your face ... Slowly she pulled a little air into her lungs, just a little more than usual, and the next instant his hand clamped across her nose and mouth.

'You fucking bitch,' he hissed. 'You never give up, do you?'

She could hear the shuffling of the man from the pub lessen and gradually disappear. Desperately she stared at the pub door, praying for it to open, but she knew full well it might be another half hour until the next mob spilled out.

'Twenty minutes before the next lot,' he said, reading her mind. 'So how about we take stock here, take a break. Maybe we can talk about our pal Danny boy. You up for that? A bit of talk about our mutual friend?'

India forced herself to give a nod.

'You make a run for it, and I'll split you wide open with this knife of mine. You know that, don't you, bitch?'

Another nod.

'I just want a little chat that's all. Well ...' He gave a dry chuckle. 'I'd like something more, but under the circumstances ... Okay, so let's keep it chilled, bitch ...'

She felt the knife ease slowly away, his grip slacken from her waist and she heard him say again, 'Bitch,' in such a satisfied tone she nearly turned on him then but she forced herself to wait. Wait until the weight and heat of him fell from her back and in that instant, fast as a cat, she planted her right foot forward and swung her body round, till she was face to face with him, his mouth opening in shock as her right knee unerringly connected high and deep in the space between the thighs that had been pressing against her all that time.

He went down like a stone.

India watched him gasping and writhing for five seconds or so, then she bent over his ashen form and said, 'See you around, *bitch*.'

Nine

It was well after midnight when India arrived at Jimbuku Bay and its smartie-bright houses scattered carefully along the beach. The wind was up, but for once she didn't care. It smelled sharp as fresh-cut limes, sliced green and clean and edged with salt, and she welcomed the sensation of purity after the past few hours.

Luckily Ellie was already in bed, so India opened a bottle of red and took it to the bathroom. She turned on the taps, peeled off her clothes and dumped them on the floor. Her right hip and knee were aching and her thigh was already turning an ugly blue-black. She had a bloody graze on her cheek and she carefully washed it with some cotton wool dipped in a little warm water and some Dettol she found in the cupboard. Once she'd bathed the blood away it didn't look as though she'd been slammed face down on to the pavement, it resembled a rash.

She sank into the bath, expecting herself to relax, but instead she found herself grabbing a cake of soap and a sponge and she was scrubbing and scrubbing her body, trying to wash away the memory of Knife-man's belly pressing into the small of her spine, his thighs against hers, his goddam *erection*.

India slugged back some wine and washed some more, cursing to herself, feeling dirty and more afraid than she wanted to admit.

After a while she let some water out of the bath, topped it up with more hot along with a generous helping of Ellie's scented bath oil. She downed another glass of wine, then lay back against the porcelain, letting the scent of wisteria and jasmine do their stuff.

Finally she allowed her mind to drift over the evening's events. After kneeing Knife-man to the ground she'd raced to the pub and, ignoring the startled stares of his mates, grabbed the chief and dragged him outside.

'You were attacked?' he'd said, looking appalled. 'You okay?'

'I'm fine, Chief, but I'm more worried about Danny. Would you mind coming with me to check out his digs?'

The Flying Angel Club told them Danny wasn't there and hadn't been all evening. She'd talked over what Danny had said about *The Pride* with the chief, who told her the ship was probably running under a flag of convenience. 'Jakarta doesn't have the regulations we do here. Australia's tight as a duck's arse, can barely move for regos, but if you're from Jakarta you can do pretty much whatever you want.'

He chewed his lip then added, 'What I can't understand is how *The Pride* came into port. Danny said they'd picked up cargo from Freo but it doesn't make sense. We only accept classified ships. You know, those who've been designated safe and seaworthy, and from what I've heard *The Pride* doesn't fit that particular bill. I don't get it.'

Nor did India.

When the chief escorted her back to her car, he suggested they went to the cops and India reluctantly agreed, praying it wouldn't take long. She was bruised and sore and could already feel her muscles stiffening.

They were dealt with by a meticulously polite Sergeant Kuteli who recorded their statements with an air of brisk efficiency. Late thirties, he was dressed in a wool jacket, nicely cut, and grey trousers, and looked fit and athletic. He had a tan that told her he spent time outdoors, and from the frayed skin around his nose and forehead, she guessed it might be sailing.

Danny's description, Kuteli told them, would be circulated, and the department would do everything they could to find him. India suggested informing the federal police about the evening's events, including the fact that *The Pride* came from Jakarta, and Kuteli made notes, saying he'd add that to his report to them in the morning, no worries.

Eventually, Kuteli put his pen down and began to push back his chair, bringing the interview to a close, but India resolutely stayed in her seat and took a deep breath. 'There's something else,' she managed.

Kuteli frowned, but he sank back into his chair.

'The man who attacked me . . .' She had to force the words out. She couldn't look at Kuteli or the chief as she spoke about Knife-man's sexual response to the attack. Afterwards, there was a huge silence. Kuteli glanced at the window then down at the floor, biting his lip, looking as though he wanted to be anywhere other than where he was.

India squirmed, and she could feel the apology rising to her lips when the chief said, very quietly, 'Christ, India, you should have said.'

She shrank a little against his look of reproach but then he was leaning across and he had taken her chilled hands between his own two warm ones and was holding them gently, carefully, so if she made the slightest movement they'd be free. But she didn't move, didn't want to break free. She felt like she had when Cuan had enfolded her in his arms on the *Kagoshima Maru.* Cared for and loved and accepted.

Still holding her hands, the chief fixed his gaze on Kuteli. When he spoke, he pushed his shoulders back, and his voice was strong and too loud for the small space of the office. It was as though he was making an oath and she was suddenly reminded of Katy's husband, William, his statement that should she ever need him, he would be there for her. But the chief's statement was somewhat less romantic, and much more to the point.

'Should I ever meet this bloke,' the chief said, voice hard and angry, 'no matter where or when, I will nail his fucking balls to the fucking floor.'

She'd given a bark of startled laughter, but where Kuteli was looking shaken, almost embarrassed, the chief's face was set like granite.

The following morning her body was stiff and achy, and as she got dressed India checked herself over and saw the bruises had multiplied and were turning a spectacular purple-blue down the length of one thigh. Her right knee looked as though it had been smeared with ink. God, Mikey would have heart palpitations. She'd have to get undressed in the dark. After downing a couple of painkillers she made a call on her mobile.

'Hey, India, got your scoop yet?'

'Er . . . Not quite. Actually, I need a favour to achieve that little goal.'

'How big a favour?' Scotto sounded guarded.

'Do you know anyone in Jakarta?'

'Why?'

'That's where the ship that rammed *Sundancer* comes from. She's called *The Pride of Tangkuban.* Ninety metres long, four derricks and one big hatch.'

Silence.

'I'd go myself, but she's probably at sea and could remain there for months. I need someone who lives there, who can scout around and ring us when she turns up.'

'Are you sure it's *The Pride* that whacked you guys?'

'One hundred per cent.'

'I'll find someone.' Scotto sounded determined. 'No problem, India. I'll get on to it today.'

Propped by the kettle – which Ellie knew was India's first port of call in the morning – she found a note saying Ellie had gone to stay overnight with her parents but would be back for supper the following day, around six p.m. A PS informed her that Katy and William had invited them to a barbecue the following week, and that she'd better not forget or she'd be boiled alive by the lot of them.

Smiling at the prospect of seeing her friends again, India made herself a pot of coffee, then checked out the *Yellow Pages.* Danny had mentioned taking some stuff on board *The Pride* at Freo from a company with Harris in its name, and she hoped she'd get a clue . . . Five minutes later she gave a groan and shoved the slab of *Yellow Pages* aside.

There had to be over thirty companies containing the name Harris in the area, covering anything from clothing stores to motor accessories. Jesus, she'd be driving around the state for the next two weeks if she did her job properly. An advertisement in the phone book may announce what each company did, but it wouldn't give her the clue she was looking for. She'd only get that by scrutinising each firm and making sure they were who they said they were. As Mikey had said, she liked to see the whites of their eyes. Still groaning to herself, India re-read Ellie's note and wrote one back.

Gone for days if I do what I'm meant to do. Don't send out a search party until the end of the week, just send supplies. A case of Bombay Sapphire wouldn't go amiss.

Feeling slightly depressed, she stood by the kitchen window and stared outside. The sky was raw, a shrieking blue between fast moving clouds, and the bottle brushes and banksias, the feathery bracken ferns, were being lashed from side to side. Three rosellas sped past, flashing red and green, and as she followed their flight she saw a cop car cruise down the street. There were two cops up front, and they were craning their necks left and right and looking at house numbers. Gradually, the car slowed and, to her dismay, parked right outside. Her heartbeat went into overdrive when both cops put on their caps and walked up the front pathway, rang the doorbell.

'Miz Kane?' the taller officer asked.

'Yes.'

'You've a couple of minutes?'

Her mind was speeding, evaluating and absorbing the two cops. Faces neutral. No tension. Hands relaxed and by their sides. Guns in their holsters. No handcuffs that she could see.

'Sure,' she said. 'Come in.'

She led them into the kitchen and offered chairs. Both preferred to stand. Putting on the kettle, she asked what they'd like. Two teas would be lovely, thanks, if it's not too much trouble. India fetched mugs and milk, grateful for the distraction to hide her nerves bundled and sharp as barbed wire.

Voice calm, polite as can be, she said, 'How can I help you?'

The taller one introduced himself. Sergeant Block: middle-aged, medium height and build, a plain face scored by lines which suggested he'd been biffed around by life a bit. Shorty was Constable Thomas, young and muscular with sandy hair and a tentative handshake.

While the kettle rumbled, Block consulted a notebook. 'We've a statement from you stating you were at the Dolphin last night.'

A sense of dread uncurled like a snake awakening in her belly.

'Yes, that's right.'

'You spoke with Danny Fawcett.'

'Danny . . .' She swallowed. 'Is he all right?'

'Er . . . did you know him well?'

The snake in her belly gave a long shiver, then lay still. 'Oh, God,' she said, and briefly closed her eyes. 'He's dead, isn't he?'

Small silence. Then Block said, 'Why would you think that?'

Her eyes snapped open. 'You said *did.* Past tense.'

There was a pause while the two cops cleared their throats and shuffled their feet, then Block spoke. 'I'm very sorry.'

'Me too.' Her fingers were trembling so she turned away and concentrated on making tea. Handed them their mugs. Nodded when they said, thank you, very kind, then she lit a cigarette. She'd promised Ellie she wouldn't smoke in the house, but this was an emergency.

'How did he die?' she asked.

'He was stabbed.'

The snake awoke, writhing into coils of nausea. She could smell the bitter herbal breath of the man who'd called her *bitch* and feel the steel of his blade against her neck, the stiffness of his erection.

'Oh Jesus,' she said.

'Would you like to sit down?' the constable asked. He was watching her anxiously.

'I'm okay, thanks.' She took an unsteady pull on her cigarette.

'I know you've already made a statement,' Block said, 'but if you wouldn't mind, we'd like to run over it with you. When was the last time you saw Danny?'

India knew the drill all too well. First, establish the movements of the victim until their death. Second, confirm the last positive sighting of the victim. She reckoned she was probably the last person to see Danny alive. Aside from his killers.

'Last night, at seven p.m. On his way to The Flying Angel Club.'

'You walked home with him?'

'No. I just wanted to see where he was staying, for the Maritime Safety Authority guys in Canberra. You see, I'd been talking with Danny about the Greenpeace incident . . .'

As she spoke, the constable made copious notes while Block interjected with the odd question. She was on her third cigarette when Block's gaze narrowed.

'Tell me about the man who attacked you.'

She described Knife-man in as much detail as she could. His jeans and fleece, neat brown hair, big boots, maybe Timberlands. Clean shaven. Mid-forties or so and fairly fit. A squashy-looking face, no angles. Pale eyes, not brown, maybe blue or grey. A mole on his right cheekbone.

The constable seemed impressed. 'You've a good eye for detail.'

India nodded, saying it certainly helped her in her job, but Block was studying her intently. 'Mid-forties, you say.'

'Yes.'

'Not early twenties?'

She shook her head. 'No way.'

Block was staring at her so hard, she decided to change the subject. 'Where was Danny's body found?'

He ignored her question. 'You say he had brown hair.'

'Dark brown. It was difficult to tell with the streetlights. But it wasn't black like an Asian guy might have, and it wasn't grey.'

'Not blond?'

It was her turn to stare back at him. 'Absolutely not.'

'You mentioned he was fit just now. What did you mean by that?'

'He ran fast, and when he caught up with me he wasn't breathing particularly hard. He had a wiry build. Strong and muscular.'

'Timberlands,' was Block's next prompt.

'Big boots,' she agreed. 'Heavy.'

'Not sneakers?'

'Are you trying to trip me up here?' she asked him sharply.

Short silence.

'Can you remember who took your statement?'

She felt her eyes narrow into slits the size of matchsticks. 'Don't tell me you can't.'

'I just want to confirm who you spoke to, that's all.'

'Sergeant Kuteli.'

The constable started and glanced across at Block, who looked as though he'd bitten on a stinging nettle.

'Is there a problem with Sergeant Kuteli?' she asked.

Huge pause while Block stared at the piece of paper in his hand and the constable chewed his lip.

'No problem,' the sergeant eventually said, and then he ran through what else she could remember. Any details of the car she'd seen, other vehicles in the street, bikes or vans, makes and number plates, and when he ran out of questions, she repeated her own about where they'd found Danny's body, not really expecting him to answer but unable to prevent her innate persistence.

To her surprise, he said, 'It was unearthed on a municipal dump out of town.'

'When did he die?'

'The forensic department reckons he was killed last night. Between eight and two.'

She tried to hide her shudder, but Block caught it. 'Those two men,' she managed.

'Yes,' he said. 'I'd like to talk to them.'

Ten

After the cops had gone, India cleared the mugs and washed the ashtray. She opened the windows, and went and smoked another couple of cigarettes in the shelter of the porch. Last night she'd been glad of the wind, its biting clarity, but today she wished it would ease off a bit. She couldn't hear properly and anyone could come up behind her or to her side without her knowing. It made her jumpy.

She hadn't liked the way the sergeant had intimated Knife-man was a totally different guy to the one who had attacked her, and wondered if he hadn't got someone else's statement mixed up with hers. It wouldn't surprise her, not all cops were great on paperwork, Mikey being a classic example. Rolling her cigarette between her fingers she considered their response to her asking if there was a problem with Sergeant Kuteli. Both cops had been extremely uncomfortable with her question. Which meant what? That they didn't like the guy? That there was some internal politics between them? Or was it something else, something deeper? Shit, she didn't know. Cops had their own agenda, she knew that, and she was on the outside.

India turned her mind to poor Danny, murdered by Knife-man and his mate. Why? Because Danny had talked to her? Had they seen her in the pub with him? Or were they going to kill him and when she'd yelled, decided to come after her?

Maybe we can talk about our pal Danny boy. You up for that?

She took a pull on her cigarette and exhaled, the wind

snatching the smoke the instant it left her lips. Why had Knife-man wanted to talk? To find out who she'd confided in and maybe go after them as well before killing her? God, talk about stepping into a pit of vipers. Would Knife-man come after her again?

Wind blew hair across her mouth and she pulled it free, turning her head into the wind. Across the street she saw a flock of cockatoos being buffeted past the trees, and a dishevelled woman walking along the pavement. Her steps were unsteady, her movements slow, and for a second India thought she was an old woman, someone in their seventies or eighties struggling to the milk bar for a newspaper, a pack of cigarettes, and then she took in the woman's lean tan, the cropped salon-streaked hair and thought, Jesus, she's the same age as me. Is she ill? India was watching anxiously when the woman stumbled and fell to her knees.

India immediately flicked her cigarette aside and raced across to help. Bending over the woman, she said, 'Hey. Are you okay?'

The woman didn't respond. She was staring at her feet, tears leaking down her cheeks. Her clothes were clean but rumpled, her shirt half tucked into her faded jeans, and her hair a tangled mess.

'Can I help you?'

'I can't . . . want . . .' The woman seemed to have trouble speaking.

'Maybe I can ring for a cab. Get you home.'

The woman looked up at her and said, 'Home,' as if she'd never heard the word before.

'Where do you live?'

The woman wiped her eyes then seemed to find some strength and added, 'Number twenty-two.'

India brightened. 'You're nearly there, you know.'

'I was . . . needed some milk.'

'I think you'd be better off at home,' India suggested. 'I can always run down and get it for you.'

'Kind,' the woman said, and rallied further. 'That would be very kind. My husband should be home soon but we've run out of milk. Sam wants Weet Bix, you see . . .'

'Here.' Holding both the woman's hands, India heaved her upright. She'd thought she might have to half-carry the woman to her house, but she seemed to have recovered enough to make it there under her own steam.

Where Ellie had a bright red door, this woman had an eye-blinding yellow one, the colour of sunflowers. India watched her inside, then said, 'How many litres?'

'Three. And . . . I don't want to trouble you—'

'It's no trouble, what else?'

'Orange juice. Without the lumps. Sam hates lumps.'

'So do I,' said India with a smile. 'See you in a tick.'

When she returned, she pressed the doorbell, but nobody answered. She gave it a minute or so, then pressed again. A little boy, maybe five, opened the door.

'Hi, are you Sam?'

He nodded.

'Is your mum in?'

'She's in the bathroom.'

'I brought you some milk. And orange juice, without the lumps.'

He eyed her intently. 'Are you a friend of Mummy's?'

'Yes, I am.'

He opened the door wide, but she remained on the doorstep. Being invited in by a minor wasn't her choice for stepping into a stranger's home.

'Can you carry this inside?' She handed him a litre of milk. 'Then you can come back and get the rest.'

Clutching the carton with both hands, he trotted off, came back.

'Is your mum still in the bathroom?'

He stared at her, eyes big and serious. 'She spends a lot of time in there. She cries a lot.'

'I'm sorry to hear that,' India said gently, and handed

him the next carton, watched him do the next relay. When he returned, she said, 'Has Mummy told you why she cries?'

'Because Pippa died.'

'Pippa?' she repeated, thinking maybe it was a dog or a puppy, and she was preparing to say something appropriately sympathetic when he added, 'She's my sister.'

He trotted off again, leaving India running a hand back and forth over her face, as though she could rub out what little Sam had told her.

I thought if we named our baby after Albert . . . that they'd be safe.

Jesus Christ, what the hell was going on with this estate?

When Sam took the orange juice from her, India said, 'Your mummy's sad. Tell her I'm sad too.'

India went back to the milk bar and asked the guy behind the counter where Albert lived.

'Shoalhaven,' he said. 'Three, Waratah Road. But you won't have any luck. He hasn't been around for yonks.'

India went there anyway. It was better than sitting in a wind-blasted porch smoking cigarette after cigarette and thinking about poor Danny, knifed to death, his body left on a municipal dump out of town.

Shoalhaven, like most of the towns on this stretch of coast, was originally settled by whalers, pearlers and cray fishermen. It was a collection of fibro and weatherboard houses set between the sea and drifting white dunes. The sand was speckled with bain, a succulent, ground-hugging plant currently in full bloom. Bright pinky-mauve petals shivered in the breeze, their centres reminding India of glorious globs of clotted cream.

The main street was a dusty thoroughfare lined with a handful of fishing and grocery stores, and she drove along until she found Waratah Road. She started scanning numbers. When she realised she'd already passed the house, she made a U-turn and parked on the corner. Number three was now a tour company, offering everything from bushwalks and fishing trips to windsurfer hire, with an alley on one side and a café on the other. The front weatherboard wall was blue, the door blue, and even the shutters and window sills were coated blue. It was like a slab had been cut from the sky and plonked in the middle of town.

The words 'Blaze a Trail' had been signpainted in white across the door but the paint had blistered and great flakes had fallen away so from a distance it now read 'Baz Tail'.

A young woman looked up from her computer when India entered. Slim as a wand, she had short, curly black hair, caramel-coloured skin and enormous brown eyes that made India think of Polly.

'Hi,' said the girl with a bright smile.

So help me God, thought India, if Polly turns out half as beautiful when she grows up, I'm in for a tough ride.

'Hi.'

'We're not usually open Sundays,' the girl said, 'but if you want to book a tour I'd be happy—'

'Actually, I'm looking for Albert Jimbuku.'

The smile faded. 'My Grandma's fishing. Come back later, why don't you?'

'She knows Albert?'

'Sure.'

'Do you have any idea where Albert is?'

Sighing as if she'd answered the question a thousand times before, the girl said, 'He hasn't been around since fourteenth August, three years back. Last blokes to see him were down the pub. The Nelson.'

'Where's that?'

'Look, you really ought to talk to Ginny. Go try the jetty. You can't miss her. Just look for an old biddy dressed in orange.'

Before India could ask where the jetty was, the phone rang and when the girl answered it, she swivelled her chair around, pointedly turning her back.

India backtracked to the main street and cruised along the sea front. She'd only gone half a K when she saw a handful of motor boats moored close to shore and a couple of runabouts buzzing across the water and hey presto, there was the jetty, a line of fishermen dotted along it.

Parking beneath a Norfolk Island pine, India picked up her daypack and went to look for an old biddy dressed in orange.

The wooden jetty looked as though it had been there a while, but it was strong and firm underfoot, and stretched maybe a hundred metres over the water. She passed a pair of blokes in their late teens with beers in one hand, fishing rods in the other; a couple of kids with their parents, and an old man with cancers scabbed on his face. Everyone turned their heads and watched her pass. Halfway along, she saw a skinny old black woman flick a small fish out of the water and in two swift movements, had removed the hook and plopped it into a plastic tub on her right. She was dressed in a pair of baggy shorts the colour of marigolds and a bright orange overshirt.

'Hi,' said India. 'My name's India Kane. Are you Ginny?'

The old woman looked up, eyes creased.

'Might be.'

'Your granddaughter said you know Albert Jimbuku.'

'What you be doing asking for Albert?'

'I have a friend who lives at Jimbuku Bay,' India said. The old woman stared at her, the wrinkles on her face deepening. Then she patted the salt-crusted wood beside her, and India hunkered down to sit with her feet dangling over mottled water, deep blue, almost black, a splash of turquoise indicating a shallow just ahead.

Ginny studied India some more while India studied her right back. She had to be at least the same height as India, around six foot, and her grey woolly hair was like a shrunken, newly shorn sheep's fleece glued to her skull. Her wrists looked oversized for her arms, her knees swollen, but she wasn't malnourished, it was just that she was old and very thin, her muscles wasted, but she had an extraordinary energy that belied the fragility of her body.

The old woman suddenly dropped her gaze and took a strip of fish intestine from the block of bloody wood beside her, popped it on a hook and chucked the line into the water.

'So, you'll be wanting to know about Albert's curse.'

'Yes.'

Another silence.

The old woman shifted her buttocks until her left thigh was close to India's, so close their knees were almost brushing. One pair smoothly clad in faded denim, the other bare and wrinkled as a desiccated orange.

'Dreamtime,' the old woman said intently. 'You know what it means?'

'A spiritual linking,' India responded. 'The unity of man and nature. The essence of life and man's continued existence.'

The old woman gave a sigh, of satisfaction India thought, and said, 'Albert was trying to protect his Dreamtime, is all. You know about Neville? That bloke who ran us off our place years back?'

India felt her spirits sag. Yes, she knew Neville. Not personally, mind you, but she'd read about him. God, what a disaster. Despite having no Aboriginal knowledge whatsoever, Neville had been designated Chief Protector of Aborigines in 1905 and for the next twenty-five years anybody who wasn't white had suffered interminably. Aborigines were rounded up and stuck into settlements, children isolated from their parents in order to bring them up to follow a European lifestyle, and come the 1930s, they'd gone from being economically independent, living in the bush or on station land, or on their own station blocks, and were trapped in a cycle of poverty, malnutrition, disease and premature death.

India remembered how shocked she'd been when she learned Aborigines weren't even counted as people until 1967. Before then, they'd been excluded from the national census. Shaped into second-class citizens, they had become outcasts in their own land. India sighed. She'd bet Jimbuku Bay wasn't the only place in Australia that had been cursed by an Aborigine.

Eleven

'You all right?' Ginny was watching her closely.

'Yes,' India said quietly. 'Neville didn't do us any favours, did he?'

'It's a bloody wonder nobody shot the bloke. Nobody liked him, not back then, not now.'

They both fell silent, watching the water.

'So if you know about Neville,' Ginny eventually said, 'you'll know none of us have been about Perth much since.'

India nodded.

'Well, that's why Albert kicked up such a stink. It's a bit of a long story . . .' Ginny squinted at the sky. 'But what it comes down to is Albert's finding his roots after years of looking. His mum died giving birth to him, see, so Albert never got to ask her about his family. He was a mixed-race baby and spent his childhood in various foster homes. All he had was his surname, Jimbuku.

'When he found out his grandad was at the Moore River Camp in the twenties, he managed to track him down. It was his grandad who told him about the time before Neville, those springs at Jimbuku Bay, and how their lot had been celebrating them springs that had given them fresh water from the time man was born. Soon as he heard that, Albert set off there like a rocket, and when he saw a bunch of excavators messing up his spiritual home, well, it kind of did his head in.'

Ginny's right arm suddenly jerked, and a fish with a yellow stripe along its flank popped from the water. Two seconds later it was released into the plastic tub to join the other dozen yellowtail, which India reckoned would be used for bait later in the day. Re-baiting her hook, Ginny tossed it with an expert flick just to the edge of the turquoise shallow.

'The authorities wouldn't help. Nor the council. He reckoned they'd been bribed, so he went back to his grandad, who's a *maban* man, a type of medicine bloke-cum-sorcerer, and he told Albert to call in Jambuwal, the Thunder Man. He's a bit of a bugger, Jambuwal.' Ginny gave a low chuckle. 'He gets really pissed off if you harm him or his people, you see, so most of us stayed away that day. Not so much that we believed Albert ringing up Jambuwal and getting his help as reckoning we'd get banged up for disturbing the peace or something.'

India held herself still, not wanting to disturb the old woman as she relived her memories.

'Wish I'd had his bloody balls and been there, 'cos he got something right. He chucked those intestines to the ground, and old Jambuwal bloody heard him.'

She gave a dry laugh. 'Imagine, all those white people spooked by an Abo covered in paint he'd bought from the local hardware store. But bugger me if a bloody great storm didn't blow up out of nowhere. Gutters got torn off roofs, trees fell over the roads and we all hid like kids beneath the bloody bedclothes. Including Jack and his whole bloody family.'

Frowning, India said, 'Who's Jack?'

'The bloke who built them bloody houses.' Ginny turned her head and spat into the water.

'Where can I find him?'

The old woman didn't look at her, just made a sweeping gesture across her torso that India recognised. It was a sign to keep away evil spirits. Watching Ginny make the gesture three times, India's skin prickled as though someone had dragged a woollen blanket against her bare skin.

'What is it?' India asked.

There was a long silence, then the old woman turned her head. Gave her a searching look. 'You're the first person to ask about Jack. Most just want Albert.'

'But Albert isn't around.'

'Don't we know it.' Ginny gave a shudder. When she next spoke, she leaned close, her voice a whisper as though scared of being overheard. 'His name's Zhuganov.'

'Zhuganov?' India repeated, startled. The Chief Inspector who'd taken her and Cuan's statement after they'd been dropped ashore had the same surname. She asked Ginny if they were related.

Again Ginny made the sign against evil spirits and spat into the water. She murmured, 'They're all related to bloody everybody. Can't move for the buggers.'

'Where can I find Jack?'

The old woman raised her head and fixed her gaze on a cormorant flying with strong, steady strokes just above the sea. 'He retired out Bulimba way. Place called Goondari.'

'When did he—'

'That's all you get.' Ginny jerked her wrinkled old knees away from India's, pulled her whole body aside. It was as though India had suddenly become poisonous, contaminated. 'Just go away, will you? Let me get on with my fishing.'

India left the old woman flipping out another fish, her stick-insect limbs jutting out of her loose orange shirt that flapped around her like a religious robe. As she stepped past the old man with the cancer-scabbed face she heard Ginny call out after her, 'For Chrissakes don't tell him it was me who sent you!'

It took India two hours to get to Bulimba, a one-street town with one garage, a small supermarket and a hotel, and in that time she saw just three other cars and a single road train. Despite the lack of traffic, she'd had her headlights on the entire trip. A southerly had screamed in just after she'd left Shoalhaven, filling the air with clouds of sand and salt spray, and it was like driving through patchy fog. Sometimes a gust would shove the car, making it swerve, so she stayed well below the 100-K limit, not wanting to get blasted off the road.

She passed brick and weatherboard homes, and a little weatherboard church. Maybe sixty residents lived here, but nobody was about. It felt as though she'd happened upon the end of the world. The 'open' sign outside the garage was flat in the middle of the street, which she took to mean the place might be open, so she drove in and asked for directions.

'Keep going through town,' the garage guy said, 'you'll find Jack's place thirty Ks on, to the left. Goondari. Can't miss it.'

He was right. Jack obviously didn't believe in discretion: the sign for Goondari was the size of a billboard poster. *Goondari Stud.*

She swung down the smooth, graded track. For some time the road followed the sea, and India slowed a while to watch the surf which, like the wind, had risen fast. A steady swell was rolling in from the south-west, rising high with spewing crests before crashing against the dunes. The surrounding area was flat and barren, the colour of wet ash, and although India loved the outback, she wasn't sure she'd cope with living out here, in the teeth of the wind.

Gradually the coastal scrub fell away to sheep pasture snarled with limestone. There were thick clumps of bloodwoods, majestic spreading eucalyptus trees that exuded a dark red gum, for stock to shelter beneath, and to her right a dark streak of forest crawled into the distance. When she had to stop and open a couple of gates, she realised the wind had begun to drop. It was still blowing, but not nearly as hard. She switched off her headlights.

Ten minutes later she reached a run-down homestead, a traditional outback home raised on stumps set in the shade of a thick clump of white gums. A tree grew through the iron roof and the verandah had rotted away. It would have been a nice home, but obviously not nice enough for Jack Zhuganov, because half a K on stood another house.

The second she took it in, her foot faltered on the accelerator. Holy fucking cow, she thought, her jaw dropping.

She saw a monolith growing from the earth with angles on the north and south sides and multiple geometric layerings in between. Earth-bermed on its west side, the building had a strangely humped form, like the shoulders of a bull. Three massive square chimneys dominated the horizon, and a shiny roof reflected the dusty colour of the sky. Acres of walls were painted a harsh, cold white, reminding India of Spain, not Australia.

It's like Jimbuku Bay all over again, she thought. It wasn't that it hadn't been well designed, but it *didn't fit in.*

She drove on, feeling Ned's ute rattle over a cattle grid, seeing smart white-painted fences lining the smoothly tended track. She passed banksias ghosted with dust, horses in the paddocks on either side, heads down and ears back, backsides facing into the wind. Beneath a patch of trees was a row of immaculate-looking stables and a red-and-cream horse box. Everything was neat and orderly, except for the rubbish tip encroaching from the near-side paddock and into the front yard.

It was like seeing a pile of bulging bin bags splitting their rotting contents across the front steps of the Opera House. There were two JCBs, countless stacks of tyres, empty oil drums, old cars, sheets of corrugated iron, truck trailers, car trailers and, right in front of the unsightly mess, a shiny red 5-ton Isuzu truck with double rear doors and a pair of silver horns on its snout.

Typical Aussie mentality, she thought with a disgusted sigh. They've got so much space they never think of disposing of their rubbish the way normal people do. Just chuck it aside to rot, like the homestead behind her.

Still shaking her head, India parked at the end of a row of new-looking Nissan Patrol traybacks. She looked up at the tall walls of the monolith, trying to work out where the front door was, and decided it had to be at the top of a dramatic processional stairway dead ahead. There had to be easier access, like a tradesmen's entrance at the rear, but she knew from past experience that people didn't like to be surprised at the back door. Better to ring the front doorbell.

She was halfway up the stairway when five dogs appeared at the top, took one look at her, and broke into a run, hackles high, barking and growling. India wouldn't have minded facing down the spaniel, but no way was she going to mess with four German shepherds. She turned round and sprinted for her car.

Twelve

India slammed the door shut just as a German shepherd launched himself at her, smacking his face against her window with a thud. Undaunted, he and his pals leaped and scrabbled at her door, barking dementedly. Boy, what a welcome, she thought.

A few minutes later a woman appeared and yelled at the dogs, who fell quiet. She came across and India cracked open her window.

'Is Jack around?'

'Yeah. BB's got a bit of a leg on him, so Jack's gone to give him a shot of antibiotics. Just look for a mean black bastard, you can't miss him.'

Unsure whether the woman was talking about a horse or Jack, India cautiously opened her door and climbed outside. One of the shepherds drew back its lips and gave a snarl and the woman turned to kick it but the dog scooted sideways. 'Do that again, Satan, I'll bloody murder you,' the woman warned. 'Sorry,' she added, turning back to India. 'They won't bother you now. And tell Jack I'm off, would you? I'll catch him at the barbie later.'

India thanked the woman, and with the five dogs trailing her at a distance like a gang of recalcitrant yobs, she headed for the stables. The wind had dropped to a stiff breeze and without the murk of dust the light was hard and bright and she pulled her sunnies from her daypack, popped them on.

The stable block was the antithesis of the rubbish tip. Dotted with giant tubs of geraniums, the yard was well tended and clean, and the smart green and white paintwork on the doors fresh. Although the air was thick with the smell of manure, it was only because of the wheelbarrow overflowing with the stuff at the end of the yard, just cleared from one of the stables. Half her childhood had been spent mucking out Aunt Sarah's horses. Not that she'd minded, since in return she was eventually given her own pony. When her parents died, the only relative the social services had been able to dig up – and who'd been willing to take on a seven-year-old Aussie – was her aunt who, as it turned out, wasn't an aunt at all but a distant cousin of her father's, although she'd insisted on being called India's aunt, 'to make things easier all-round'.

Aunt Sarah was a brisk, toughened old bird of fifty who smoked like a chimney and lived in a sprawling old farmhouse north of Oxford with eleven cats, five Labradors, and no central heating. India had been terrified of her until she saw her aunt with her horses and realised she had a heart the texture and sweetness of golden syrup. It was Aunt Sarah who'd paid for her education, her school trips, the deposit on her first rented flat in London, but the first thing she'd done had been to teach her how to ride.

Once India had mastered the basics and was hankering to be allowed to jump, Aunt Sarah had whipped away the saddle and made her do it barebacked, with her arms folded. India fell off so many times she lost count, but by the time she was ten she was bombing bareback around the countryside on her pony and had never been happier.

India made a mental note to ring Sarah sometime. They hadn't spoken for a while, and she would enjoy hearing about her visiting a stud in W.A. where the horses' names were painted in gold and green above their stables: Grafton Diplomat, Grafton Jury, Sunny Side Up.

As she walked along the yard she heard a horse's enraged squeal from a stable to her left, and then there was a clatter of hooves followed by a crash resounding against wood. Cautiously she peered into the stable, pushing her sunnies on top of her head and letting her eyes adjust to the gloom. Skittering on concrete and straw, head taut against a thick rope, was a huge, dusty black horse with a white splash on its near foreleg.

A thickset man held what looked like a syringe and as he neared the horse's head it tried to bite him, but the rope was too tight and it couldn't reach. Despite its dirty coat, she knew she was looking at a prime piece of horseflesh. A stallion, no less. Perfectly proportioned he had an arrogant carriage, and beneath his fine, thoroughbred's skin, she could see the great muscles bunching and flexing with enormous power.

She could feel her throat closing in an automatic Sarah-murmur to gentle the horse as the man approached. Hey, sweetheart, settle down, she said silently, wanting to soothe the animal's distress, and suddenly the creature stopped its thrashing and stilled, swung its head her way as though it had heard her. The next instant the man gave the injection and slapped the horse's neck. The horse promptly swung its rear round and lashed out with both feet, but he'd tied the animal well and the hooves didn't come anywhere near.

With a single twitch, the man released the slip knot and the horse was free. For a second the animal stood there as though stunned, and then it came after him but it was too late. The man was already outside and had bolted the door behind him. He turned to face her, expression smoothly neutral, and with a little shock, she realised he'd been aware of her all the time.

A greasy hat topped a square brown face, chequered with sun spots. Grey stubble. Muscular forearms and hands covered in coarse grey hair. Solid chest. Strong neck and sloping shoulders like a professional boxer might have. Probably in his sixties, but still attractive in a blunt kind of way. He wore a thickly padded red-check overshirt and even though it was midwinter, a pair of shorts, and the usual pair of large, dusty boots every outback farmer wore.

Wearing her most cheerful expression she said, 'I'm India Kane,' and stuck out a hand. He didn't take it. Nor did he offer his name.

Letting her hand fall by her side, she ploughed on. 'I'm a journalist, and I'd love to talk to you about your horses.'

His expression remained the same, but something cold crawled from the back of his eyes and settled there, watching her.

'I'm a farmer,' he said, 'and I don't talk to journalists.'

All the hairs on the nape of her neck stood on end. She felt as though she'd come across an innocuous house spider which had metamorphosed into a deadly black funnel web.

'I'm sorry,' she said, trying not to flounder. 'But you've some terrific animals here. Especially your stallion. And some of the brood mares in the front paddock are seriously stunning. Are they all race horses?'

He continued to stare at her with a stillness that was unnerving, almost reptilian in its quiet patience.

She flinched when he spoke.

'Which magazine?' he asked, tone coldly polite.

'Oh, it's not a magazine,' she lied. 'I work for a publisher who has commissioned me to do a book. A big, coffee-table book, with lots of pictures covering the history of horse racing. Owners, trainers, that sort of thing, from the last century up to today.'

She thought she caught a flash of amusement on his face and her stomach went cold. Had he seen through her?

'I see,' he said.

There was a long silence while he appraised her and she tried not to fidget.

'Why the cold call?' he asked, his voice gravelly and deep, his words measured.

'Because until I'd seen it, I didn't know if the place would be photogenic enough. Most people hate being contacted and then rejected.'

'Why me?'

Still that hint of amusement that kept her entrails squirming in ice.

'Oh, *Horse Australia* magazine. They said I shouldn't miss out on you. They were right.'

He appraised her a little longer while she held her breath, and eventually he said, 'You fancy a beer?'

'I'd love one.' She was almost gasping with relief. 'Oh, I nearly forgot . . .'

But he was already walking to the mansion, obviously expecting her to follow. Hastily, India started after him.

'Er . . . a lady at your house said she had to go. And that she'd see you at the barbecue later.'

He didn't respond, but she didn't repeat herself. He didn't seem like the sort of man who would tolerate being told something twice. And, she belatedly realised, he still hadn't introduced himself, just assumed he didn't need to. God, the arrogance of the man made her want to kick him. Talk about Jack the lord of the fucking mansion.

As they approached his monstrous house she glanced at the row of Nissan traybacks. 'What's with the cars?'

She saw him slide her a sideways glance and although she kept her face purposely bland, he didn't say anything. She gave a careless shrug and concentrated on appearing calm and relaxed so he wouldn't see how much he was unsettling her.

He led her to the back of the house and through a landscaped enclosure with sculpted patio furniture, a jacuzzi, and an enormous pool with a swim-up bar. There were palm trees and thatched umbrellas for shade and sprays of bright red and orange bougainvillaea bushes. It smacked of Thailand, and India said so, hoping to flatter him but getting it completely wrong.

'Not Thailand,' he corrected, looking irritated. 'Indonesia.'

'My mistake,' she said meekly.

Feeling as though she was on a film set, she copied Jack

when he shucked off his boots and padded after him, her head craning from side to side, not wanting to miss a thing. Cool white walls and stretches of pale sand-coloured tiles along a corridor. To her right, black marble in a living room the size of a cathedral filled with heads of dead cape buffalo, oryx and kudu, the floor covered with skins of zebra and, more worryingly, lion, leopard and cheetah.

She followed Jack across more polished tiles and into a room she took to be his own. Jarrah shelves and dark wood floorboards, lots of heavy furniture and thick carpets, stacks of magazines and newspapers, but the chief eyecatcher were the pictures taking up almost the whole of one wall. Horses walking, trotting, galloping in races, but India wasn't interested in them. She was staring at the array of ornate and heavily framed social photographs strategically placed where they couldn't be missed.

Gone was the rough outback farmer and in his place was a man in tailored suits and dinner jackets looking urbane and charming, shaking hands with important-looking people . . . Good grief, Jack was with Bob Hawke in this one, Australia's ex-Prime Minister. And there he was at a barbie with the disgraced Alan Bond, who'd defrauded Bell Resources of 1.2 billion dollars. Interesting social contacts. She leaned closer to one in a hideous bronze frame to see Jack dining with a family somewhere tropical. There were guys in army green behind the diners, and at the head of the table, on Jack's left, sat the former president Soeharto.

Amazed, completely absorbed, she was waiting to see him taking tea with the Queen of England when her gaze latched on to a photograph way down, below waist height. Her heart gave a little leap.

The picture was faded, quite old, and showed a container ship chugging across a still, blue sea.

It had a white accommodation block, one big hatch and four derricks . . . My God, she thought. It could be the same container ship that had run them down, but this ship looked new. However, if the photograph was as old as it looked . . .

Jack had vanished ahead and she quickly ducked down, tried to see the ship's name, but the print was too small. She was squinting at the picture, trying to find something else to identify it, when she heard the distinctive rubber snap of a fridge opening, and she hurriedly rejoined Jack. He was standing in a broad kitchen adjacent to his den and pulling out a couple of stubbies from a fridge the size of her living room. It came as no surprise that it wasn't an Ocean Green model. She couldn't see Jack being green considering the tip outside his mansion.

Ushering her outside, Jack sat beside her on a giant, tiled verandah overlooking the front paddocks, the only concession to traditional Aussie living that she'd been able to see. They were tucked well out of the wind, but the gum trees around the house swung and swayed, the sound of their rattling dry leaves like pebbles being poured into an enamel sink.

Jack chinked his bottle against hers and she noticed his hands were sun-damaged and scarred with white ridges across the knuckles. Scars that went with the sloping fighter's shoulders.

'So, Miz Kane,' he said, 'fire away.'

Still unsure of him, she decided to tread carefully. Taking her micro-cassette recorder from her bag, she popped it between them and opened up her notebook. She was longing to ask him about the photograph of the ship but reckoned on softening him up first by talking about his horses, which he seemed happy to do. He told her that they were a hobby he'd come into late in life, quite unplanned. He'd backed BB at the Boulder Cup races as an outsider and when he won, Jack had bought him, built the stables, and shipped him over.

BB was the black stallion Jack had given the injection to, and was officially known as Grafton Statesman, but after he'd bitten a stable hand so badly he'd had to be hospitalised, the horse had been nicknamed Bloody Bastard.

She found herself tuning out as he talked about the first mares he had bought, which dams were producing the best colts, but nearly jumped out of her skin when he said the name Harris. Luckily Jack appeared so absorbed in reminiscing he didn't seem to notice.

'Harris?' she said.

'And Hewitt. They're just about the only livestock insurers in the area worth dealing with.'

'They're local?'

He paused as though thinking over whether to answer or not, and after a long pause said, 'Down Moora way. Local enough.'

She'd check them out later, she decided, although quite what a livestock insurance company had to do with a rust-bucket of a container ship, she wasn't sure. They couldn't be shipping horses to Antarctica, surely.

She took a small sip of beer. Good old Swan Lager, the state's top beverage, cold as hell and a full five per cent alcohol, guaranteed to put her over the limit if she had the whole bottle. Turning her eyes to the paddocks she saw that a couple of horses had turned broadside to the wind and were cropping the grass.

'So, before you retired happily with your horses, what did you do?'

His face grew guarded.

'I just need an example, that's all,' she said as if it didn't matter. 'I'm not trying to pry, but the readers need something to identify with. You know, Jack Zhuganov, owner of Grafton Statesman and ex-builder or architect or whatever. How about we include a couple of pictures of that fantastic place you built on the coast, Jimbuku Bay? It's incredibly photogenic.'

He didn't say a word.

'I heard there was a big storm around that time,' India

kept plugging away. 'There were rumours it had something to do with a curse. Now that would be a terrific human-interest story.'

His eyes scuttled. India started to sweat.

Desperately wanting Mr Jack I-love-my-horses to return, she hurriedly pointed at an elegant yellow mare in the nearest paddock that had her rump still turned to the breeze. 'She looks Arabian.'

He clicked his eyes to the mare then back. 'Top drawer for my boy.'

'Lucky BB,' she said, and she felt the muscles in her neck relax when the scuttling stopped. With a crack of his knees, Jack got to his feet and waved his empty beer bottle at her. 'You fancy another?'

'I'd love one, but I'm driving,' she said. 'Sorry.'

Jack gave a derisive snort. 'The only bloke on patrol along the coast is a cousin of mine. He won't dob you in if you say you know me.'

Without a beat, India said, 'In that case, I'd love another beer.'

While he was inside India tried to calm herself. Her breathing and heartbeat were up and she didn't want Jack to know how much he was unnerving her. He had an extraordinary charisma about him, she realised, but when he did that creepy thing with his eyes she just about turned around and fled with her tail between her legs. She wanted to jump into her car and never return, but she had to push a bit further, and push Jack too.

When he returned she let him talk some more about his horses and when they were on their third beer, she pulled up her courage from the tips of her toenails and said, calm as can be, 'What's with the photograph of a container ship in your house? Were you into shipping?'

He didn't blink or show any surprise at her question. Just flexed his jaw once and said, very quietly, 'I think it's time you were going, don't you?'

Thirteen

India drove back down the coast slick with sweat. She didn't think she'd interviewed anybody who had scared her so badly before. She knew she'd been treading a fine line when she asked Jack about the ship, and although he'd ushered her to her ute with meticulous politeness, she'd felt as though she'd got away with poking a grizzly bear on the muzzle.

At least she'd learned two things: Jack Zhuganov didn't want to talk about Jimbuku Bay or the ship. Was the ship in the photograph the one that had run them down? After all, Danny said it came from Jakarta, and Jack had that photo of himself dining with Indonesia's former president, Soeharto. Perhaps Soeharto owned the thing, or one of his children. From what she knew they owned just about everything in Indonesia's capital.

She tried to think more laterally but her mind felt fuzzy from the beer sloshing around her system. Hurriedly she checked her speed and slowed to a steady 70 Ks. It wasn't that she might lose her licence so much as should a kangaroo jump across the road, her reflexes would be so slow she'd probably hit it.

She knew if she'd refused Jack's beer he wouldn't have allowed her to stay for as long. It was the way things were out here. You stuck to a glass of water while your companion drank beer, you became an outcast. You drank what they drank, you were a mate. Not that he thought of her as a mate, she thought, especially not after her questions.

When she reached the stretch of road overlooking the sea, she saw the surf was still crashing over the dunes, but where the scrub and brittle, bleached grasses had been flattened to the horizon earlier, they now sprang upright. Sure, they were quivering a lot, but the gale had passed, thank God.

India was coming into Shoalhaven, bang on the 60-K speed limit, when a cop car cruised past her from the opposite direction. She double checked the speedometer then her eyes were on the rear-view mirror as she watched the cop car go. And just as she turned her gaze forward, a ute pulled out from a driveway, right in front of her. The driver wore an Akubra type hat, his passenger a frizz of grey hair, and a car was in the other lane, no hard shoulder, she had no choice but to slam her foot on the brakes.

With a screech of rubber, her vehicle fishtailed towards the rear of the ute and at the last second she raised her foot off the brake and twitched the steering wheel right, regained control for an instant but it was too late. She slammed into a streetlight.

'Shit, fuck,' she said.

The ute continued down the road, the driver oblivious, and vanished from sight.

Unbuckling her seatbelt, she checked her rear-view mirror.

'Shit, fuck,' she said again.

The police car had done a U-turn and was heading her way.

She hurriedly buckled up and picked reverse, but then she saw the cop car had flipped on its lights. She was busted.

India was outside and calmly surveying the damage when two cops approached. Not that there was much damage. All the streetlight needed was a bit of sanding down and a splash of paint, Ned's roo bar a bit of straightening out.

'Hi, officers,' she said.

One was large and bulky with an alcohol-reddened face, the other looked like he was just out of school.

'Licence and reg please,' said the schoolboy.

She handed them over. 'A ute with two old folk pulled out right in front of me, no warning. I don't think they even saw me. Since there was traffic coming the other way, I took evasive action.' India gestured at the streetlight.

'You been drinking at all?' asked schoolboy.

She considered denying it, but she knew if either of them took one step closer they'd smell the beer on her breath, so she said, 'I shared a beer over lunch, that's all.'

'Just the one?' His voice was sarcastic.

'Yes. I shared it with a friend.' She took a breath and decided to go for broke. 'Jack Zhuganov. He had half, I had the other.'

Huge silence.

'You agree to be breathalysed, ma'am?' asked the bulky cop, a hard edge to his tone.

Deep breath. She knew she'd lost her licence.

'No need for that.' Schoolboy handed back her papers. 'Half a beer isn't a problem,' he said with a smile. 'So long as you and your car're okay, we don't have a problem either.'

'We fucking do have a problem,' his colleague said violently. His face had flushed so hard he looked like he was going to have a heart attack. 'I'll bet you a hundred bucks she's over the limit and I don't care who she's sleeping with, you or your whole fucking family, I'm going to breathalyse her and—'

Schoolboy grabbed the bulky guy's arm and twisted him aside, said something India couldn't hear.

Bulky guy's shoulders slumped, but he wasn't giving in totally. He was muttering loudly, cursing mothers and dogs and a whole lot of wildlife in between, but in the end he backed down. He reminded her of Mikey pushed to the edge and having to draw back. Schoolboy turned and came to her, raised a forefinger to his hat and flicked a salute, saying, 'Safe journey now, Miz Kane.'

'India, please,' she said, and stepped forward to shake.

'Bryce Zhuganov,' he supplied, and gave her a wink as he added, 'Always glad to help a friend of the family.'

It took two hours to get to Jimbuku Bay and the wind was buffeting Ned's ute from side to side when she turned up. Climbing outside, her hair whipping around her face, India felt the same strange shock she'd experienced when she'd first visited the place. That peculiar sensation of being in a fashionable part of the city, feet on immaculate paving, shiny glass and designer chic all around, and then the roar of the surf, the smell of rotting sea grass, sand gritting between her teeth.

Nature intruding, making herself known.

The smell of dead grass and salt followed her up the path and inside the house, and she gave a shiver. The temperature felt as though it was below zero. Going to the cupboard at the top of the stairs she checked the hot water heater, saw it wasn't on, and rectified the problem. With a soft belch the hot water heater kicked into gear, and she padded downstairs to the sound of the air-con unit humming in the hallway, the wind rattling against the windows.

As the house warmed, India pulled out a carton of milk from the fridge and started to make herself some hot chocolate, half watching the news. More stuff about Iraq. A volcano that had erupted in South America. No matter where the news story was in the world, there were always armies involved, or emergency services, people dying, getting massacred. God, it was depressing.

She'd switched channels to pick up a re-run of *Blade Runner* and was pouring hot milk into her mug when it happened. Her heart seemed to stop and her breathing jammed. She felt like she was having a seizure. She dropped the pan, fighting to catch a breath, but her lungs didn't seem to be working. *There was no air.*

Stumbling, mouth working, she fought her way outside. As she felt the sea-laden wind slap against her face she fell to her knees, her lungs gave a single great heaving gasp, and she was breathing again. Panting and choking, her body convulsed in relief as she felt the blissful rush of oxygen in her veins. She knelt there for a while, cautious of moving and setting whatever it was off again. She waited until her breathing was steady and calm, her heartbeat absolutely level, and then she got to her feet. Waited some more. Patted herself down. All limbs functioning and seemingly in working order. She took a deep breath down into her belly and released it.

She cleaned up the spilt milk and washed out the pan, thinking about Albert's curse and Pippa's death. India gave a shudder. She didn't believe the estate's illnesses had anything to do with a curse, or her sudden inability to breathe. There had to be a rational explanation for both. Too many metals in the water or asbestos or something. She considered having a glass of wine to steady her nerves, but didn't dare in case it set her off again. Instead she went to bed with one of the travel books Mikey had bought her for Christmas, a guide to Guatemala with lots of glossy pictures of Mayan ruins set amidst thick jungle. Where some people read novels or magazines for relaxation, India read travel books. One day she'd get to see some of the places she'd read about; but in the meantime it was wonderful escapism.

Eventually she slid the book on to the bedside table. Her breathing was free and easy, her heartbeat right on the nail.

For God's sake, she told herself as she snapped out the light, the writing's on the wall, okay? You've got to give up smoking.

The next morning India forewent her usual Marlboro for a piece of toast drenched in honey and, still munching, booted up Ned's computer to discover he'd put in a password that she couldn't break. She tried everything from Albert and Jimbuku to Ellie, whales, minke and *Sundancer*, and, intensely frustrated, dumped her sticky plate into the sink and headed for Shoalhaven which, apparently, had the only internet café within a fifty-K radius.

Set on the beach front, the Whizz Internet Café was a crumbling single-storey building with a patchy lawn of buffalo grass poking through sand. Salt caked its windows and there was a broom set on the front step that she reckoned was meant to sweep the front step of sand, but nobody seemed to have used it for a while. The drift was four inches thick.

Inside, it smelled of fresh coffee and doughnuts and India was pleased to see she was the only customer. The young guy at the counter poured her a coffee and set her up at a computer overlooking the beach. It took her a while until she hooked into something useful, and the first thing to pop up was a five-year-old newspaper report. Apparently Regent Enterprises, owned by Jack Zhuganov, had been given several Government building contracts and a rival firm had accused the development commissioner of cronyism. Which wasn't surprising, India thought, considering the commissioner was married to Frank Zhuganov, Jack's elder brother. Frank, she read on, was in the transport business and had two sons, Jimmy and Bobby, who were 'angry' and 'upset' at the allegations against their mother.

Several more newspaper pieces followed, all fairly small and running along the same vein, accusing the family of corruption and nepotism, but nothing ever came of them. They'd flare up briefly, and a couple of days later, died. There were some wild guesses about how much Regent Enterprises was worth. AUS$30 billion was widely quoted, but nobody really knew.

India dug a little more into Regent to discover the

company had interests right across the state, from Zhuganov-owned skyscrapers in Perth to a Zhuganov-owned taxi firm in Broome. She learned Jack had never married, had no kids, which was surprising given the fact he was one of seven himself. Usually people from big families liked to have big families themselves, but as she scrolled on, she realised she'd got him wrong. He *did* have a big family, just not under the same roof.

Jack had four brothers and two sisters. His siblings had had seventeen children between them and, if the information was accurate, those seventeen children had produced twelve more kids, all under the age of eleven. Two of Jack's brothers had emigrated to the United States and set up businesses in Los Angeles, but the rest of the family were firmly rooted in Western Australia.

India leaned back, her mind reeling from the dynastic proportions of the Zhuganov family. No wonder they're being accused of monopolising the state's business, she thought. They couldn't help it, they practically had a relative in every town across Western Australia. Which reminded her. She quickly asked for Harris & Hewitt, Jack's livestock insurance agents, and after a lot of digging around, managed to glean that David Harris was third cousin once removed from Jack, and nephew to Steve Harris, the state's health minister.

Steve Harris's website told her he had pledged to introduce heroin-injecting rooms into the state, and that every hospital and clinic would be supplied with ground-breaking new refrigerants from Ocean Green out of his $20 million budget. Steve was, he said, proud to be doing something for the environment.

India was further amazed Jack didn't have an Ocean Green fridge, but she'd bet one would find its way to his mansion soon, having fallen off the back of the proverbial family lorry.

The café fly-screen door slammed and she glanced up to

see a leathery old bloke in a workshirt and bush hat come in and take the computer next to her. He was tanned the colour of jarrah and his nose and ear tips were scabbed, the lines around his eyes scored from a lifetime of squinting into the sun and wind.

'G'day,' he said.

'Hi.'

India rubbed her eyes, and glanced at the clock. Jesus, she'd been at it for over two hours. Getting up, she got herself some more coffee, did some stretches, and settled back down again, a pile of doughnuts to hand. This time, she changed tack.

An hour later, India sat back, her back aching, her neck like a block of wood, her mind buzzing. What a family! Talk about fingers in every sort of pie imaginable. There was a Zhuganov industrial cleaning service, a Zhuganov bottling company, and even a Zhuganov at the top of the pile in governmental safety checks on manufactured products.

They were heavily into regional and local government, but what interested her was the leader of the liberal party, Jack's youngest brother, Don. From what she'd read Don looked poised to topple the current Labour leader at the next elections. A Zhuganov as the Premier of the state. And what would happen if they decided to advance on national government? The thought of a Zhuganov as Prime Minister didn't sit well with her. Not after all those allegations of cronyism.

'Friends of yours?'

India turned to see the young guy behind the counter had disappeared, and that the old man was watching her.

'I'm sorry?'

He gestured at her screen. 'The Zhugs.' He pronounced it *Zoogs*.

'Not particularly.'

'What does that mean in English?'

India considered him briefly, the curiosity in his eyes and

smiled. 'That I wouldn't trust them as far as I can throw them.'

He gave a dry laugh which ended up in a hacking cough, tears leaking into the deep folds around his eyes. 'Too bloody right. Jack stiffed my son-in-law a couple of weeks back, the bastard.'

'Stiffed?' she prompted.

'Yeah, poor bugger owed Jack sixty grand but Jack wouldn't wait for him to raise the cash so he ended up giving him the cars off his own forecourt. Worth two hundred grand, not sixty.'

She stared at the old guy. 'They weren't Nissan traybacks, were they?'

He frowned. 'How'd you know that? You in the transport biz like our Joe?'

India shook her head and was going to tell him, no, but something he'd said had stuck in her brain like a bur. Transport, *transport.* The newspaper report had said that Jack's brother Frank was in the transport business. Her spirits rose a little. Maybe this included ships.

'What do you know about Jack's brother, Frank?'

A blink of surprise.

'Frank's dead,' he said.

'You knew him?'

A grunt at the back of the throat, which she took as a yes.

'How did he die?'

'Cancer.' His voice dropped to a rasping murmur. 'Rotted the bugger inside out.'

'I heard Frank had a transport business.'

'Never thought of it like that, but he had loads of trucks. Made his money dealing with our rubbish, see. Collecting and disposing, even got into recycling at one point. Did all right too, considering he was worth twenty-one million bucks before he kicked the bucket.' He shook his head. 'Wish I'd gotten into that game when it started. Bloody goldmine.'

Danny's body, she thought. *It was unearthed on a municipal dump out of town.*

She asked the old guy about Albert, and she heard another tale of gutters ripped from walls, cars spun in circles and trees toppled. 'Where's Albert now?'

'Nobody knows.' He shook his head. 'Last time I saw him, it was at the Nelson. Right after he'd called in that bloody storm. Wearing one of his godawful floral shirts. You'd never get me dressed like that.'

'Did he go home when he left?'

'Home? Nah. He left when Jimmy turned up . . .' To her annoyance he paused when the young guy reappeared.

'Jimmy?'

He flicked a glance at the guy behind the counter and turned back to his screen. 'Wrong time to be asking these sorts of questions,' he murmured.

'Who is he?' she whispered.

He held up a hand until the young guy ducked behind the counter making clattering sounds with mugs and plates.

'Steve Marsdon,' he whispered back.

Disappointed, she said, 'He's not a Zoog?'

The old bloke leaned close, eyes wary and fixed on the counter. 'One hundred per cent. That mob have changed their names all over the place. Lot of 'em don't like being thought of as foreign. You've Reillys, Grants and Marsdons. They're all related.'

'Thanks.'

When Steve Marsdon straightened up, the older man swung back and started tapping on his keyboard, then paused when she pushed back her chair.

'Nice meeting you,' he said.

'You too.'

India walked out of the café and kicked at the pile of sand on the step and scowled. Despite the mountain of information she'd gathered, she hadn't found a single reference to Soeharto or Jack or any of their relatives owning or having anything to do with a container ship.

It was dark when India parked outside Ellie's and walked up the little path, searching for her keys. The breeze was coming from the south and the air was damp and briny with the scent of the sea and salt bush. She was still digging in her daypack when she reached the porch. One day, she thought, I'll have a bag the size of a matchbox so I can bloody *find* things in it.

Her fingers had just brushed her mobile phone and she was thinking she must ring Mikey and Polly as soon as she got inside when she heard footsteps behind her. As she started to swing round a man launched himself at her, smacking her against the door, forcing her left arm high between her shoulder blades. She opened her mouth to yell but a hand clamped over her mouth. She kicked backwards but stopped when her arm was squeezed higher and she moaned. The pressure eased a fraction.

'Hi, bitch,' he whispered into her ear. 'You been missing me?'

Fourteen

India shook her head.

'Oh, but I think you have. Why else have you been sniffing around, asking about stuff that isn't any of your business?'

She rolled her eyes left and right, looking for help, but she was in the porch with her face jammed against the door and she couldn't see a thing.

'You look very fuckable when you're asleep, you know. Can't say as much for your fat friend. Pregnant cows don't do it for me.'

A ball of panic lodged itself in her throat. *He'd watched her and Ellie sleeping.*

He ratcheted her arm up a fraction and she yelped a protest, but he didn't soften his grip.

'Now, I want you to listen very carefully. I thought I was pretty restrained last time we met, but my patience is wearing thin. So I think you should know that if I hear you chatting to AMSA, the chief or the feds about any sort of ship – a fucking runabout or the HMAS *Adelaide* – I'll be back and I won't be quite so polite.'

She could smell the bitter antiseptic of rosemary as his words punctured the air. 'Oh, and no more going down to Shoalhaven and pumping the general population about things that don't concern you. So no more chit-chats at the internet café, or with Grandma Ginny. My family's got fuck all to do with you, get it?'

Her mind was unravelling like a ball of string. Sweet Jesus, how did he know so much?

'I want you to fuck off home. Message understood?'

She nodded furiously.

Keeping his hand against her mouth, he dropped her arm and yanked her against him, sliding a hand down the front of her jeans. His hand was warm on the bare skin of her belly and as she struggled he pulled her even closer, and then his hand was creeping into the waistband of her knickers, reaching for the first curls of pubic hair and she could feel his chest, his thighs and his dick grinding against the small of her back.

'I'll miss you, bitch,' he whispered, and licked the back of her neck.

'Bastard!' she muffled against his hand and jabbed an elbow for his sternum, hoping to make him catch a breath, even wind him, and amazingly it connected and his hand slipped.

Quick as a flash she opened her mouth and grabbed the fleshy part of his thumb between her teeth. She bit down, hard. He yelled, his other hand coming up to hit her. She dropped his thumb and spun round and for a split second they were facing each other and she did something she'd never done for real, although she'd been shown how. She headbutted him straight in the face.

There was a dull *crunch* and he staggered back, and then he was yelling, 'You fucking bitch!' and she was running for the street, sprinting for her life, when a shadow materialised from behind the banksia and something whacked her behind her ear. Pain exploded behind her eyes and she was folding to the ground, dizzy, blinded, her hands fumbling for a rock, a stone, a branch to stab into his eyes, her penknife, *anything*.

A boot thudded into her ribs making her breath whoosh from her lungs, another in her kidneys and she was groaning, curling into a ball, trying to protect herself against the assault.

'Christ, Jimmy,' a man said. 'Not now. We've got to get out of here.'

Thud. 'Fucking bitch.' Thud.

'Jimmy, let's *go*.'

'Let's do her now.' Thud. 'Save us a load of hassle.'

'It was meant to be a *warning*. Jesus, Jimmy—'

'Forget warning her.' Jimmy gave an hysterical laugh. 'She'll only be back. You've seen what she's like.'

Where was everyone? India wondered frantically. Surely someone must have heard them.

'But Bobby told us *not* to.'

'What does he know? He's nothing but a wet fucking rag.'

India desperately tried to clear her head and gather her energy. She had to get up. She had to move, to get enough strength to scream. She rolled her eyes around and squinted through her pain to see a man lit by streetlights standing beside Jimmy, fists clenched. A man she hadn't expected to see. A neatly dressed, athletic-looking man. Sergeant Kuteli. Sweet Jesus. No wonder her description of Jimmy hadn't added up. Jimmy sure had the right friends in the right places.

'She's recognised you,' Jimmy said, sounding pleased. 'You really want to let her go now? Report you? I know it won't come to anything, but do you really want the hassle? You'll get suspended. Have to face all sorts of crap.'

'*Shit*.' Kuteli ran his hands over his head.

India pulled a lungful of air against the screaming agony and opened her mouth to shout for help. She caught a movement out of the corner of her eye. She pulled her head around just in time to miss her cheek getting mashed by Jimmy's boot. Her shoulder took the brunt of it but the shock of pain sucked the breath from her: she couldn't even groan.

'See?' said Jimmy. 'She never gives up.'

'Okay,' said Kuteli, sounding brisk. 'Let's do it.'

He jogged away then came back. Hands grabbed her and she tried to fight, but she was too weak against their double strength. She saw the car's boot was open and a wave of fear poured through her, giving her a surge of strength. She gave a violent buck and felt Kuteli's grip slip but then she got hit on the back of the head so hard it almost knocked her out. She didn't know what had hit her, but it wasn't a fist. More like a block of wood or a cosh. The energy left her and with a rush they lifted her and carried her to the car, threw her in, and slammed the boot shut.

Panic gripped her and she tried to push at the boot lid with her hands and knees, but her limbs were weak, and the back of her head where she'd been hit was numb.

With a jolt, the car started to move. India writhed on to her side in the pitch black of the boot. Groped with her fingers for the lock, but the mechanism was hidden behind a wall of plastic, and she searched for a purchase to yank it open, but when she felt the nubs of screws bolting the boot lining into the metalwork, she realised she had no chance of accessing the lock without tools of some sort.

She lay there, panting and sweating, aware the air was turning stale already. Would she suffocate? Surely not. Car boots weren't hermetically sealed, she told herself. She had to fight the hysteria she could feel building. She closed her eyes. She must remain calm. There had to be a way of surviving this.

The car gave a bounce and she groaned as her hip smacked into something metal beneath her. Feeling around, she recognised the hard rim of the spare tyre. And usually where there were spare tyres, there were tool kits.

India started groping around the tyre, hoping the tool kit would be tucked inside and that it wasn't buried beneath the thing. Nope, nothing there. Carefully she checked the rest of the boot, feeling for a compartment that might spring open and reveal a handful of DIY goodies, but found nothing. She didn't believe Kuteli would travel without a car jack and a handful of spares, and knew with a sick feeling he'd buried everything beneath the tyre; she obviously wasn't the first person to get chucked inside his boot.

Okay. How to move the tyre? Wasn't it held in place by a bracket of some sort? Fumbling some more, she realised Kuteli has decided on only the most rudimentary of precautions. There was no bracket, and the tyre was set on a single metal post secured by a wingnut. Simple. Untwist wingnut and pull off tyre. Except that she was crammed in a space the size of a post-it-note and the tyre weighed a ton.

She tried to shift the tyre so she could feel underneath, and her head suddenly exploded into a blossom of red. India collapsed on top of the tyre. The air was hot and heavy, like sucking in a wet flannel. Rest for a bit, she told herself. Just a bit.

She didn't have any idea how much time was passing. The tyres were humming and whining, with the occasional small *click* of a stone, and she knew they were on bitumen, but that was all she knew. Aside from the fact they wanted to kill her.

At one point she passed out. When she came to, they were on a rough track, lurching from side to side. The motion must have jolted her awake. Had they turned off a main road on to dirt? God, how long had she been unconscious? They might have travelled hundreds of Ks by now. The thought galvanised her. Rolling over, she manoeuvred herself over the tyre. She made a vow to yank it free in the first effort. First time, or nothing.

With a grunt, she gave an almighty great heave. Pain lanced her neck and behind her eyes, but she kept heaving. Got it balanced on top of the bolt. She was panting heavily and she wanted to rest, but she daren't, a sudden lurch of the car might topple the tyre back. So she gritted her teeth and pushed through her pain to shove the tyre to one side, as far as it would go. Then she stopped, gasping, sweat pouring, until her breathing levelled. She shoved her hand in the pit.

One plastic-bound tool kit, a jack and a tyre lever. She hefted the weighty metal in both hands. Terrific weapon. She could belt Jimmy with it and break his jaw. She wished. Unrolling the tool kit, she could feel a couple of spanners, a screwdriver and a wrench. Okay, she'd better make a plan. When they opened the boot, she'd spring out, whack them and run away. What if they were armed? Kuteli was a cop and probably had a gun. Okay. She'd prise her way out of here, jump outside and run like hell before she got shot.

Screwdriver in hand, India tackled the first screw holding the boot lining in place, but with the lurching of the car and unable to see, unscrewing more than two was going to be virtually impossible. Plan B. Rip the goddam boot lining off.

Scrunched up in a tortured, hunched position that had her muscles screaming, India wedged the point of the screwdriver between the lip of the plastic and the metal-work and yanked down hard. The plastic gave a little and, encouraged, she worked her way towards the first screw, and to her amazement it popped out first time. India grabbed the plastic rim with both hands and pulled. The plastic popped another screw and she forced her hand into the two inch gap, searching for the lock, the release cable, *anything*, but all she felt was air.

She shifted her concentration to the near side of the boot, the driver's side, and the screws there. Her hands were sore, her muscles aching, but she kept up her determined heaving and tugging . . . She almost gave a shout when she felt the plastic give. At last, the boot lining gaped open.

India thrust her arm inside, searching for the cable that would pop the lock from the driver's position. There! She hooked her fingers round the slender wire and pulled it towards her. There was a small clunk, and for an instant she couldn't believe it. The boot lid slowly swung open and stayed there, bobbing up and down with the motion of the car.

India waited for the car to screech to a halt, but it didn't. Whoever was driving wasn't looking in their rear-view mirror. Why should they? It was dark, they weren't on a major highway, so there wouldn't be much to see. Except for her escaping, that was.

Shoving a handful of smaller tools in her pockets, clutching the tyre lever, she glanced outside. In a single second she saw scrubby bush on either side of the dirt track. The stars were out. The wind was freezing, desert cold. She hurriedly peered down at the ground. It seemed to be going past terribly fast, but even so . . .

Don't think. Just do it.

She manoeuvred herself on to the rim of the boot, her breathing coming fast. Tucked her head in. Crossed her arms across her chest. And tumbled outside, shoulder first.

Almost immediately, the breath knocked right out of her, the tyre lever flung aside, she didn't know where, she was scrambling up, ignoring the pain roaring through her shoulder and moving as fast as she could for the bush. She crashed through the undergrowth. She couldn't see any details, just an outline of obstacles, lit by starlight. And for an amazing, wonderful second, she heard the engine note still cruising away and thought she'd got away with it, but suddenly there was a violent squirt of gravel and then the whine as the car reversed. Fast.

India tried to get as far as she could before they got out of the car. Once they were outside, she'd have to remain utterly quiet, utterly still. Branches tore at her clothes, thorns scratched her skin. She was gasping like a fox on the run. Would they find her tracks? No time to worry, the engine had stopped. She fell on to her front and wriggled behind a tree trunk. A ghost gum. She could see the headlights cutting through the dark. Heard two doors slam.

'When?' Jimmy demanded. His voice carried easily in the still, cool air.

'I only just noticed.'

'Jesus Christ! Are you telling me she could have jumped out twenty Ks back?'

Silence, which Jimmy obviously took for assent.

'You stupid cunt!'

'Shouldn't we look around here, just in case?'

'What's the fucking point? We're never going to find her. It's dark, in case you hadn't noticed. You got a torch?'

'Sorry.'

Jimmy let rip with a stream of curses. 'Turn the car round, then. Use the headlights instead. Let's see if we can find where she got out.'

'If we can't find her . . .' Kuteli said hesitantly. 'Well, it's not like she's got a survival pack or anything.' His tone brightened. 'Maybe it's not such a bad thing. You think she'll survive out here?'

'You'd better fucking hope not.'

Both doors slammed again and slowly, infinitely slowly, they began driving back the way they'd come.

India lay there. She was alive. She had no food or drink, her body felt wrecked, but, for the moment, she was alive.

Fifteen

India limped back down the dirt track. She didn't think Jimmy and Kuteli would return and besides, she had no intention of getting lost out here. She'd follow the track until she hit the bitumen, and then she'd flag down a car and take it from there. What had Jimmy said? Twenty Ks? It wasn't that far. She should be there by morning.

Occasionally she checked her watch, trying to gauge the distance she'd covered. The starlight was so bright she could even see the second hand. Incredible. A couple of times she heard a crash in the bush and she'd jump a mile, only to relax a couple of seconds later at the soft thud-thudding of startled kangaroos.

Her limp eventually became a slow hobble. Her shoulder was throbbing, her ribs sore, and she felt shivery and ill. Come two a.m. her feet were barely moving, so she stopped for a rest. Moving well off the track she tucked herself in a sandy gully. The sand was cold and damp, but she fell asleep almost immediately.

She awoke after an hour, shuddering with cold, layered with dew. She lay there, aching all over, in too much pain to move. Morning seemed such a long way away, but she was still petrified Jimmy might come back and find her, so she forced herself to get up.

India shuffled along the track with her hands under her armpits, hugging herself, trying to get warm. The track suddenly started to climb. She had little enough energy for a flat road, let alone a hill, but she didn't have much choice. She was sweating and staggering when she got to the top.

Time for another rest, she thought, and slumped on to a rock. In the distance, near the curvature of the earth, she saw a hair's-breadth strip of crimson split the blue-black of the sky. Dawn. She couldn't be far from the main road now.

India sat and waited for the sun to rise a little more, so she could get her bearings. She was thirsty and hungry and in need of a soft bed and some super-strength painkillers. A knot of anxiety tightened in her chest. Where were any lights from towns or homesteads? Headlights, streetlights, traffic lights? Swivelling her head three-sixty degrees, she realised with horror that there were no lights whatsoever.

In her painful exhaustion, she must have missed a turning. Maybe she'd even walked across a crossroads that the car had turned left or right at while she'd been unconscious. Dear God. When you're lost in the bush you're meant to back-track to your last known point and start again. She didn't even know where she'd started from.

You think she'll survive out here?

She refused to give in to the tide of fear gushing through her and hurriedly turned her mind to practical things. First up, water. As the horizon broadened into blue, she studied the endless stretches of desert and scrub, looking for any sign of life. There! A flock of cockatoos flying low, heading west, towards the sun. India watched their steady flight until she could no longer see them, and then she got up, and followed them.

She didn't find any water that morning, but she did find some djuk bushes. Looking closer, she saw some tiny orange-red fruits were ripening on the outer stems, and blessed God that she'd learned a bit about bush tucker a couple of years back, and that the native cherry could pretty much fruit at any time of the year. She stripped the bushes, which harvested two handfuls of berries which she ate immediately, and another handful which she pocketed.

Her spirits lifted, she walked on, watching the flight of

any birds she saw, tracking the sun, making sure she was on a trail that headed west all the time. She certainly didn't want to walk east, and into the baking interior. Towards the west she at least had a hope of coming across a homestead. God willing. And she wasn't that thirsty yet. The temperature had been around the sixties and she hadn't sweated much. Yes, she could have downed a litre of water in an instant, but it wasn't debilitating. More like a nagging need, a warning. She had loads of time. So long as she found water by tomorrow, she thought cheerfully, she'd be fine.

It didn't take long for her hopes to crash to earth. She remembered the flippant note she'd left Ellie, telling her not to send out a search party until the end of the week. Nobody would be looking for her, not that they even knew where to look. She pictured her bones being found by some bush walker, picked clean by bush animals and ants, her clothes rotted away.

Get a grip, she told herself. You're not dead yet. And look, the sun's going down, so concentrate. Sure enough, twenty minutes later, a bunch of little brown birds scooted past, chattering. Cementing her bearings firmly in her mind, India followed them off the track and into the undergrowth. The birds settled briefly in a gum tree before setting off again. India worried she might lose them, but then four cockatoos flew past.

Five minutes later, she came across a creek. A small creek, hardly flowing, but there was plenty of water in the rocky pool. On all fours, India bent her head and scooped handfuls of water into her mouth. Water dripping down her throat, she put her little remaining energy into making herself a nest to sleep in. She gouged out a hollow in the sand and collected heaps of dried grasses to crawl under for warmth. Already it was getting dark, so she pulled the tools she'd taken from the boot of the car from her pockets and shoved them beside a branch she'd recognise in the morning.

Snuggled into her bush bed she tried to ignore her stomach's growls, her crushed muscles and aching ribs.

You will get out of here, she promised herself. And you will make Jimmy pay.

The next morning she found another creek heading west. Occasionally it disappeared underground, but not for long enough for her to lose it. She followed its winding course across the flat expanse of scrub, praying it would lead her to a farm or station, some human habitation, but then it disappeared. She searched for hours but couldn't find its on-going source again. She wanted to scream but knew it wouldn't help, so she sat on a rock and tried to think what to do. There was no point in following it back to where she'd come from, and no point in staying with it until she died of hunger. She had to go on, and hope she'd find more water on the way.

By mid-afternoon the next day, India was frantically thirsty, so she sucked on a stone as she walked. Got to keep going, she told herself. There are birds around, not many, but they're around, so there's water here somewhere. Just got to find it, that's all.

The first indication she was nearing the coast was a straggly, spreading shrub with succulent, grey-green leaves. A sea berry saltbush. Red-eyed wattle appeared along with the smell of savoury sword sedge. The ground turned soft, into grey sand, draining each step, but when she came upon some wheel ruts she followed them west. Always west.

The sun had set and was draining light from the sky when the wheel ruts split. One went right, the other dead ahead. She went dead ahead where she could hear the roar of surf, and came to a beach. She skidded down a dune and shucked off her boots and went and bathed her poor, blistered feet in the sea. Scooped salt water against her face, desperate to drink it, but not daring to. Water trickling down her neck, she looked up and down the coastline. She couldn't see any creeks spilling fresh water on to the beach. No people, no beach buggies or shacks in the hollows. Just a single, rusting tin boat set high in the dunes. She considered where it was in reference to the wheel tracks she'd followed, and clambered back up the dune. Followed the wheel ruts to where they turned left. The sand was cool beneath her feet. She was so slow, so weak, she wondered if she'd be able to carry her boots much longer. They felt as heavy as lead.

A fenceline. A grove of tuarts. The wheel ruts joined a gravel track. Wagtails and honeyeaters fluttered and hopped in the fading shadows of paperbarks. She stumbled on. And then she saw it.

A house.

The back door was closed behind the insect screen. She went round to the front. No car in the gravel driveway. No sign of life. Crows cawed from a clump of casuarinas.

On the verandah was a tattered, overstuffed armchair and a wooden table covered in plates, beer bottles and cigarette ends. She limped to the front door and knocked even though she was pretty sure nobody was home. Tried the door handle. Unlocked.

She fell inside. Dust motes spun in the disturbed air. She staggered into the kitchen. Turned the ancient rusty tap. Oh, thank God. She dipped her head and drank straight from the cool, clear flow. She let it sluice over her face and her neck, relished its pouring between her breasts and across her belly, soaking the waistband of her jeans.

Switching on the lights she began opening cupboards. Found tins of soup and beans, packs of tea and coffee and cocoa, sugar, packets of cereal. Ripping open a pack of cornflakes, she ate handfuls as she checked out the house. An old dresser with cracked china plates. Aluminium tables and chairs. Little bowls of ratsack in every corner. Phone lines that looked as though they'd been ripped off the wall. Shelves of towels in the laundry. Fishing gear and a chart by the back door. Band-Aids and sunscreen in the bathroom.

It felt like a house abandoned in a hurry. The essentials packed, everything else left behind. Her legs were softening, ready to collapse as she came to the last room: a mattress on the floor.

Fear of trespassing didn't enter her head. The last thing she heard was the distant, lonely moan of a crow.

India crawled awake when the sun was high in the sky. She blinked several times until the room came into focus: weatherboard walls, a threadbare rug of indeterminate origin, curling posters of motorbikes, big trucks and large-breasted women.

She lay there a long time, thinking about what she knew.

Jimmy had come to warn her off her investigation into *The Pride* and talking to people about his family. He'd told her not to talk to the chief, AMSA and the feds. Jimmy had to be Jack's nephew; he was obviously Jack's bully boy.

The Zhuganovs must have followed her initially, searching her office to see what she had found out about the container ship, but when she hadn't had any luck, dropped their surveillance. Witnessing Danny's snatch had brought the Zhuganov searchlights to focus back on her. Jimmy had killed Danny. He didn't want Danny to talk about the ship he'd crewed on, the ship that had rammed *Sundancer*.

Jack had a picture of what looked like the guilty container ship in his house. Jack and his family were growing more and more powerful in Western Australia, even preparing themselves to win the next elections.

It was, she thought, little wonder that if they owned the guilty ship they wanted it kept quiet. It would damage the family big time that their master hadn't stopped to help them, that they hadn't come clean and compensated the families of those who had died. Nobody'd vote for them once that came out.

India wondered why, if they had so much money, they hadn't owned up to the collision. She was pretty sure they could have afforded it. Maybe they were protecting something else, something that would explain why *The Pride* had been so far away from the normal shipping routes, and had ignored Ned's calls on channel 16.

Whatever the answer was, she had every intention of finding out what they were up to, and why they'd been driven to kill Danny and come after her.

Pushing back the blankets, she limped to the hot water heater and switched it on. Then she went to the bathroom, stripped off her clothes, and stood under the shower. Lots of hot water, shampoo and soap. Bliss, aside from the fact she was grindingly sore. Her ribs still hurt like hell and she reckoned Jimmy might have cracked a couple. She'd fractured a rib once, falling off her pony years ago, and she knew there was little she could do about it except pop painkillers and let them heal of their own accord.

When she was clean she went back to the bedroom and opened cupboards and drawers. She put on a baggy sloppy joe and shorts that were too big for her. She tied them around the waist with string from the laundry, then she went and studied the fishing chart stuck to the wall beside the back door.

The scuffed mark on the paper, from having a finger prodded at it over time, indicated the house. The nearest habitation was a little scattering of houses just outside the thumb mark. Cape Cray. India scanned the chart carefully, looking for something she recognised, but it still took her a good five minutes to realise she wasn't as far north as she'd thought. Perth wasn't exactly around the corner, but it wasn't impossible to get to either.

Exhausted and in need of another twelve-hour sleep, she took a bowl of Weet Bix drowned in long-life milk on to the verandah and sank into the tattered armchair.

She was just finishing up when a guy in his twenties came into sight, walking barefoot for the house. There was no point trying to hide, he'd already seen her. She'd have to brazen it out. He stopped in front of her and pushed back his salt-stained cap with a finger. His eyes ran over her too-big clothes then came to rest on her face. He didn't look angry, just puzzled.

'You a mate of Stewie's?' he asked.

'Not really.'

He looked at her nearly empty bowl, then at the scratches and bruises all over her legs and on her arms, and gave a disgusted grimace. 'No respect for women,' he said. 'Makes me sick.'

It took her a second to realise what he meant. He obviously thought she'd been beaten up by some guy, probably her husband, and was hiding out.

'You all right?'

'Yes,' she said. 'Thank you.'

He nodded. Looked around a bit. His shorts and shirt were standard Aussie wear, his feet filthy and his fingernails bitten to the quick.

Tilting his head at the house, he said, 'You wanna rent it for a bit?'

God, she thought, *brilliant*. Jimmy would never find her here.

'I'd love to,' she told him. 'But what about Stewie, won't he mind?'

'Nah. Took off a few weeks back under not very favourable circumstances. He won't be coming back for a while.' He raised a hand and had a quick chew at the corner of his thumbnail, appraised it, let it fall. 'If ever.'

'I see.'

'He was always getting into trouble. It's been real quiet without him.' He sighed. 'I'm his brother. Everyone calls me Chew.'

'India.'

They shook and India told him to sit. Chew sat. He said she could have the house for a hundred bucks a week, but if Stewie returned she'd have to get the hell out. Fine by her, she agreed. India asked if she could hire a car around here, and he put his head on one side and said she could use Stewie's ute if she wanted, since he'd taken the Valiant. For a hundred bucks a week, of course. Cash.

'Deal,' she said.

Chew dropped off the ute late afternoon, when the sun had just hit the water and taken the warmth from the day. With a fleece of Stewie's over a pair of his trackies, she drove barefoot to Cape Cray, parked outside the roadhouse. She got out and looked around at the settlement wedged between the sea and sand dunes. A bunch of tin sheds near the water. Weatherboard houses, a bait shop, and from somewhere she could hear the drone of a diesel generator. Down on the jetty a couple of boats were being winched on to trailers. There was no pub, no café. People bought their meat and beer from the roadhouse and held their own parties.

Inside the roadhouse, freezers rumbled and heavy metal played on the radio. A man in a pair of greasy overalls gave her a wave and she asked him where the phone was. He pointed behind her.

'Scotto?' She spoke quietly, not wanting to be overheard. 'It's me. Could you do me a favour?'

Sixteen

India signed for Scotto's parcel at the roadhouse two days later, and took it to her home in the dunes before she opened it. There was a list of phone numbers he obviously reckoned she'd find useful, including her bank manager's, fifteen hundred dollars in cash, her passport for identification, and a mobile phone and charger. But the best surprise was a company credit card. Once she'd set up the phone – highly relieved she had a signal – she rang Scotto and thanked him.

'No staying at the Hyatt, okay?' he told her. 'It's too expensive.'

'Two hundred bucks a week all right by you?'

'So long as you don't bring any bed bugs back to the office.' He gave a little cough that she knew meant he was worried. 'Are you sure you're okay?'

She wasn't going to tell him she'd spent the last forty-eight hours munching Aspirin and sleeping, and assured him she was fine.

'Right,' his tone turned brisk. 'I've got the contact you asked for. His name's Greg Elsden. He's an ex-boyfriend of Sally's.'

'Sally?' India didn't know what he was talking about.

'India,' he said, exasperated, 'she's only been our receptionist the past ten months.'

'Oh. That Sally.'

'Anyway, they met backpacking last year, and when Sally came home, he didn't . . . He now lives and works in Jakarta. Teaches English to rich families. He said he'll check the docks twice a week for us, starting today. We've worked out a rough fee for him, and he gets a pretty nice bonus if he gets one of us over to see *The Pride*, so he's pretty keen. He's got your number, but I'd better give you his.'

She hastily punched it into her mobile.

'That's brilliant, Scotto,' she told him.

'Even more brilliant if we actually get to catch the sucker.'

India rang Mikey briefly, and gave him an abbreviated account of the past few days. She didn't say a word about Jimmy and Kuteli's plan to kill her. Mikey would only demand her to drop her investigation and come home, and since Jimmy probably thought she was dead, she had no intention of giving up the perfect opportunity to do some digging around when he wasn't looking for her. Despite her best efforts, however, Mikey knew something was up, and it took her a good five minutes of hearty reassurances before he let her hang up.

Lighting a cigarette India tried to work out what to do next. She reckoned she'd gleaned as much as she needed about the Zhuganovs and wondered how to find a back-door route to link the family to *The Pride* without tipping Jimmy off. Danny had said that they'd loaded gear from a company with Harris in its name on board *The Pride* at Freo, and the only Harris she could link to Jack for sure were his livestock insurers, Harris & Hewitt, which was run by a distant cousin of his.

It was a pretty tenuous connection, but since it was the only one she had, she may as well start there. Besides, she might get a brighter idea on the way.

The tyres on Stewie's ute weren't great, but they had enough tread to make them legal. The oil was thin and black and stringy, indicating a change wouldn't go amiss, but otherwise the car looked in pretty good shape.

She picked up the highway south, listening to the radio

fade in and out. Traffic was light, the bitumen smooth, and after a while the desert began to give way to sheep pasture, then smaller plots. Hobby farms, a couple of pine plantations. A handful of garden centres sprang up and she knew she wasn't far from Perth.

At the next gas station she filled two forty-litre jerry cans with unleaded and managed to get a guy filling his Holden to strap them in the back. Then she went to a sports store across the road and bought a pair of binoculars, some rope and a torch. Next store along, a daypack, notebook and pens, a baseball cap, bottled water; chocolate bars and biscuits.

Swallowing another couple of Aspirin, she pulled the map on to her lap and had a quick look. Fifteen minutes later, she was driving through the gates of Harris & Hewitt, Veterinary Group and Livestock Insurers.

Since the visitor spaces were full, India parked around the back and between two utes emblazoned with *H & H Veterinary Group*. It was a pretty big outfit all up, and included a warehouse selling pet foods and accessories along with a bunch of smaller stores specialising in anything from pet crematoria to pet-sitting services. There was a saddlery and country store along with a harness maker, saddle fitter and bridle repair service. Vitamins and supplements for your sheep or under-the-weather cow. If she owned an animal in the area, Harris & Hewitt appeared to provide for its every need while it was alive, and take care of it when it was dead.

The receptionist – Linda, according to the badge on her lapel – greeted India with a cheerful smile.

'How can I help?'

India introduced herself – Jenny Morris from *Your Little Treasure* magazine – and told her she was doing an article on pet insurance. 'I don't suppose Mr Harris is around, is he?'

'Nah. Dave's gone to see a client out at Dundilla. Lost a

bunch of alpacas, we don't know why yet.' She pulled a face. 'Shouldn't be farming them things over here, it's too bloody hot. If I had my way I'd send the whole lot back to the Andes. They'd be much happier back home.'

Not having a clue about the average alpaca's quality of life in W.A. compared to South America, India settled for murmuring a neutral agreement, which got her a smile.

'If Dave's out . . .' India said, purposely hesitant. 'I've a deadline, you see. I don't suppose you might be able help?'

Linda looked dubious, but said, 'I'll give it a go.'

'You insure horses?' she asked.

'Along with everything else. We had an anaconda last week . . .' A truck rumbled past, making the office shudder. Both India and Linda glanced outside to see an enormous Mac grinding down its gears, and right behind it was a bright red Isuzu truck with a pair of silver horns on its snout. India stared at it, stunned, and watched it turn around the corner of the building. It was the truck she'd seen at the front of Jack's rubbish tip.

'Linda, I'm sorry,' she lunged for the door, 'but my dog's jumped out of my car . . .'

Linda said something but India didn't hear what it was because she was already racing outside. Belting around the corner, she screeched to a halt when she saw the Isuzu back up to a roller-door at the rear of the veterinary surgery fifty yards down. Panting more from the pain hammering through her ribs than exertion, India watched a man climb out: plain overalls, heavy boots, clipboard. He went through a rear door, and a couple of minutes later the roller-door clattered up.

The man began loading what looked like sacks of rubbish into the back of the Isuzu. The plastic bags were tagged with bright yellow strips and the yellow caught at her, as though she'd seen a wasp, and she headed over to have a look.

When the man returned, two more yellow-tagged bags in each hand, she gave him a bright smile. 'Hi,' she said.

He looked her up and down, gave her a smile back. 'Hi.'

'Look, I work in there,' she waved a hand at the veterinary surgery, 'and I've lost my wedding ring. I don't suppose it would be in any of these, would it? I've been going mad looking for it, and I thought maybe—'

'Sorry, love. I can't have you rummaging through this lot. You might get stabbed by a needle or something.'

'Damn. Isn't there any way . . . ? Where's it going?'

'Back to base. They sort it there.'

'Where's base?'

His face clouded. 'Ring 'em, why don't you? See if they can help. Sorry.'

'Thanks anyway,' she said. When he'd disappeared inside the loading bay she climbed into her ute and started it up, drove round the corner, parked and watched the truck in her rear-view mirror. Finally, with another five bags loaded on board, the truck reversed, then the engine changed gear as he picked drive, then he was off.

It wasn't difficult to follow him, since he didn't appear to be in any sort of hurry. He went to another veterinary surgery to pick up some more bags flashed with yellow, then the rear of a company called Pharmacy Plus. She tagged along for the ride to his next stop, a reprographics firm, and she watched the van driver and a young girl from inside load up with what she reckoned was a forest worth of waste paper.

The truck stopped a couple more times and by the time they trailed into the centre of Perth, it was late afternoon. Behind the endless low-rise of roofs and roads, several silver towers rose like bamboo shoots towards the sky. India counted eight tower blocks to denote the city's financial heart. It didn't seem much compared to other capitals in the world, and she felt a sudden surge of affection for the place.

Buzzing down her windows, India let the air tug at her hair. She could smell the briny scent of the sea and what she took to be chicken frying. What an incredible city, she thought. I'm on a major arterial road striking right through its heart and the traffic is light and I can smell the goddam sea. Maybe I should move out here. It would help my stress levels heaps, and it sure would help Mikey's.

When the truck started to slow, she drew back. It was indicating left for an industrial park, and she slowed further, waited for it to turn. As it turned, her mobile rang. Fumbling for her bag on the passenger seat, eyes fixed on the truck, she swung carefully after it, keeping her distance.

'Hello?' she said.

'Hey, India.' It was Scotto. 'Look, Ellie's been doing her nut trying to get hold of you. Ring her, would you?'

'God, sorry, I should have done it before, but—'

'You've been absorbed in more important matters.' His voice was dry.

'Damn right.'

Hanging up, she immediately dialled Ellie's mobile.

'India! Where the hell have you been?'

'Oh, working. You know how it is. Sorry I haven't rung.'

'I assume you're on your way. I mean I told William and Katy that just because you hadn't been in touch didn't mean you weren't coming. You are coming, aren't you?'

India's mind did a scrambled backtrack. Oh, hell. Katy was hosting a barbie for them all – and it was tonight.

'Hello? India?'

'Give me a sec. Traffic's gone mad.'

Could she go to the barbecue? She couldn't see why not. After all, it wasn't being held at Ellie's, but at Katy and William's, well south of the city. Jimmy wouldn't have Katy's house under surveillance any more than he would his own, surely. She doubted he knew Katy even existed. India checked her rear-view mirror, but she knew nobody was on her tail because she'd been checking all day. Even so, she dithered. She didn't want to bring the Zhuganovs to her friends' doorstep.

'India, India?' Her mobile was squawking.

'Yup.'

'We've done a pig spit.'

India's mouth instantly watered. She'd been so glad of the cupboards of canned foods and cereal when she'd arrived at her house in the dunes, but a pig spit? She could almost taste the crackling now.

'I'm on my way.'

Three minutes later the red Isuzu pulled into a forecourt and she drove past cautiously to see the driver climbing out and stretching his arms. She headed to the top of the street, to a T-junction, and did a U-turn. On her way back down she saw three men in overalls unloading the van – casual, uncaring, just doing their job – saw the big sign at the forecourt's entrance. Kemble Environmental Services.

She drove past, not cruising but not hanging around either, like she was someone heading home after a long day's work, but when she hit the highway she spun the wheel hard left and gunned the engine. Shit, she'd better get a hoof on. She was miles away.

Seventeen

India's eyes kept flicking to her rear-view mirror the whole way. She even stopped at one point on a length of empty road for a good ten minutes to make sure nobody was following her. Two vehicles drove past and kept going, one oil truck and a ute overflowing with straw, but otherwise there was no traffic. Relieved, she stepped on the gas, suddenly looking forward to seeing friends. It felt like weeks rather than days since she'd been in safe company.

When she arrived the sun was lowering and turning the sky pink, the air cooling rapidly. She climbed out of her car and scrutinised the track behind her, looking for a tell-tale plume of dust. Nothing. The air was still and silent.

All at once she was surrounded by six dogs of inter-mingled breeds with wagging tails and shrieks of delight from Katy that India told her could be heard in Darwin.

'Who cares? I can't believe you're here!'

'Neither can I,' she admitted, looking around and trying not to show her amazement. Penselwood Farm wasn't a farm at all, but a zoo. There were lush green paddocks with oxen, donkeys, water buffalo and camels. A handful of sturdy antelopes with black stripes down their faces stood beneath a clump of gum trees, swishing their tails. She could hear the moaning of crows and the high-pitched screeching and chattering of parrots.

'This is Billy,' Katy told her as she gave her a whirlwind tour. Billy was a koala who'd suffered from a nasty virus but had luckily made a full recovery.

'And this is Digger and family.' She pointed out several

wombat earths in the ground. 'The first pair we had dug a tunnel almost a K long and escaped, but since they're nocturnal it took us a while to realise it. We kept putting food out which kept getting eaten, but it wasn't our precious wombats at all, just the local mice and rats having a field day.'

Wild birds were everywhere; currawongs and galahs, pigeons, parrots and white-tailed black cockatoos.

'Half our wildlife are volunteers,' Katy said with a chuckle. 'Even the roos and wallabies try to break in for a free feed.'

It was like being in a different country. Here the ground was red, nothing like the white sandy soil up north, and instead of coastal scrub there were turf farms and dozens of horses and long-legged Holsteins grazing on the hills beyond. She'd guessed the Hugheses wouldn't live in a slum with William's millions, but even so, their house . . . India tried not to turn green, and failed. Beautifully renovated, the old building was raised on stumps – to take advantage of the circulating cool breezes in the summer – and had spacious verandahs, shutters on every window, and a long sloping roof of green, newly painted, corrugated iron.

She could hear William's voice as they approached the back yard and tried to drag her fingers through her hair but it was a clogged and tangled mess after having the car windows open. She had no make-up on, hadn't showered since this morning, and she had no doubt she looked as grubby and untidy as she felt. Some guest, she thought. She may have washed her jeans and shirt, but after her trek in the desert they looked as though they'd been dragged behind a galloping horse for a week. Stained with dirt at the knees and elbows, they were covered in little tears and rips, and had threads of cotton hanging free. She was glad Jimmy hadn't managed to hit her face. At least nobody could see the cuts and bruises under her clothes.

'Sorry I'm late,' she announced, taking in the underground lighting, heated pool, gazebo, and riots of native plants: orange and yellow wattles, pink rainbows, fringe lilies, red kangaroo paws. It was chaotic and colourful and, like the house, gorgeous.

'You're always bloody late,' Ellie grumbled, and India was smiling, walking to meet her friend, when William came at her in a rush and to her complete surprise, hugged her close. It took all her effort not to shout as her ribs howled in protest.

'So good to see you,' he said, voice muffled against her shoulder.

'Hey, good to see you too, William,' she said, and hurriedly disentangled herself, patting his back like she would an over-friendly Labrador.

'Sorry.' He stepped back, looking abashed. Flicked a glance at Katy approaching with a glass of wine. 'I'm not normally so . . .'

'Demonstrative,' Katy finished for him as she passed India the wine. 'But considering you worship the ground she walks on since she saved my life, I'll forgive you.'

William managed a weak grin.

India and Ellie hugged, both checking the other over. Ellie looked great, big belly and all, and India was smiling at the thought of Ellie's baby, *Ned's baby*, until she caught the look in Ellie's eye. Ellie knew something was wrong. Her tattered clothes probably gave her away, along with her awkward gait, favouring her bruises. She was glad Ellie didn't say anything, not even when India told her she wouldn't be staying with her for a while. Just put a hand against her cheek and told her to be careful.

To prevent herself falling on to the suckling pig slowly spitting over the fire and devouring every inch of crackling in sight, India lit a cigarette, took a gulp of wine and groaned with pleasure. No cheap casks for the Hughes household but something vintage and deliciously expensive.

'You've an amazing place,' she said to William as she took another glug from her glass, glad to feel herself winding down as the alcohol and nicotine kicked through her veins. God, it was good to be with friends. 'A *zoo*, for heaven's sake,' she added.

'I call it my financial big black hole,' William grinned. 'But it makes me laugh. Like when a python broke in last week and ate one of the birds, but couldn't get out because his body was so bloated.'

Dying to know how he came to be so wealthy, she decided on the direct approach. 'You're obviously incredibly successful,' she said. 'Do you mind me asking how you got started?'

'Officially,' he said, eyes creasing at the corners, 'I was curious why eco cleaning products didn't do the job as well as normal brands and were twice the price, so I hired a scientist, Brian Derry, to create our competitively priced, eco-friendly Get Active range.'

'Unofficially?'

'It's a gravy train.'

She gave a snort of half-shocked laughter. 'Are you telling me you're not Mr Green after all?'

'Don't tell Katy,' he rolled his eyes dramatically, 'or she'll divorce me.'

'You're as green as the jolly green giant,' she told him tartly. 'Stop denying it. You invented Ecopac.'

'Brian invented it, not me. I just stumped up the funds for his research.'

'You obviously have a thing for big black holes,' she laughed. 'Research is a classic, a never-ending financial bloodsucker.'

'Tell me about it.' His voice was dry as he brought his beer up for a swig.

'So how did you get the money to fund the research?'

William's hand paused mid-air. His whole body went still.

'God, sorry,' she said, cringing at her relentless curiosity. 'It's the journo in me, I'm afraid. Inherently nosy. Just ignore me.'

He took a long pull of beer then raised his head to watch a handful of black crested cockatoos fly past, screeching. The sun had bled out of the sky and stars were beginning to shine in the arc of darkness above.

Since you ask,' he said in an even tone, 'I got a loan.'

Holy cow, she thought. It must have been huge. Squillions at least, to create something as incredible as Ecopac.

'I take it you've repaid it. I mean, God, William, I'm sorry. It's the wine. I'm not normally so intrusive.'

He was still staring at the space where the cockatoos had flown and India's scalp crawled at the look on his face. It was peculiarly withdrawn, almost fearful.

'No,' he said quietly. 'I still owe them.'

'Food's up!' The magic words broke the spell between them. William abruptly turned away and, seeing the tension in his shoulders, India decided to let him be and get her priorities straight. Like leaping for the pig spit and piling her plate high. She was glad when Katy ushered them all inside because she was tired and hungry, which in turn always made her feel cold.

India made a beeline for the open fireplace where great logs of jarrah were burning. The lights were low, the sitting room warm and welcoming with plump couches, thick colourful rugs over old wood floors and pictures of wildlife on the walls. Munching on tender, juicy pork, she took in a David Shepherd painting of African elephants, and realised it was an original. Her gaze then latched on to a collection of photographs of horses displayed on a baby grand piano: sleek horses in parade rings, horses with their necks stretched out as they crossed the finishing line; horses steaming and sweaty in the winners enclosure.

'You own racehorses?' she asked Katy.

'William's hoping to win the Melbourne Cup next year.'

Where William's horse pictures were beautifully framed in silver, Jack's had been a haphazard collection in heavy, ornate frames in every colour you could think of, but there was the same pride, the same passion in their display.

Interesting, she thought, how two very different men used their riches in creating their homes. Jack had built a gleaming white monstrosity of a mansion filled with marble, trophies of dead animals and a pseudo-Indonesian pool area, while William had taken a traditional home and renovated it to the hilt, styling it sympathetically with class and elegance. Talk about chalk and cheese, even in great wealth.

When Katy and Ellie cleared the plates into the kitchen, India glanced at the horse pictures, then at William, sipping wine on the sofa. He looked as contented as only a happily married man with a full stomach could. Would he know Jack? she wondered. Could William give her the lever to open another avenue she could follow? The Melbourne Cup was in a different league from the races Jack entered, but you never knew.

'I was talking horses with someone last week,' she ventured. William turned his head in polite enquiry. 'Heard about one that sounded pretty hot. A stallion called Grafton Statesman.'

If she'd shot him in the foot she couldn't have been more surprised at his reaction. He bolted out of the sofa and across the room to her, expression frantic, wine spilling from his glass.

'Christ, India,' he pleaded. 'Not here.'

'Oh my God,' she said, stunned. 'You know him, don't you? You know Jack.'

'Shhh.' William shoved his glass aside, not seeming to notice it had soaked his wrist, his cuff. He was staring at the kitchen door.

'How do you know him?'

He was making urgent dampening motions with his hands, gaze still fixed toward the kitchen. 'I don't want Katy to hear, okay?'

'Okay,' she whispered.

William hunkered beside her, eyes flicking back and forth between the kitchen door and herself. 'How the hell do you know about that horse? What's going on?'

'I think Jack's the owner of the cargo ship that hit *Sundancer*.'

The blood left his face so fast she thought he might faint. 'You're kidding me.'

'Nope.'

'Are you sure?' he asked. '*Absolutely* sure?'

She wasn't at all, but she made her tone firm. 'Yup.'

'Oh, Jesus. What are you going to do? You can't go after him . . .' His eyes darted around the room, to the windows, the fire, but always returned to the kitchen door. 'I mean . . . oh, God, India. People have tried in the past and regretted it big time. His reputation . . .' William swallowed. 'He's ruthless. Powerful as hell. He'll crush you like a bug beneath his shoe. Can't you drop it?' He gave her an imploring look. 'I don't want you to get hurt, and it would kill Katy. She thinks of you like a sister after what you've been through.'

'I'll be careful, I promise.'

But her words didn't seem to convince him. 'India, I know you want to avenge Ned, get justice for *Sundancer*, but Jack isn't your normal sort of guy. He's violent and callous and has the soul of an iceberg. Everyone in the city knows it.'

'William,' she said gently, 'how do you know Jack?'

He turned his head aside so she couldn't read his face. 'Business,' he said dully. 'Just business.'

And then Katy and Ellie were coming in with coffee and cake, and William went to his wife and put his arms around her waist, pulling her close, kissing her neck, her hair, and

Katy was laughing, half-protesting because they had guests, but melting all the same and kissing him back, clinging to him.

India smiled as she watched them, recognising that they probably slept like Mikey and she did, like shrimps glued together, but something inside her felt cold and uncertain. She couldn't stop hearing herself badgering William earlier in the evening, asking him how he'd got the money to fund the millions of dollars to research his Get Active range and Ecopac.

I got a loan.

I take it you've repaid it.

No. I still owe them.

Eighteen

Back at her house in the dunes, India was smoking her first cigarette of the day in the kitchen when her mobile rang. Normally she'd smoke it on the verandah, but the wind was up and whistling through the walls, leaving little piles of sand on the floor.

'Is that India Kane?' a man asked. Australian accent, surprisingly high-pitched voice.

'Who's calling?'

'Oh, Greg. Greg Elsden. Scotto passed me your number. I'm in Jakarta. I've got your ship here.'

She nearly dropped her Marlboro on to the floor. 'You *what*?'

'*The Pride of Tangkuban.* She's here getting some repairs done. From what I gather she'll be here about a week.'

'What does she look like?'

'Er . . . well, she's pretty big. Looks quite old. Lots of rust.'

'Is she a tanker, or a container ship?'

'Oh, a container.'

'I'll be on the next flight out. I'll ring you when I get there.'

India punched the line free and stood there, her mind a frantic jumble. Could she ring AMSA now? Tip them off? What if Kuteli found out? She'd bet he had contacts in the feds. And what about the International Maritime Organisation? Then she recalled the photograph of Jack dining with Soeharto. Talk about having seriously high contacts in Indonesia. With a shudder she realised she couldn't tell anyone official without the Zhuganovs discovering that she was alive.

She had to go to Jakarta alone.

Ringing Scotto, she got his go-ahead. After all, he was the guy who paid her expenses, and she knew he'd never breathe a word. And nor would Mikey. He might hate it when she was on a mission, but you'd have to rip out his fingernails before he'd give her away. And more.

'I know you hate it when I say this,' he said when she had filled him in, 'but *please* be careful. The Foreign Office are advising all nationals not to travel there and the way you attract trouble . . .' Mikey trailed off and she knew he was biting his lip to stop himself from having a go at her. 'Sorry,' he added. 'You know I can't help myself sometimes. I happen to quite like you. Sometimes.'

'I think you're okay too. Sometimes.'

'Enough to tie the knot?'

'Sorry, Mikey. I've got to go. Love to Polly.'

Pushing all thoughts of marriage, white frocks and her terror at the word 'wedding' aside, she went and rigged up a system that would tell her if anyone had come to the house while she was away. Then she packed her daypack with minimum supplies, grabbed her passport, and drove to the airport.

The guide book India bought warned her that Jakarta was a squalid, overpopulated and dirty city that most travellers tried to avoid and she could see why. The heat was incredible, as were the pollution and the noise. A mix of engines belched fumes all around; motorbikes, public minibuses, *bemos*, and three-wheeled scooter cabs, *bajajs*, that careered about trailing blue smoke. Children ran through the alleys and women threw water on the ground to dampen down the dust. People shouted and whistled, dogs barked, and pop music blared from just about every rickety roadside shop.

Through the open windows of her taxi, she could smell frying garlic, and then the air was full of diesel exhaust and the cloying undertone of human excrement. It was crowded to the point of bursting, the air fetid beneath an anaemic glow of yellow sun trying to pierce the thick haze of pollution, but India felt her spirits rise. She loved being somewhere new, especially a place so foreign to her, and her nerves were tingling in a combination of curiosity and expectation. She felt renewed. As though she was on the brink of a revelation of some sort.

India paid off her taxi at the docks. She had originally hoped Greg might have come along to be her interpreter, but had changed her mind once she met him. She'd gone to his apartment, small and cramped with cane furniture and potted plants, and, without even saying hello, he'd demanded the money, counted it laboriously, then demanded to be her guide for a fee that would have paid for Polly's entire education. Greedy wasn't the word for it.

At the entrance to the dock were two army lorries. Soldiers in camouflage uniforms, rifles hanging loosely at their sides, were checking papers. One of them checked her passport and spat a fat red gob of betel juice on to the ground as he handed it back.

'Kelapa office, over there.' He waved a hand at a low-slung building blurred to brown due to the pollution. 'They book your ship.'

India found the Kelapa office, with advertisements for berths on commercial ships plastered all over its windows. Three Swedish-looking backpackers were discussing whether they should take a tanker to Sumatra or go straight to Singapore. India walked on. The air was thick with heat, and the humidity made her clothes stick uncomfortably to her skin. Swigging mineral water as she walked, India passed a ship loading up and dock workers shouting to one another as derricks swung containers inside its holds. There were piles of timber that scented the air with a sweet resin and India wondered if they'd been illegally logged. Barely anyone took any notice of her as she passed, they were obviously used to seeing foreigners searching for a cheap ride.

India had been walking for well over two hours when she saw a container ship with rust streaking her flanks like bloody claw marks. She had a four-storey block, painted white and topped with filthy windows, that was the bridge. Tears of corrosion streaked from the windows and down the peeling paint. There was no ensign, nobody around that she could see.

Heartbeat picking up, she moved towards the ship, studying the bow, but her port side was clean. India studied it for a while, then studied the starboard side. The port side was *too* clean. It could well have been repaired.

Going to the rear of the ship she saw a dent in the transom, just like the footprint of a man's boot in mud. Her stomach swooped and for a second her ears were filled with alarms sounding, the air-horn blaring, she could hear Cuan's voice, tinny over the tannoy, instructing everyone to get into the inflatables, the life rafts, the ship was going down . . .

She hadn't told anyone about the dent, she realised, because she'd forgotten. It was only seeing it now that it all came back to her. The deafening howl of metal tearing, groaning and screeching, the icy water closing over her head and that grinding sound going on and on.

Sweat drenched her neck and shoulders as she studied the ship's name above the dent. Although there was barely any paint the letters were carved, standing proud of the metal, and in the sunshine it was clear as day.

The Pride of Tangkuban.

She'd found the ship that had rammed *Sundancer*. She'd bloody well found it.

*

India felt a surge of anger so sharp and deep inside her that it felt as though she'd swallowed a sword.

How dare you? she wanted to shout. How dare you do this to people who are decent and kind? How dare you sit there and pretend nothing happened?

The container ship sat, unmoving as the lump of man-made machinery it was. Silent and without comment. So India marched off to try and find its master. A crew member. Anybody who could give her an answer as to why it had collided with them. Why they hadn't stopped. Why they hadn't answered Ned's radio calls and had been running without lights.

Another hour later, she found a handful of offices, but they were all closed, so she headed back to the Kelapa office, where she'd seen the Swedish backpackers.

'Hello, misses,' an excruciatingly thin Indian man greeted her as she stepped inside. He was smoking a long thin cigarette resembling bay leaves, and had a smile yellow with nicotine. 'You are looking to go to Singapore? Maybe Pedang?'

She hadn't a clue where Pedang was, but gave a vague nod. A big ceiling fan wafted round and round, doing nothing but stir hot air against her face and make the sorry-looking pot plant on top of a filing cabinet clatter its leaves against the wall.

'You are wanting to see the boat? Meet the captain?'

'Oh, yes please.' India took the plunge. 'I'd like to look at the ship called *The Pride of Tangkuban*.'

The man placed his skinny cylinder of bay leaves on an overflowing ashtray and turned to a large folder on his desk. Flicking through the folder, he said, 'I am not knowing this ship.' He frowned. 'She is taking passengers?'

'So I've heard.'

He lifted the receiver of a phone and dialled. He spoke in Hindi, quite fast, waited a while, listened some more, then hung up.

'This ship is not taking passengers. Is there not another you would like to take?'

'No. I'd like to see *The Pride.* And if it's possible, meet with one of the crew.' Delving into her money belt she withdrew a US dollar bill from the stack of twenties tucked beneath her passport, and placed it on his desk. 'Obviously,' she said, 'if I talk with someone like the chief officer, or even the master, it would benefit you further.'

She saw his gaze flick to the note, and his eyes lit up. Immediately he got to his feet and shook her hand vigorously. 'I am Batuan, I am very happy to be helping you in this matter.'

India glanced at the dollar bill rapidly disappearing into his pocket. Oh, for goodness sake, she thought. Why did the Americans make all their dollar bills nearly identical? No wonder Batuan's gasping to help. Instead of giving him ten bucks, she'd handed him a hundred.

Three phone calls later he hung up, beaming. 'I am having a very good success for you . . .'

He paused when the phone rang, picked it up. His beam vanished. Another fast conversation, and then he did a lot of listening. He glanced at the pot plant then at her, and rattled off some more Hindi, and when he looked at her again her heart missed a beat. She thought he was discussing her with his caller, but then he averted his head and finished the conversation.

Hanging up, his smile returned. 'So,' he said cheerfully, 'you shall be meeting with a representative of the ship. He will be here shortly.'

The Pride's representative was a young Indonesian man dressed in a pair of clean shorts and an artistic-looking black and orange T-shirt with two cockerels fighting on the front. He introduced himself as Halim, and then they were walking down the acres of concrete wavering in the dense heat, India raising her hair off her neck in a vain attempt to cool down. In the distance she caught the faint chanting wail of an *azan*, calling the faithful to prayer. She lifted her head to watch the slim yellow disc of the sun struggling to break through the veil of smog staining the sky.

'*Panas*,' Halim said with a smile. 'Very hot.'

'Very,' she agreed.

Halim asked her where she was staying, and when she said she hadn't booked anywhere, suggested a cheap, family-run hotel town. 'The Puri Mango,' he said. 'It is a very small losmen, but very nice, and very clean.'

He told her where he lived, and that he didn't work at the docks, never had, but helped run his family's batik shop in town.

Puzzled, India said, 'I was hoping to have a look around *The Pride*. How is this going to be possible if you don't have access?'

'My cousin is the bosun. I will translate for you. His English is not so good.'

Wow, thought India. A hundred bucks went quite a way here. The bosun was third in line behind the master and should be laden with information. If he was willing to share it, that was.

Halim's cousin was ten years older with a wrench sticking out of his rear pocket and wary eyes the colour of black marble. His muscles were hard and twisted like knotted rope. When he shook Halim's hand, India caught the flash of cash palmed between the two men, and wondered if he was a cousin at all. Not that it mattered, not now she was on board.

Flakes of rust crunched under her feet as she followed the men along the narrow steel deck and headed for the white-painted block at the stern. The bosun dragged open the door at the bottom of the block with a screech of exhausted metal, and they went up a flight of stairs through a stale smell of ancient cooking odours and sweat. She was shown the galley, thick with years of grease and its ceiling coated black, and then some of the crew cabins. Each had copious clippings from porn magazines sellotaped to the walls, and reeked of filthy toilets and disinfectant. All the portholes were wide open.

'Do you have air conditioning?' she asked the bosun.

'Not for a long time,' Halim translated. 'The generators are broken.'

She thought of the icy wastes of the Southern Ocean. 'Heating?'

The bosun laughed, showing two gold teeth before answering.

'He says no, but he hopes it will be working for their next voyage. This is why the ship is now in port. For repairs.'

They headed for the bridge, a long, dark room running the width of the ship with a wheel, a radar and radio. A sextant sat on the far port side of the bridge, next to the chart table. Most of the equipment was filthy and looked as neglected as the rest of the ship; cracks radiated from the corners of the window frames. She could see a procession of ants walking across the floor. Indicating the radar, India raised her eyebrows into a question. The bosun picked up a pair of binoculars, shook them at her.

'You're kidding,' she said, unable to keep the horror from her face.

The bosun grinned and shook his head.

India pointed at the auto pilot and the bosun gave another grin. 'Also broken,' he said, beaming. 'I am autopilot!'

In disbelief, she said, 'Does the radio work?'

Halim smoothly stepped into his translator's role.

'Of course. How else would we know when to move?'

'Who instructs him?'

'The owner.'

'And who is that?'

'He doesn't know.'

'Has he ever met him?'

'He says no. The owner instructs the master directly by radio transmission.'

'So the owner could be anywhere in the world?'

Small break while Halim talked to the bosun.

'This is how it works, yes.'

'What about the ship's agent, would they know the owner?'

'He says not necessarily. The agent is only responsible for servicing the ship when she comes into port. He arranges supplies for the crew. The owner's representative would be better. He would know.'

Before she could ask her next question the bosun interjected and Halim added, 'No, he doesn't know the owner's representative.'

'Okay. What about the cargo? Wouldn't companies shipping their goods know the owner?'

'Yes. Along with the broker. The broker arranges the price of disposal, puts the cargo owner in touch with the ship owner.'

'Who's the broker for *The Pride*?'

'Sorry,' said Halim, 'my cousin doesn't know this.'

India watched a seagull wheel past the grime-smeared bridge window and alight on one of the derricks.

'What is this ship's registration number?'

'He doesn't know.'

'Is he saying it's unregistered?'

Silence while the bosun picked at his oil-blackened fingernails and Halim studied his feet. India took this as, 'Yes.'

No wonder the bosun was looking abashed, she thought. Unregistered meant unregulated and unclassed. No safety inspections. No checks run on the seaworthiness of the vessel, and she bet they never had a fire drill.

'Could you ask your cousin when and where he sailed in January?'

The bosun gave Halim a narrowed look, then studied India.

'Chennai,' translated Halim. 'Madras.'

'I don't believe him. I *saw* this ship. It rammed us in the Southern Ocean and left us to sink.'

When the translation came through the bosun flinched and glued his eyes to the floor. His whole posture reeked of guilt and he was hanging his head like a dog that had been caught raiding the rubbish bin.

'I see.' India took a deep breath, wrestling to keep her anger under control. 'What was the ship carrying?'

The bosun was hesitating, so she brought out a twenty-dollar bill and his expression perked up. 'Cargo,' she said directly to him. 'Last trip, what cargo?'

He glanced at Halim then back at the floor. He shook his head.

In for a hundred, what was another twenty? she thought, and gave the bosun the note anyway. She was rewarded with a smile that warmed his eyes into liquid black treacle. He said something, but Halim didn't translate.

'What did he say?'

'It is his daughter's birthday tomorrow.'

'Tell her happy birthday from me.'

Another smile from the bosun while India feverishly lined up her next questions. 'Is *The Pride* part of a fleet? Does her owner have other ships?' She gestured through the filthy bridge window at the ship moored ahead.

'Oh, very many. There is *The Pearl of Kupang*, who is at sea at present, and her sister ship, *The Glory of Surakata*.'

Three ships, she thought. Quite a fleet.

'But there are many more,' Halim continued. '*The Prince of San Diego* and the *King of New York*. The *Monarch of Miami*.'

She said, 'They're American names.'

'That is because they are American ships, operating out of America.'

A chill swept over her. If Jack owned this shipping company, his business was not just contained to Jakarta and the Southern Ocean, it stretched to the other side of the globe.

'Do these other ships sail to Australia?'

More shrugs.

'And he can't tell me anything about the cargo?'

Long consultation.

'He thinks they had some machine parts last trip. Maybe some chemicals.'

'Can he remember a company name? Any name will do.'

The bosun studied Halim for a second, then shook his head firmly.

She decided to change tack. 'Could he tell me who pays the crew?'

'The master.'

'Who employs the crew?'

'The master.'

'I'd like to meet the master. Where can I find him?'

The bosun gave another firm shake of the head.

'The master is away,' Halim said. 'This is impossible.'

Halim was glancing at his watch and heading for the stairs, so India thanked the bosun and made to follow him, but stopped when the bosun put an oil-stained hand on her arm.

'Thank you,' he said very carefully, patting his front pocket where the twenty-dollar bill lay.

She gave him a smile. 'How old will your daughter be?' She held one finger up, then three, and cocked her head to one side.

His eyes crinkled as he held up one hand, all fingers spread.

'Five,' she said.

She could hear Halim's footsteps clattering downstairs on metal and as the bosun glanced at the stairwell, the smile left his face. He said quietly, 'Reenpeese. I very sorry.'

Despite the heat she felt a rush of cold over her skin. Every hair on her body stood on end. *Greenpeace?*

Nineteen

'Greenpeace?' she said out loud, her heart beating fast.

'Shhh.' The bosun put an urgent finger to his lips.

'You know what happened?' she whispered.

He gestured at the binoculars and looked miserable. 'No good. Not see . . . How you say . . .?' He put both hands over his eyes.

Blindfolded, she thought and said, 'Fog.'

'Fog,' he repeated, nodding. 'No radar. I autopilot.'

'But we radioed you. Didn't you hear?'

'I hear radio.' He looked ready to weep. 'You see me. I not see you.'

Sweet Jesus, she thought. He'd heard Ned's radio call and realised there was another ship near by, and assumed, quite rightly, that since he'd been called up his ship was on their radar, so he'd be safe. He'd continued to sail in the same dead line so that *Sundancer* would take evasive action. But Ned had collapsed before he could change course.

She put a hand on his arm. 'It was an accident.'

He gulped convulsively. 'Master not want stop. I see people in the water. Many, many people.'

India refused to give in to the vision he was now reliving. Emma thrown into the sea and Joe diving for her. Others lying in the freezing ocean unconscious, some frantically swimming for lifeboats, the Zodiac's outboard roaring and churning, desperately trying to save them all.

'Master is boss,' she said. 'You bosun.'

Unhappy nod.

'Bosun did good job,' she said firmly. 'In very bad conditions.'

'Bosun very bad,' he agreed.

'No.' She gave his arm a little shake. 'Bosun very good.'

He gave a wan smile, but the misery didn't leave his face.

Both of them flinched when they thought they heard a tap on the metal staircase. Not a footstep, just a tap, like someone had knocked their watch against a railing. Distant. Nothing to worry about.

'Tell me, cargo? Any name of cargo.' She quickly passed him another twenty bucks and he pocketed it fast, expression earnest.

''Stralia?'

'Yes, from Australia.'

'Big cargo?'

'Yes, your biggest client would be brilliant.'

'Kemmal,' he said. 'How you say? Enronment . . . Like Reenpeace.'

A swoop of excitement. 'You mean Kemble Environmental Services?'

He nodded vigorously.

'What were you doing out there? In the Southern Ocean?'

He looked blank.

'What you do,' she amended, 'before hit Greenpeace?'

His brow cleared.

'Cargo,' he said, and as he took a breath to continue—

A crack! like a bullwhip lashed past her ear, and at the same time the bosun's head disintegrated into a bloody pulp. For a second she stood, motionless with shock, but as his body began to crumple, her mouth stretched open and then she was yelling, flinging herself sideways.

Shoulder down to absorb the blow of the deck, her legs were pumping to keep her moving when she hit the floor, and she gave another yell as a violent shot of pain wrapped around her ribs. She heard another crack! but she hadn't been hit, and she was forcing herself for the bosun, wriggling behind his body for cover, and there was another crack! and she felt a stinging sensation on her upper arm as though someone had sliced her with a knife.

Tick-tick, her eyes went round the bridge. Only one escape route, down the stairwell. A man was advancing on her, pistol in hand. He had a thick black moustache and a stripe of grey hair running from his forehead to the crown. His skin shone as though it had been layered with grease. Batuan was behind him making terrified moaning sounds, his face ashen.

'Rajiv!' Batuan cried. 'No, Rajiv!'

Rajiv didn't respond to Batuan's pleas.

She could feel the warmth of the bosun's body against hers and although she knew he was dead she longed for him to rise up and defend her.

The man called Rajiv pointed his pistol at her, looked her straight in the eyes. His mouth was open and he was panting. His hands had blood on them and his shirt was soaked with sweat and the ripe stench of him made her want to gag, but time was slowing to a pinpoint and he was stepping close, gun aimed at her head, his whole posture and expression telling her he had won, when she said, 'I know all about your cargo.' Purposely she slurred her words, as though it was an effort to speak. 'Police,' she added. 'I told them about your cargo.'

Rajiv swung around to yell at Batuan.

That was all she needed. In one movement she grabbed the wrench from the bosun's back pocket and launched herself at him. She heard Rajiv shout something but it was too late. The wrench connected with his head and she didn't wait to see if he dropped, she was going for the stairwell. For freedom.

Wrench still in her hand she charged Batuan blocking her exit. She didn't know whether he had a gun or not, but she still went for it. Screaming at the top of her voice like a wild banshee, her black corkscrew hair streaming behind her, she bolted straight towards him.

His eyes widened and he was yelling, and then he dived sideways and vanished, she didn't know where, because she was suddenly in the stairwell with the smell of stale cooking in her lungs, belting down the narrow metal steps, slipping, skidding, trying to keep her feet. She let the wrench drop with a clank. Five floors to go, she told herself, her breathing frantic, her ribs lancing white-hot. Just five.

At the bottom she hurdled Halim's body. No point in stopping. His head had been almost severed with a piece of wire.

She burst outside and raced along the narrow deck, then she was on the dock, a glorious runway of long, smooth concrete that she could run along for ever without tripping, and she could see startled dock workers follow her flight but she didn't care, she had to get away.

She heard a man shouting behind her, urgent and angry.

Frantic look over her shoulder. Rajiv was coming after her. But what filled her with horror was that he wasn't alone. Dock workers were joining him, running in pursuit.

Desperately India looked for somewhere to hide and spotted a line of army trucks just ahead. Each had a canopy over their backs. A handful of soldiers were up front, leaning against the bodywork of the lead truck, rifles over their shoulders. None of them seemed to hear her, or look her way. She swung out of their line of vision and sprinted for the last truck in the line. There was nowhere else she could go. No other cover.

Fingers fumbling, she undid four toggles and pushed back the canvas. She put her foot on the tow bar and heaved herself into the back of the truck then pulled the canvas back into place. Inside it was dark and hot and airless, and smelled of gasoline. Her breathing was out of control, gasping and wheezing, and she leaned forward, desperately trying to ease the screaming of her ribs, but she forgot all about her pain when she heard the sound of running footsteps.

She held her breath, heart hammering. She heard voices calling to each other, and then they faded a little. But not far. They were talking to the soldiers. What if they searched the trucks? They'd find her in two seconds and then she'd be arrested and slung into jail, accused of the bosun's murder and she'd never get to see Mikey or Polly again . . .

India groped her way to the front of the truck, hoping she might be able to access the cab and see what was going on. She found a hatch and was about to open it when, to her horror, she heard footsteps. There was a click, then the truck gave a small shudder as the door was slammed shut. She heard a hawking sound and then a man spat. Oh, shit. Someone was inside the cab.

She inched to the corner, trying to make herself small, but she knew if anyone peered inside they'd see her.

She heard the rumble of a truck ahead, and then another engine started up. With a rough, choking roar, her driver started his truck. There was a long, agonising crunch as the stick was forced into gear. The truck moved forward, ground into second gear, and just behind them, a man gave a shout. Footsteps ran their way, the man still shouting.

Her mind flew into panic. It sounded like Rajiv. Oh, God. Had he seen the toggles of the canvas were undone? Guessed she was inside?

The truck slowed a little, but it didn't stop.

India moved to crouch at the rear of the truck, readying herself to bolt from cover should the soldier decide to let Rajiv check the back of his vehicle. The truck started to slow. Rajiv was still yelling. And then she heard the driver hit his horn and yell back. He yelled at the top of his voice, well and truly pissed-off. Metal was thumped, as though Rajiv was pounding the bodywork.

The driver blasted his horn again and, still yelling furiously, shoved his foot on the accelerator. India careered backwards, hitting her elbow on metal and making her give a muffled groan. Above the roar of the diesel engine she heard Rajiv still shouting, but her driver wasn't stopping.

India wriggled to the corner and peeked through a half-centimetre gap in the canvass. Nothing. Just a length of concrete dock. The truck began to turn left and then she saw them. Rajiv and about ten men determinedly jogging after the convoy, obviously convinced she was inside, and obviously not about to give up.

She willed the truck to speed up, but it continued at the same steady pace behind its mini-convoy. At this rate, Rajiv would soon catch her.

Clunk, the truck was in fourth gear. Doing maybe thirty Ks.

India peeked outside again to see the distance between her and Rajiv had increased, but they were still hanging in there. The truck rolled along for maybe half a K, Rajiv and his mob now the size of ants in the distance, but still plugging away. After five minutes or so, she peered outside again to see they were passing the Kelapa office and approaching the dock gates. Then, to her dismay, the truck slowed down and stopped. The engine was switched off and the driver got out of the cab and slammed the door. Walked away. She heard more doors slamming. The convoy had come to a halt.

Heart in overdrive, she wondered what to do next. She couldn't stay here and wait for Rajiv to catch up with her. She had to get away.

She took a quick look outside. A couple of dock workers were walking her way, but nobody else. She waited until they'd passed, then clambered outside. Her nerves were strung tight, but nobody shouted, nobody came for her. Sliding to the edge of the truck she peered round, saw soldiers talking, scuffing their boots and lighting cigarettes, their movements relaxed, unhurried.

India took a deep breath and walked for the checkpoint,

forcing herself not to run, to stay calm. She covered her bloody right arm with her hand and kept walking. It didn't hurt. It must be the adrenalin acting as an anaesthetic. One of the soldiers raised his head and she recognised him from earlier, the guard who had spat betel juice on to the ground. She gave him a nod. He nodded back, and without any fuss she was through.

The *bajaj* driver who picked her up charged her twice the going rate but she didn't argue. She sat in the back clutching her upper arm, blood wet between her fingers as he beeped and swerved his way for the centre of town, thanking God she had anything of value in her bum bag: her money and her passport, as well as her airline ticket. Her daypack, however, was still on *The Pride*, so she stopped off at a general store and bought an overshirt to put over her bloody clothes. Then she got her driver to take her to a shopping mall. She did a quick shop in a pharmacy, then hurriedly bought some new clothes and a handful of supplies: shampoo, soap and cigarettes. Finally, she asked her driver to take her to the Puri Mango losmen.

The Puri Mango didn't have phones in the rooms, or en-suites, but, as Halim had said, it was clean and pretty, had a tiny dining room, and an Internet café comprising a bar, a small pond filled with carp, and a single computer.

Rajiv wouldn't look for her here. He'd expect her to go straight to a big Western-style hotel with luxury amenities as well as telephones. She booked a double room under the name of Mr and Mrs Drew and gave the girl behind reception a cash deposit. Once inside her small, simple room she gritted her teeth and peeled off her shirt, half-expecting to see a massive bullet-shaped hole on her arm. But all she had was an inch-long gouge, as though she'd been raked by a lion's claw. No wonder she hadn't noticed it hurting. The bullet must have just skimmed her. It wasn't that deep and although she reckoned it could have done with a couple of stitches to reduce the size of the scar, it wasn't anything serious and already the blood was clotting. She washed the wound with mineral water from a bottle on the bedside table, then fixed it up with a sterile dressing and some crêpe bandage.

India sagged on the bed, suddenly feeling weak, and guessed it was her body's reaction to the stress. After all, she hadn't lost much blood. She wavered between calling the Indonesian police or not, and decided against it. Not only did she want to avoid being overheard by anyone on reception, but she didn't trust the cops not to shove her in a police station for days of questioning while *The Pride* sailed away scot-free. She needed someone with political weight in Australia, and decided on Cuan, *Sundancer*'s expedition leader. The Australian government would have to respond to information from Greenpeace, and get working with the Indonesian authorities.

After she'd set up a Hotmail address she emailed Cuan, then went and washed away the reek of sweat and fear in the communal bathroom. Instead of a shower or a bath, there was a mandi, a large water tank from which you scooped water with a dipper, which made it easy for her to keep her bandage dry. In clean, new clothes, she checked her Hotmail to see Cuan had responded.

All systems go. Keep in touch.

She spent the rest of the afternoon dozing, aches and pains preventing her from falling into a deep sleep. As evening drew in she forced herself to get up, and although her nerves had taken away her appetite, she managed to eat a plate of *nasi goreng*, fried rice with vegetables and chicken and topped with two fried eggs. Fresh Indonesian coffee followed, thick and tangy.

Returning to her room she found a gas lamp set on the floor, casting a warm glow over her narrow bed. The mosquito net had been released from its knot in the ceiling, and a single frangipani flower sat on her pillow. A fresh bottle of mineral water stood within reach of the bed. Although she was pretty sure Rajiv wouldn't track her to the losmen, she went to bed in her trousers and shirt.

Twenty

She awoke with a jerk, eyes wide, unsure where she was. Polly? she thought. Scrambling upright she saw a tangle of sheets around her feet and it was then she took in the light spilling through the slatted window. It was barely dawn but she could see it wasn't a hard, Aussie winter light, but yellow and hot. Outside a rooster called and pots and pans clattered. It sounded as though someone was washing up in the carp pond. The air was humid and unbearably sticky and her mouth felt as though it was packed with sand. She fell back on the bed feeling flat and tired, her limbs barely able to move.

Ten minutes passed before she downed a couple of Panadol and clambered out of bed, clothes rumpled and sweaty. Then she stumbled for the Internet café.

It's sorted, said Cuan. *We've the equivalent of a police commissioner on our side. Where can he pick you up? He's ready to go now!*

India checked the inner-city map on the reception wall, conveniently marked with shopping centres and varying accommodations.

Outside the Karya guesthouse in forty minutes. It's on the corner of Jalan Jaksa and Jalan Cikini.

Good luck!

She'd chosen a place away from her losmen in case she needed a safe bolt hole to return to. The equivalent of a police commissioner. Shit.

In the bathroom she saw her wound had scabbed over nicely and she washed carefully, keeping it dry. As she combed out the knots in her hair, she realised she felt brighter, much less tired, and knew the painkillers were doing their stuff. More energised, she got changed. Smart loose-fitting oyster coloured linen trousers, and matching overshirt. Soft leather shoes, nice and flat should she have to make a run for it. Silk batik scarf. Nothing that might offend, yet smart enough to be taken seriously.

The second she stepped outside the hotel she saw them: two uniforms on motorbikes. They started up their engines and executed a slow turn in the road in order to follow her. A handful of cars slowed and parted around them like a cautious shoal of fish would a pair of sharks.

Her stomach cramped. They wore green uniforms and round white helmets. Military cops. Jesus, what was going on? She knew she'd stirred up a hornet's nest, but this was scary. They were following her slowly, keeping their distance. Could they be protecting her? Or were they waiting until nobody was about so they could gun her down and obliterate any evidence that Indonesia was harbouring the container ship that had destroyed Greenpeace's *Sundancer*?

She wondered how long they'd known where she was staying and reckoned probably most of the night. They'd obviously pulled the stops out the instant Greenpeace had stuck a rocket up their government's backside and arranged hundreds of telephone operators to ring every hotel and losmen asking about a tall, wild-haired woman. Not for the first time she wished her looks weren't so distinctive.

When she reached the Karya guesthouse, firmly shut at six-thirty in the morning, she watched the bikers swing in a circle, checking out the area. One biker raised a finger to his helmet to which the other nodded, and they both halted at the side of the road, sat astride their machines and watched her. Engines running and ready to go.

Her nerves were jangling like windchimes in a storm, but

she steadied herself with the thought that the two uniforms hadn't attacked her, just followed her to the meeting place.

It was cool and relatively quiet. For Jakarta, that was. Several *bajajs* buzzed past, then a bus, already crowded. A weary *becak* driver trundled his three-wheeled pedicab slowly past. A flock of grey Java sparrows squabbled in a clump of banana trees near by, and suddenly, way in the distance, she heard sirens wailing. Lots of sirens. Then she heard a helicopter's clatter and looked up to see it hovering high in the sky, slap bang above her.

A cyclist glanced over his shoulder and wobbled so violently he nearly fell off. She could see why. A motorcade of black, window-darkened Mercedes was approaching.

For a second she considered legging it out of there, but she'd get ten yards before one of the bikes would get her. Best stick to her guns and go for it.

The stream of shiny black cars braked to a hard stop. Dozens of soldiers jumped out, all armed. Pistols, MP5s, sub-machine guns. She could feel her heart thumping, strong and hard, but she didn't move. Whoever the top dog was in the middle of all this hardware, they could bloody well come to her.

Finally, a man stepped out of one of the middle cars – a limo with blackened windows and a miniature red-and-white flag of Indonesia fluttering on its bonnet. He wore an olive-green uniform with lots of gold braid and medal ribbons. Army-cropped black hair with grey stripes above his ears. Reflective sunglasses and shoes so shiny she could use them to put on her mascara. Two guys in uniform on either side, he walked briskly towards her. He was a foot shorter than India, and she knew he hated it by the way his mouth pursed when he looked up at her.

The guy on his right asked, 'You are Miss Kane?' He had a slight lisp and a mole on his cheek.

She said she was and looked straight at Medals' sunglasses, waiting for an introduction.

'We go now,' said Lisp.

No intros, no explanation, no small talk, no mention of Greenpeace or government co-operation, but the Indonesian authorities were here, and that was, after all, what she had wanted. Wasn't it?

As Lisp gestured her forward, towards the limo, a rocket of panic blasted through her. What if I get inside and they shoot me and dump my body in one of their stinking canals? Mikey'd never find me and I can't leave Polly, I *can't*.

Mouth dry, she was desperately trying to think what to do next when she heard her name being yelled. Looking to the rear of the motorcade she saw a collective fuss that made her spirits soar. TV cameras and reporters were jostling with military police, and she could see two journos waving at her. She had to repress the urge to wave back. Her relief was cosmic. If the Press were here, she'd be okay, she had to be.

She gave Lisp a very slight nod, a bare inclination of agreement that she was ready to go, and as Medals turned and walked for his car, Lisp and the other uniform took up position on either side of her and escorted her in his wake.

The Press had obviously been told to stay put, but since she knew they could have been filming the inside hairs of her nostrils if they wanted, she kept her head held high and shoulders back.

Climbing inside the limo, icy-cold with air conditioning, she sat on the back seat with Medals. Luckily it was big enough to give them lots of personal space. She thought he needed it. So did she. Lisp took the bench seat opposite. Gave her a nod. She wasn't sure what it meant, whether it was supposed to put her at ease, or if it was just an acknowledgement she'd done the right thing and climbed aboard without protesting.

Then someone hit the siren button and they were off. Nobody said a word the entire journey. Medals sat, legs planted firmly on the floor, hands folded in his lap, and stared outside. India followed suit, trying to appear unconcerned, as though an army came to pick her up outside a Javanese losmen every day of her life. She gazed at the variety of streets unwinding through the window, and the chaos they left behind; cars and buses shouldered to the side, bicycles dragged randomly into shop fronts, people staring after them, their brown faces fearful.

She couldn't work out why the army had been hauled in. She knew the Australians had an arrangement whereby they could exchange information between the maritime authorities of different countries; did this mean the army was the equivalent of the Australian federal police?

They arrived at the docks and roared past the soldiers at the barrier, sirens still blaring. She caught sight of one young soldier, barely out of his teens, face pale, watching them go.

'Where is this ship?' asked Lisp. 'Please, show us.'

The next ten minutes were mayhem. The limo relayed her instructions by radio, the army cars trying to keep Medals and herself in the middle and protected. One second the Press was at the rear, the next they were passing them when they had to do a U-turn. If she hadn't been so unnerved, she would have been hooting with laughter. It was like the keystone cops on a bad day.

Marines in powerful inflatables bobbed about on the harbour along with a couple of cop boats. She couldn't see a single dock worker. The entire place had been cleared. And when they got to *The Pride*'s berth, India didn't feel a prick of surprise to see she had gone.

The motorcade came to a stop and they all climbed out, army guys getting tense with the media getting too close, the media getting tense with the army guys fingering their guns. Medals and India stood on the dock where *The Pride* had been moored. The cameras and mikes were close this time. She could see a mike labelled CNN and one from Channel 7.

'The ship was here, you say?' Lisp asked her. '*The Pride of Tangkuban*?'

'Yes. She was here yesterday, at one p.m.'

'There is no record of this ship being in this port. Could you mean the *Tangub?* The names are all very similar and I know you are not familiar with our language—'

'No,' India interrupted firmly. 'She was called *Tangkuban*.'

Lisp talked her through what had happened. When they reached the part when the bosun had been murdered he gave a little sneer.

'And you do not know his name.'

'No. But it should be easy to find out who the bosun—'

'Of course. If the ship was here,' Lisp loaded the word *here* with disbelief, as if he was talking about a UFO, 'everything would be so much easier.'

'The bosun had a daughter,' she said. 'And, believe it or not, it is her birthday today. She's five years old.'

Huge silence.

'Tell me,' India's voice carried over the crowd, 'where is the little girl's daddy?'

Everyone was still. Then Lisp gestured at the cop boats and the marines, saying, 'They have been searching ever since we heard you thought you had identified the ship which sank your Greenpeace boat. They have found nothing.'

'I didn't *think* I'd found the ship,' India said fiercely. '*I had found her*.'

More silence, then Medals murmured something to Lisp, turned his blank gaze on her.

'You said there was a man from the Kelapa office on board this ship.'

'Yes. A man called Batuan.'

'Nobody works there of that name.' Lisp gestured a terrified-looking Indonesian forward. 'This is the manager.'

The terrified manager confirmed nobody called Batuan had ever worked in his office, that he didn't know anybody of that name, never had, and at the first opportunity, bolted out of sight.

Lisp said, 'We go now.'

And off they went again. They cruised around a bit as though they were on another mission. They stopped beside Merdeka Square, a barren and deserted field with a gold-tipped monument in the middle, then swept to the railway station. Nobody said a word throughout. India knew Medals was dragging out the whole process. A wild goose chase, he was saying to the world. This journalist is wasting our time.

Eventually, they turned up at the airport. Lisp rapped on the driver's window and clicked his fingers. The driver passed Lisp a plastic carrier bag, which he then passed to India. Her stuff from the losmen. Bandages, bloody shirt and all. The motorcade halted. Lisp opened the door and India climbed out, followed by the entire entourage.

In the departure lounge, Lisp handed her a one-way, business-class ticket back to Perth, told her it had been a pleasure meeting her, and not to worry, they had settled her bill at the losmen. Medals didn't say a word.

Turning to the media, Lisp added, 'We shall be making every effort to find this ship, *The Pride of Tangkuban.* Just because we had no luck today, does not mean we will stop looking.' He continued in the same vein for another few minutes, a load of waffle about international co-operation and government resources while India stood there grinding her teeth. She was nothing but an embarrassment, hence the whole exercise. An international exercise in a brief blast of propaganda to show Indonesia was up front and looking into the *Sundancer* catastrophe, and as Lisp talked she knew he was implying there wasn't a microcosm of evidence that supported India Kane's story but nobody could say they hadn't tried.

She was almost glad to get on board the plane. Lisp followed, wishing her a pleasant trip and making sure she was buckled up and had a glass of orange juice in hand. The instant he left, the plane door was closed and the captain came on the address system, apologising for the delay, but now they had their VIP on board, they were at last ready to go.

As the aircraft pushed back, her neighbour gave her a curious look. 'Hi. I'm Howard. Just wondering what—'

'Sorry,' she said, and pointedly picked up the in-flight magazine. 'I don't mean to be rude, but I really don't feel like talking.'

Twenty-one

When India disembarked at Perth clutching her paltry plastic carrier bag of bloody clothes, she was as jumpy as a cat. She'd seen a Channel 7 mike in Java, and one from CNN, and she could almost hear the reports in her mind.

India Kane left for Perth at four-fifteen today.

Would Jimmy be waiting for her? She kept looking over her shoulder and if anyone bumped into her she flinched as though she'd been stuck with an electric cattle prod.

A gaggle of journalists greeted her in the arrivals hall along with a small group of greenies, who waved their banners and gave a cheer. She found it hard to smile as she scanned the area. No Jimmy, no Kuteli, no man with a pony tail that she could see. But she had no doubt they'd be here somewhere, waiting.

Skin tight, she gave the journos a good ten minutes, reiterating she had found the right ship, but that it had vanished and she doubted they'd now find it. '*The Pride* is the ship that hit *Sundancer*,' she repeated, 'but what she was doing all the way out in the Southern Ocean still remains a mystery.'

The journos seemed happy with what they'd got and as they departed, the greenies moved in. India answered lots more questions, her eyes darting beyond them, to the periphery of the arrivals hall, past the restrooms, along the escalators, then back to the broad windows overlooking the car park. Still nothing, but it didn't mean they weren't there.

One of the greenies, dreadlocks, a bolt through her

eyebrow, pushed a small tissue-wrapped parcel into India's hand. 'For you,' she said. 'A prezzie.' And then the girl was pushing her way back through the crowd, head ducked, embarrassed.

Startled, India called out, 'Thank you,' but the girl didn't acknowledge her and India slid the gift into her plastic bag.

The greenies didn't look as though they were going to depart of their own volition, so India took the initiative and walked for the door, stepped outside. Immediately she started to shiver. The sun was out and it had to be around 15 degrees or so, but she was tired and her blood felt sluggish and cold.

Dare she head for Stewie's ute? Would they be watching her? Of course they would. She looked around for a taxi and then a car was pulling up right in front of her with a squeak of brakes, a grey Holden station wagon, nothing unusual about it, but the passenger door was being flung open and she was backing away when she saw a man leaning across the passenger seat and waving an arm urgently at her. An arm that was big and muscular and had a tattoo that looked like a dove carrying a banner in its beak.

'For God's sake, woman, get in,' the chief said. It was Hank Gregory, the harbour master.

India chucked her plastic bag into the footwell and jumped inside. The instant she slammed the door shut, he gunned the engine.

'Hi,' she said.

'Hi.'

He drove fast through the car park for the gate, pushed a pre-paid ticket into the machine and then barrelled down the road, eyes clicking to his mirrors, to the road, and back again.

'Well,' she said, and cleared her throat, 'this is a nice surprise.'

He gave a grunt, and at the next intersection, jumped a

red light and swerved left, narrowly missing a brand-new Prado who blared its horn at them. India belatedly buckled up. She sat with muscles tense as iron as the chief conducted a set of fast, extremely worrying manoeuvres, and then they were charging into a garage forecourt full of cars and sliding to a stop. The chief sprang out of the car saying, 'Quick! Get in the Shogun! The white one!'

India did as he said, and then they were whizzing past the garage showroom and taking the rear exit. The chief swung the Shogun north and stepped on the gas, still checking his rear-view mirror, fists tense on the steering wheel. India kept quiet.

After they'd made a couple of turns, spent a tense ten Ks threading their way through various suburbs, the chief pulled over outside a nondescript red-brick suburban house with a patch of lawn and a driveway with a tin boat parked inside. He was red and sweating and breathing hard.

'Sorry,' he said.

'But I love being picked up at airports,' India said.

'Sorry,' he said again, and reached out a hand. India took it and gripped it hard. He was trembling.

'I'm not brave,' he said. His words were jerky. 'I'm a coward really. I'm scared of spiders, hate snakes, and I only get into fights when I've been backed into a corner I can't get out of. I may be big, but I'm pretty useless really.' He pulled his hand free and ran it over his forehead, wiping away the sweat. Took a breath. 'Two blokes came to see me a while back, jumped me when I was walking home from the pub. One of them had a knife. He scared the crap out of me.'

Jimmy, she thought.

'They killed Danny, didn't they?' he stated.

'Yes.'

'Christ.'

They both looked through the windscreen at a woman hanging out her washing, then the chief continued.

'They told me that if you ever contacted me, I was to let them know immediately. Where you were. When. And if they found out that I hadn't dobbed you in, they'd . . . Well, put it this way, I wouldn't be walking for a while, if ever. Same story if I went to the cops about their visit.'

'I'm sorry, Chief.'

He massaged the bridge of his nose as though he could rub away the memory. 'I didn't report it. I just hoped I wouldn't see you again. Which went against the grain a bit since not seeing you wasn't exactly on my wish list.' He managed a faint smile. 'But there you were, in full technicolour, on my goddam TV.'

'Ah,' she said.

'And I knew if I'd seen you, they would have too.'

'Hmm,' she agreed.

'So I thought I'd get to you first.'

She looked across at him and said simply, 'Thanks.'

It was after midnight when the chief dropped her back at the airport, to pick up Stewie's ute. The car park was still, silent.

As they'd arranged, the chief followed her to the Brand Highway, to keep an eye out should anyone be following her. Nobody did. When it came for them to part, India for her house in the dunes, the chief for his semi in Fremantle, they beeped one another, flashed their lights. She felt sad to see him go. What a friend he'd turned out to be.

It had been his idea to wait until the airport was quiet before she collected her car, so it would be easier to spot a tail, and when he'd suggested supper at his place to kill time, she'd been only too happy to comply.

The second she was inside the chief's house – lots of polished wood floors and luxurious rugs, golf trophies on the mantelpiece, pictures of him putting, swinging clubs on various greens – she asked if she could use his phone and was passed a hands-free unit which she immediately took outside. Mikey would be going mad for news of her.

She'd dialled Mikey's mobile, got his answering machine. She started leaving a message, reassuring him she was fine, then quickly amended it to she was exhausted, knackered and in need of a stiff drink, because she knew it would settle his concern more than if she was 'just fine'.

'I'll be home as soon as I can,' she finished up, 'I've a couple of things to do first.' She wanted to add something warm and loving but knew if she did her voice might give her away and he'd know everything wasn't fine at all, and the next second he'd be out here and putting himself into danger, so she hung up.

Sipping a deliciously expensive chardonnay that the chief had whipped out of the fridge, India had popped herself on a stool in his kitchen and watched him cook. It felt strange being cooked for by another man. Since she had trouble even boiling an egg, Mikey did all the cooking at home, and she felt a deep pang inside her as she thought of him.

'You okay?' the chief eyed her narrowly.

'Once you get that food on my plate.' She pointed at the lobster tails sizzling under the grill.

'Coming right up.'

India eyed the perfectly tender lobster, the olive-oil-dressed wild-leaved salad with parmesan shavings, the tiny new potatoes drenched in butter and finely chopped flat-leaved parsley. Then she looked up at him. His statuesque physique, bright blue eyes and wild curly hair. She cleared her throat, said, 'Is there a Mrs Chief?'

He paused. 'Not yet. Haven't found anyone I wanted to ask.'

India parked on the wheel tracks in the scrub well away from the house and approached it barefoot. It was cloudy and still and dark as the inside of a broom cupboard. She could smell dead grass and salt, hear the soft slide of surf on sand, but she couldn't see a thing. Shielding it as best she could, she clicked on her torch, but she knew if anyone was looking out for her, they couldn't miss it. Still, she studied the tyre marks in the sand, looking for fresh tracks, and checked the small branches she'd put there before she'd left for the airport.

All were in the same places, unbroken.

Slowly, carefully, India padded to the gravel approach to the house and checked the array of twigs she'd placed there. Then the final tests: the little shreds of paper she'd torn from brown paper bags and wedged into the back and front doors that would drop to the ground when the doors opened. All were just as she'd left them.

She moved into the house, her footsteps creaking on the floorboards, but nobody jumped out at her, nobody rammed her face into the woodwork and stuck his dick in her spine. All lights blazing, India made herself a cup of cocoa. A rich, soothing drink that she reckoned she needed. She took it outside and smoked a cigarette looking into the half-circle of scrub and sand the house lights illuminated.

When she finally collapsed on her mattress, she slept as though anaesthetised.

The sun woke her the next morning, slanting across her eyelids where she lay. Reluctantly, she clambered her way up through the blankets, testing her body for pain. She got up slowly, taking her coffee to the verandah, and collapsed onto Stewie's comfy chair. She felt sluggish and knew she'd need another couple of nights' sleep before she recovered from her Indonesian sojourn. Her fight-or-flight system had been severely tested and needed time to recuperate.

Come eight a.m. she was washed and clean and slightly more energised, but it still took a big effort to climb into Stewie's ute and turn the ignition key. Engine rumbling, she looked over the beige bonnet at the sandy track and wondered if she shouldn't leave it for a day or two. The bosun had told her Kemble Environmental Services were *The Pride's* biggest client, so that was where she should start, but what if she met Jimmy? She'd manage a ten-yard dash on adrenalin, and then she'd be wasted and he'd rape her and slit her throat with his knife.

Starting up the ute she drove it to the front of the house and switched off the ignition. Just twenty-four hours, she promised herself. Besides, I need to do some washing, sort myself out. She grabbed the plastic carrier bag Lisp had given her with her bloody clothes inside, and trailed to the laundry. Upended the bag on top of the washing machine. Jeans, shirt, undies and shampoo and soap tumbled out and she lunged for something falling to the floor, caught it just in time.

A small, tissue-paper-wrapped parcel. The present from the girl at the airport with dreadlocks and a bolt through her eyebrow. With the chief acting like Bruce Willis she'd forgotten all about it. Unceremoniously, India tore the tissue open to find a small wood-carved bracelet, decorated with tiny white and yellow dots, shadows of brown that could be roos, could be dogs or porcupines.

It had been snapped in half.

'Mikey?' She tried to temper her tone, keep the panic from it, but he still heard.

'What's wrong?'

'Where's Polly?'

'Right here. Just getting ready for school.'

She slumped against the wall and closed her eyes. Thank you, God.

'Mikey? Does she still have her bracelet?'

Small silence, then, 'How the hell did you know about that?'

'She lost it?'

'No, she didn't. Some fat kid came up to her after school

and demanded she give it to him. Clever girl didn't argue, just handed it over.'

Oh, sweet Jesus. The woman who'd followed her. She'd had a fat kid in tow. An overweight boy who had pinched Polly's bracelet, which eventually found its way to her to scare her half to death.

'What's going on?'

There was no way she could keep this from Mikey. Not when Polly's safety was involved.

'India, at least tell me—'

'I'll call you later.'

Before she could change her mind, she hung up. Stared at the phone. She had to tell Mikey. She *had* to. But she didn't want to. She wanted to hunt Jimmy down and see his carcass hanging off a meat hook. How dare he threaten her family?

The walls seemed to press in and suddenly the house felt small and dusty and claustrophobic, so she fled outside, broke into a run. And as she ran she felt something loosen inside her, like she'd been in a strait-jacket and been freed of the constriction.

When she came to the beach she shucked off her boots and rolled up her jeans. The sand sucked at her feet, cold and damp, and the dunes were bright white in the sunlight, making her scrunch up her eyes. Sword sedge pricked at her ankles as she scrambled for the ocean's rim. As soon as she felt the sand packed hard and firm, she broke into a run again, wanting to shout and lash out at someone, but no one was here, she was alone with just her rage and tearing guilt for company. *She hadn't told Mikey.*

A wave rushed in just ahead and she charged through it, uncaring she was getting soaked. Run, run, run, her mind told her, don't ever stop, because if you stop you'll face your demons and they're red and bloody and dark and deep and you don't want that.

India ran until her breath was hot in her throat, her ribs

aching, before she finally stopped. She didn't want to run from Jimmy. She knew from past experience running from things that scared you didn't help in the future. To have Jimmy possessing her subconscious, howling in triumph over her capitulation, would be intolerable.

Slowly, retracing her route along the low-water mark, she tracked the scalloped edges of the sea, thinking hard.

Back in the house, she rang Mikey and told him.

Shocked pause. 'He's *threatening* us?' There was a roar of rage followed by a lot of cursing and what sounded like the side of his fist hitting the wall.

'I'm going to bring him down,' she told him.

'No, India. You take the next flight home—'

'Take Polly somewhere safe. I'll ring you soon.'

She rang off before she could change her mind and headed straight to the ute, her tiredness swallowed beneath a wave of determined resolution, her anger burning bright and hard as sunlight falling on polished steel.

Twenty-two

India cruised slowly past Kemble Environment Services, searching for the perfect surveillance point. She had to settle down and watch the place, gather details and routines, and maybe get evidence of a connection with *The Pride.* Knowing she might be there for some time, she needed a spot where she'd be hard, if not impossible, to see. Opposite the warehouse was a cemetary. There were rows of white headstones and copious rose bushes, pruned well back for winter, and a little rise crowded with trees and dense thickets of shrubs that looked perfect for her needs. Dressed in neutral-coloured clothing, she would be well hidden in the gloom of foliage, and the slight elevation would give her a good view of the warehouse.

She parked the ute in the cemetary car park, one of seven vehicles there. Nobody would think anything of it. Just a grieving relative visiting. She checked around to make sure she was alone, and walked casually for the shrubby thicket. As she neared, she saw a woman appear at the far end of a row of headstones, but her head was bowed, and she wasn't looking India's way.

India turned and pushed her way through thick clumps of parrot-bush, the spiky fan-shaped leaves snatching at her clothes. When she was comfortably settled against a white gum, she allowed herself a mental pat on the back. She had a terrific vantage point, almost opposite the warehouse and where she could see vehicles approaching from half a K away. Everyone on the estate drove. Utes, vans, trucks and traybacks drove into forecourts and out, drove to the café at the end of the street to collect their lunch, drove back.

Using her binos, she saw the two-storey building looked relatively new, made of pinky-grey brick, and was surrounded by eucalyptus trees. Out front was a car park, filled with delivery trucks, and a loading bay, where a couple of guys were forklifting crates out of the trucks and into the building's dark interior. Jack's red Isuzu was there, along with a Diahatsu, a Subaru and two Toyotas. Nothing flash, just normal cars for normal people.

She made notes of trucks delivering to the warehouse, the cars parked in the forecourt. She should have hit the Internet first, she realised, and found out exactly what Kemble Environmental Services did, but she'd been so filled with anger she hadn't been thinking straight. She'd just wanted to get here and see the place for herself. *The Pride*'s biggest client.

Magpies squawked and chattered, playing tag through the trees. Currawongs burbled, white butterflies danced. Above her floated that big, blue, endless Western Australian sky. After a while she realised that the trucks delivering to Kemble Environmental Services were unmarked. They came in a variety of makes and colours, regos from Queensland, Victoria and New South Wales but each one was clean of advertising. A whole fleet of assorted, anonymous-looking trucks from all over Australia.

She swung her binos to a Nissan Patrol pulling up. A man got out. Beeped on his alarm. Walked inside. Easy, long-legged stride. Nice suit.

India felt as though the breath had been sucked from her lungs.

Holy crap. It was Jimmy. She stared at the door where he'd vanished as if it was about to explode.

Chest aching with tension, India sat and watched the door like a petrified rabbit, but adrenalin only lasts for so long, and soon she had shaken off her initial shock and was taking down his Nissan's registration, studying the car for any dings and dents – none that she could see – and then she rang Mikey's mobile.

When he answered she said, 'Hi,' but he didn't respond.

'Mikey?'

'What, India?' he snapped.

'Could you run some plates for me?'

He mumbled something that sounded like, God give me strength, and she was cringing, remembering her last call when she'd asked him to look after Polly, and his reaction to Jimmy – a fist slamming against the wall.

'Sorry,' she said, pleading. 'But could you?'

Small silence, and then he said okay, and repeated the numbers back to her. His voice was unnaturally cold. His cop voice.

'Where are you?' she asked him.

'Where the fuck do you think?'

Her mind went blank.

Then he said in the same hard voice, 'Can I have your number? Your other one doesn't work.'

She gave it to him and she was about to ask him how he was, how Polly was, maybe apologise for messing up his life and Polly's while she went after Jimmy, but he'd hung up.

India watched trucks coming and going through her binos, and it was only when a thread of spider's web floated past her lens that it clicked. Of course she knew where Mikey was. And Polly. The safest haven they all knew. A weatherboard house on the edge of an outback town deep in the desert, where a friend of theirs kept a tarantula as a pet. It was where they'd all first met. Her and Mikey and Polly.

She gave a sigh of relief, wondering how she couldn't have known it immediately. Of course that's where Mikey would take Polly. No one would ever find them there.

More trucks arrived and departed, and just after lunch-time, Jimmy came out and drove off in his Nissan. She didn't follow him. There was no way she wanted to come within a hundred yards of him without a gun of some sort, preferably a Magnum .45 that would blow a hole the size of a frying pan through his chest.

At three p.m. Mikey rang her.

'Ready?' was all he said to her bright hello, his voice still cold.

'Um . . .' She was going to ask him to send her love to Polly, but he was already in full flow, and she was scrambling for her notebook.

'All the trucks are owned by Jack Zhuganov. The Nissan, James Zhuganov.'

'Jimmy.'

'If you say so.'

'Mikey, that's brilliant, thanks—'

'When you've finished whatever you're doing,' Mikey interrupted, tone like ice, 'perhaps you and I can have a talk. See how we feel about each other.'

Without another word, he hung up.

India felt as though she'd been slugged with a sandbag. She tried to ring Mikey all afternoon but he had left it on message receive, and although part of her was grateful to Mikey for taking himself and Polly somewhere safe, the other part was small and cold and frightened. Mikey didn't want to marry her any more, and who could blame him?

Tears scalded her eyes. Tears of rage, of love, and grief. She couldn't stop now. She had a crowd of people living in her soul. They stood in a ragged line watching her every minute of every day. Ned and Emma and the other four Greenpeace crew. To the side were the bosun and Halim, and always, right in the middle stood Danny with his spaniel eyes.

She couldn't let them down. Not even for Mikey.

Before she headed to her house in the dunes, she ducked

into the city and checked the Internet. Kemble Environmental Services' website informed her it was a recycling firm with procedures and regulations in place to ensure that it met its statutory obligations.

'Where possible,' she read, 'we seek to reclaim or recycle material for reuse or manufacture into another product. When disposal is the only option we will explore all available routes to remove your waste at the most competitive cost.'

They played a key role in waste minimisation, pollution control and effluent treatment. They recovered scrap metal, recycled glass, plastic and paper, and were signed up to lists of legislation, including the Environmental Protection Act and Use of Transportable Pressure Receptacle Regulations, whatever that meant.

India then went for the company's records and business portfolio, share holders, board members, and eventually found what she wanted.

She let out a 'Yes!' and punched the air with her fist, making the young girl next to her jump.

Kemble Environmental Services used to be owned by Frank Zhuganov, and when he died, his brother Jack had taken it over, along with Frank's son, Jimmy.

The next morning she woke to rain lashing the windows and surf crashing outside; a violent southerly in full flow. A steady drip-drip led her to the corridor where the roof was leaking. On the hunt for a bucket, she came across another four leaks and popped a variety of bowls beneath each one. The house was like a sieve in the wind.

She didn't rush to leave. It was a Saturday, so no doubt the entire industrial estate would be quiet as the proverbial grave, but when she got there, she found she was wrong. Kemble Environmental Services were flat out. Trucks were arriving like a swarm of ants homing in on an open jar of honey. Where on earth were they all coming from? They didn't seem to be picking anything up from the warehouse, just delivering. Hoping to see something unusual with all this activity going on, she parked the ute just inside the cemetary gates and glued her binos to her face.

She watched truckers delivering barrels and crates as the weather worsened. Wind blew in horizontal gusts and trees groaned and hissed. She could barely see a thing through the windscreen even when the wipers were on.

By five p.m. India was cramped and cold and bored, and when a skinny bloke in overalls started up Jack's red Isuzu truck, she decided to follow it. Hurriedly she scraped back her hair and stuffed it into a baseball cap, then pulled on an old padded jacket of Stewie's, and turned up the collar. It wasn't much of a disguise, but it was better than nothing.

India had only been following him for twenty minutes when he pulled into a large Esso service station-cum-shopping centre with a KFC, sports bar and grog shop. India parked outside a subway shop, selling baguettes the size of railway carriages, where she could keep an eye on the Esso's exit. Forty minutes later the truck reappeared and she slotted behind it, praying he wasn't looking to be tailed. The traffic was light at the weekend, making it hard for her to hide.

The clouds remained dark and angry as night began to draw in. Wipers thumping, headlights on, she followed Jack's truck on to the Roe Highway and headed north. The road was newly built, flanked by bare, low sandy banks turned grey by traffic pollution, and it was almost empty.

They were barely fifteen Ks from the city centre when, to India's surprise, the truck swung off the highway and down Welshpool, gunning for the countryside. Ahead were long damp green hills and small paddocks filled with huddles of cows and sheep, and when she glanced hastily at her map, she saw they were nearing Bickley's Brook and acres of walking trails.

Finally, the light left the sky, and because she was so far

behind, she nearly missed the truck turning down a private road and she dithered briefly, wondering if it was safe to follow. She'd stick out a mile and there was no way she could drive without headlights now, it was almost black, no moon.

She decided to wait and see if he returned, and if he didn't, do a recce in daylight. Glad there weren't any fences, she bumped her ute off the road and splashed into a rough field. Parked behind a bunch of trees. Turned off the engine and pushed down the central-locking button. God, it was wet out there. Swollen raindrops lashed against her windows, sending the trees into a shivering frenzy. In the distance she could see a scattering of tiny lights flickering on what she reckoned was a hill. Eleven of them, well spaced apart. People's homes. She pictured them making dinner, chatting, maybe watching TV.

She glanced at the luminous digital clock on the dash. Seven ten. She listened to some light jazz on the radio. Unwrapped a Violet Crumble and ate it more out of boredom than hunger. Wriggling in her seat, she changed the radio channel to catch the news. Mikey was addicted to news, it was as though if he didn't know what was going on in the world it might fall apart. She wondered what he was doing and hoped he wasn't getting drunk. He tended to hit the bottle when he was upset. Or was he completely sober and rehearsing the speech that would tell her it was all over between them?

Rain drummed even more heavily on the car roof, miniature waterfalls cascading down the windscreen. She wiped the windows of condensation, peered around. Nothing but dark murk.

By eight-fifteen she was wondering who on earth would want to be a private eye. Sitting around waiting was so *dull*.

Ten minutes on and a pair of headlights appeared on her left. She waited until the tail lights winked out of view, then followed the truck across the Tonkin Highway, and when it picked up Roe again, she realised it was returning to base and she peeled away to take another route. Map on her lap, interior light on, she belted west on Orrong Road, eventually picking up the Leach Highway which took her straight to the cemetery, and she was parked, lights out, when the truck arrived.

Despite the foul weather and the lateness of the hour, the place was busy. The forecourt and warehouse were brightly lit, and she counted five guys in rain-slickers helping four trucks unload. Jack's truck had six crates that needed a forklift to handle them into the warehouse. Two crates had a big red X marked on each side, but the others were plain.

India watched until the last crate had been shifted and the trucks parked in a neat row, the guys in their own cars and heading home, before she did the same.

After a shower, she took a big pack of nuts and a bottle of red to the big window by the verandah, rain drip-dripping in the various bowls around the house. The southerly was still blowing strong and she could hear the dull boom of the waves as they broke against the dunes. Mikey and Polly loved storms. If they were here they'd be on the lip of the dunes, watching the sea crash in.

India downed the first glass of wine fast, wanting to dull the emotions rising. Mikey had to wait until later. *Please, Mikey, don't abandon me.*

Twenty-three

First thing on Monday, India retraced the route Jack's truck had taken. Wattles and gum trees slumped low on either side, still dripping, as she splashed her way down the private road. In the distance, she saw a thin streak of blue breaking up the grey canvas of sky and she thanked the Lord the southerly had blown itself out. The road broadened and the trees fell away. Quick glance at the dashboard clock. Nine ten. A large, modern complex loomed into view, walls shiny with rain. White sign with royal blue letters. Blue Park PLC.

The name suited the place, given the fact it was built out of blue brick. Lots of glass and steel poles gave the buildings a smart and efficient air. Thanks to a decent landscape architect, concrete was kept to a minimum whereas trees and shrubs were plentiful. There was a little park with a stream running prettily beside it, and tables and benches set along its banks. Not a bad place to work, out of the city and where you could hear the sounds of the bush. There were a couple of ducks quack-quacking and somewhere she could hear the mournful caw of a crow.

A security guy took her details and directed her towards reception. Obediently she did as he said and parked in the space provided. Scanning the vehicles around she saw a mix of utes and sedans, Holdens and Fords; nothing special. Reception was small but smart, and the girl behind the desk small and smart as well. India apologised that she'd mislaid her Press card, and handed the girl her *Sydney Morning Herald* credit card as identification instead.

'You don't have an appointment?'

'Sorry, no.'

Frowning, the girl said, 'They're all very busy, but I'll ring round and see if someone can see you.'

India gave her top marks. Polite, cautious on behalf of her colleagues, but helpful. While the receptionist started making calls, India flicked through a glossy Blue Park brochure.

Blue Park PLC manufactures high-quality plastics . . . Over forty years of experience . . . Stringent specification product lines . . .

A limited company that made plastics. Her stomach sank. How in the hell was she going to wing this one? Frantically she racked her brains for a plausible reason for her being there but came up with nothing.

Behind her the girl said, 'Leo's on his way. He's our disposal manager.'

'Thanks.'

Eventually a harassed-looking man in his early thirties came in. Grey trousers, white shirt and a tie with a golf club motif. Curly brown hair. He cheered up a bit when he saw India.

'Beth tells me you want to do a feature on us?' Unsurprisingly, he looked puzzled. Plastics weren't the most exciting thing to write about, but then a sudden flash of inspiration hit her so hard she felt her face split into a huge grin. He grinned back. Her glee was obviously catching.

'What I'm interested in is today's plastic against tomorrow's. You've heard of William Hughes's invention? Ecopac?'

His face cleared. 'Ah. I see. Let's go to my office. Would you like a tea or something? Beth will bring it in for us.'

'Coffee would be great. Black, two sugars.'

Leo's office was cramped and claustrophobic, and she was surprised. She'd expected something nicer given the exterior of the place and put it down to some accountant squeezing office space in order to cut costs. Leo waved her into a chair and took up position behind his desk. The instant she took out her notebook, he leaned forward and steepled his fingers in front of his face, expression serious.

'Thanks,' she said. 'I really appreciate this.'

He gave a nod.

'Do you mind if I start with a bit of background on your company?'

'Not at all.'

'I've done a little research, but I'd like to hear in your own words what it is you produce, where it goes, what it's used for.'

Leo went off like a clockwork toy. She learned Blue Park supplied the industrial market as well as making accessories. They produced conservatories and fascia boards, polycarbonate roofing and guttering, and also windows and polypropylene for engineering plastics. Silicones and cladding. Polycarbonate sheets, perspex and adhesives and cements. He took a breath when Beth arrived with coffee. Instant, in two mugs with the company logo on their sides.

'Thanks,' India said as Beth disappeared and, taking a sip, she tried her best not to grimace. It was probably the most disgusting coffee she'd had in her life. That penny-pinching accountant had a lot to answer for.

'You've a lot of plastic on the market. Do you think William Hughes could be a threat to your business?'

'Not really. He's going to produce cartons, as far as I know. For milk, orange juice, wine. That's not our field.'

She asked him a bunch of questions about his clients, none of whom she recognised, and quickly ascertained that Blue Park supplied the home market only and delivered all their products.

'You don't have any clients who collect?'

He blinked. Leaned back in his chair. 'I can't see what these questions have to do with William Hughes and Ecopac.'

He was more switched on that she'd thought. Rapidly she weighed up her options. She could go the nice route, which would lead her nowhere, slowly, or she could take the direct route which might backfire and get her thrown off the property, but if she was on the right track, and this was the upfront, honest guy he appeared to be . . . she may as well be bold.

Closing her notebook she leaned forward, turned her tone low. 'Look, Leo, I'm not supposed to do this, but . . . I like you, so I'm going to put my cards on the table. I'm also going to trust you with what I'm about to say, because if it gets out—'

Alarmed, he said, 'If what gets out?'

She took a theatrically deep breath, blew it out. Watched his whole body tense in expectation.

'We've a big investigation going on. An exposé about Kemble Environmental Services.'

Leo stared at her. 'KES? You're *investigating KES*?'

'Yes.' She kept her face serious, sombre. 'And although we know you, Leo, aren't personally involved, things are moving really fast here and the cops are itching to bust in and take everyone down.'

'You're kidding me.' His jaw was almost on the ground. 'They're in trouble? KES? I mean, what's going on? If it's that serious . . .' He frowned. 'I'm not sure about this. Shouldn't you have brought someone official with you?'

She scribbled Scotto's name and the *Sydney Morning Herald*'s number on her notebook, tore the page out and pushed it across. 'Call my editor. He'll put you in touch with the cop heading the investigation if you like.'

He looked at the piece of paper and turned it over and over between his fingers, and glanced at the phone.

'If you'd prefer me to wait outside,' she offered smoothly, 'I'd be happy to.'

'No. It's okay.' Without looking at her he picked up the phone and dialled. Asked for Scotto Kennedy.

India sat with her fingers crossed while Leo spoke with Scotto, praying Scotto would pick up the ball and bat it hard.

'Hi,' said Leo. 'I've an India Kane here investigating KES. I just wanted to ... Right, I see ... yes, I understand you can't say exactly what on the phone ... Who's the investigating officer? Right, Sergeant Johnson.' Long pause while he listened. 'Yes. Yes, of course I'll do what I can.' Leo hung up, his expression shaken.

'Christ,' he said.

India exhaled in relief. Thank God for Scotto, and she hoped her little ruse wouldn't cause him any trouble. It wasn't exactly legal, but since she knew Jimmy didn't do things by the book, she didn't see why she had to.

'Look, Leo, we saw an unmarked truck picked up eight crates on Saturday, seven-thirty p.m. Two crates were marked with red crosses.'

'I'm sorry?' He looked blank.

She repeated what she'd said.

'No, that's not possible.' He was shaking his head. 'We don't work Saturday.'

'Believe me, it happened.'

'No, no. You must be mistaken.'

'Leo, we *filmed it.*'

He picked up a file, gazed at it blankly, then dropped it back on his desk. His hands were trembling.

'Jesus,' he whispered.

'Look, if you could tell me what was in those crates, it'll help you ... well, when it comes to court.'

Leo gulped. 'Well, I've got a pretty good idea, but ... okay.' Swinging to his computer he tapped on the keyboard.

'Eight crates, you say.' He was tapping away, expression tense, and when one of the phones rang he snatched it up, listened briefly and said, 'Sure. Give me five.'

'I've got them,' he said after a while. 'Picked up by KES on Monday. Signed and sealed.'

He leaned back, looking relieved.

'What was in them?'

'Waste.'

A brush of apprehension made the back of her neck tighten.

'What sort of waste?'

'Stuff that can't go down the drain or be thrown out with the garbage. We have to dispose of it responsibly.'

'You're saying it's toxic?'

'Well, not necessarily toxic, but it isn't like throwing a paper bag away.' He shifted uncomfortably. 'There are dozens of regulations, you know, and one thing you must realise is that we meet all our statutory obligations. We know exactly where our waste is at any time, and although it costs us over half a million dollars a year, we dot every I and cross every T.'

'So where are those eight crates now?'

Small pause while he looked at her and she gazed back. He took a breath, picked up the phone, dialled. 'Hi, Nicky. It's me. Look, the eight lots of waste you collected on Monday, could you tell me where they are now? Sure, I'll wait.' Leo covered the mouthpiece with his hand as he spoke to India. 'We've total batch traceability. I'm sure you'll find it's just some sort of mix-up . . .' He turned back to the phone. 'Oh, hi. Right. I see. No, er, that's fine.' He gave a slightly hysterical laugh. 'That's what I have too. Sorry to bother you.'

He hung up, looking sick.

'Leo,' she said, 'what did Nicky say?'

His Adam's apple bobbed up and down.

'Leo,' she warned.

When he spoke it was almost a whisper. 'She doesn't have any record of them.'

Twenty-four

India let a long silence develop.

'So where did they go?' she asked. 'You're the disposal manager, you should know.'

'Fuck.' The look in his eyes turned wild. 'They can't dump that shit anywhere. Not P24. It's got to be contained. They *can't*.'

'Leo, have you ever had to follow up any waste with KES before? Checked that it left you on the right day, arrived at KES when it should?'

'There's no need! They're fully regulated in transportation and disposal, that's their job, *not mine*.' He gulped, adding, 'The only time I check is when the inspectors turn up. We tally KES's records with mine ...'

'And they've always been accurate?'

'Totally!'

'Hmm,' India said and took a pretend sip of disgusting coffee, trying to give a sense of normality, calm him down. 'If your records are in sync with KES's, then my guess is someone's pulling a fast one in the middle. Somebody from your company, and someone from KES.' Her tone turned musing. 'I wonder who they could be?'

Both of them jumped when the door opened and a woman stepped inside.

'Sorry, Leo,' she said, not sounding sorry at all. 'I thought you said you were going to be a couple of minutes.'

Leo looked at India like a wallaby fixed in the glare of a roo-hunter's spotlight.

'I was just going,' said India, and quickly slipped her notebook and pen into Stewie's surfer-stickered daypack.

'Er, Elaine, sorry,' he gestured weakly at India. 'I was, er . . . busy.'

'So I see.' The woman's tone could have seared a steak.

Slim as a toothpick, sharp suit, tightly permed hair, India reckoned the uptight cow would need three bowls of prunes to help her mental constipation through the day.

'I'll just see her out, I mean . . .' Leo shot India a terrified glance.

'It's okay, Leo,' India assured him, 'I know my way. And thanks for the advice. You're a great friend.' She patted her flat belly. 'My little one thinks so too. Thanks.'

She left his office to Elaine's blink of surprise, Leo's shoulders slumping with relief, and walked along the long blue corridor to reception.

Giving Beth a smile, she went over saying, 'Thanks for the coffee.'

'No worries.'

'Look, I wanted to write Leo a thank-you card. Could you let me have his address?'

India left with not only Leo's address but his home telephone number as well as his mobile.

Driving back into the city, she felt the familiar roll of excitement as everything started to fall into place. Jack's brother, Frank, had made his millions in the rubbish business, and either he or Jimmy had obviously expanded into the illegitimate market. Jack's trucks were collecting waste from companies who didn't want to go the official, highly expensive route of disposing it legally, and she'd bet her last dollar Jack and Jimmy were shipping the lot off to Chennai at half the expense. She thought of Greenpeace's fight against dumping the world's toxic waste in Asia and gave a shudder.

Turning her mind to KES, she wondered whether she

had the courage to break into their offices, see if she could confirm the scam. If it was a cash business she doubted she'd find much. They wouldn't keep ledgers of their dodgy dealings.

India stopped to refuel the ute, then headed back to her shrubby rise in the cemetery. Aside from a gardener trimming the lawns with a strimmer, nobody else was around. A quiet day for mourners. She watched a couple of trucks unloading crates into KES's warehouse, and, an hour later, Jimmy turned up. Natty suit, shiny shoes. He stayed for exactly two hours and twelve minutes, and then left.

A little later, India saw a blue truck pull into the loading bay. It had a big white logo on its sides, OG, the letters formed by dolphins swimming nose-to-tail. She hadn't seen it before, and quickly made a note of its registration. Crossing her fingers, she called Mikey, and left a message with a lot of pleading and begging for him to check the truck's rego, she'd owe him big time, and she was sorry for being such a pain in the backside, she didn't mean to be . . . She hung up as she felt her throat start to close.

Barely twenty minutes later, he called back.

'Got your truck owner.'

His tone was arctic. India swallowed, said, 'That was quick.'

'Bobynin Zhuganov.'

Interesting, she thought. Bobynin was the first Russian-sounding Christian name she had come across.

Mikey hadn't hung up, so she said, 'Thanks, Mikey.'

Small silence, then, 'I take it he's a rellie of Jack's. The guy who owns all those trucks.'

'Correct. And you ought to know there's a Detective Inspector Zhuganov along with a constable called Bryce Zhuganov.'

'Christ, India.' The cold tone melted into horror. 'Don't tell me you've unearthed some Australian mafia. Look, do you want to fill me in?'

Did she ever. But just as she began to talk, she saw the blue truck back up to the dock.

'Mikey, hang on a sec.'

Raising her binos, she stopped breathing. Two crates were being loaded inside. Both had big red crosses on their sides. They were Leo's. Blue Park's waste. Boy, did she want to see where they ended up. The next second the roller-doors were slammed shut and the blue truck started up.

'Look, I've got to go,' she hurriedly told Mikey. 'I'll ring you tonight.'

She'd only been following the truck for twenty minutes, when she checked her rear-view mirror. Her stomach swooped. There was a cop car right on her tail. Sweat sprang on her skin and she quickly indicated right, intending to pull into the outside lane to overtake the truck, accelerate and disappear.

Please God, she prayed, don't let it be Bryce.

She checked the rear-view mirror again, ready to see the cop car flash its lights and pull her over, but it was indicating left. *It was exiting the highway.*

Limp with relief, India decelerated and edged behind the truck again. God, she hoped she wouldn't panic quite as much every time she saw a patrol car. Lighting a cigarette, her nerves began to settle as she continued to track the truck, but she kept a sharp look-out in her mirrors for cop cars, as well as Jimmy's grey Nissan.

They'd just passed a sign for the Cannington Greyhound Racetrack when the truck indicated left and plunged into another industrial estate. Plumbing and drainage specialists, auto parts, wreckers and truck sales. Swinging left again, she followed it down a long street with parked cars on either side. Five hundred metres on, the truck turned through a set of factory gates belonging to a company she recognised.

Ocean Green, producers of the most eco-kind and expensive refrigerant known to man.

She paused at the gates, engine running, eyes clicking

from her mirrors and back in case she was holding up traffic, and watched as the truck reversed to a dock at the far end of a huge forecourt. Within seconds Leo's crates had been forklifted inside.

What the hell would Ocean Green be doing with Blue Park's waste? Swinging right, India pulled over and inched her ute between two sedans. Then she picked up her mobile.

'Leo?' she asked. 'India Kane here.'

'Er . . . Hi.' He swallowed audibly.

'Look, a quick question. What use could your waste be to another company?'

'What do you mean?'

'Well, you remember I mentioned two of your crates with big red crosses on their sides?'

His voice went faint. 'P24.'

'What use could P24 be to a refrigerant firm?'

Silence.

'Leo?'

'*They're using P24 in refrigerators?*'

'Well, nothing's confirmed, but—'

'Oh my God. They can't do that!'

She could see his face clearly in her mind, completely panic-stricken.

'Leo, please, I need you to be *calm*. Talk me through what P24 is and how it could be used in refrigerants.'

Small silence where she hoped Leo was regaining some control.

'Okay.' He cleared his throat a couple of times. 'Right. Um . . . well, do you know how a fridge works?'

'Not really.'

'Oh. Well, there's a gas inside the fridge, and as it expands, it uses energy, making everything around it cold. Refrigerators and air-conditioners used to use CFCs as they were efficient in absorbing the heat, but since they're ozone eaters they were banned. I guess P24 could be used to produce a new, more efficient gas, but it's *illegal* . . .' He trailed off then said, 'Are you *sure* they're using P24?'

'Yes,' she said firmly.

'That is such a bad idea.' She had no doubt he had his head buried in his hands.

'Why?'

'What if it *leaks*? You wouldn't even know! It's odourless, evaporates easily . . . It could *kill* you.'

A rush of ice swept over her.

'Say that again?'

'P24 attacks the lungs,' he said, and he was talking about masks and protective clothing but India wasn't listening. She was reliving her dropping the milk pan in Ellie's kitchen. *There had been no air.*

The pathologist's voice. *His lungs were constricted and filled with inflammatory cells.*

Ellie's Dad. *Sick as parrots a lot of them. They've lost five in the past year.*

It wasn't Albert's curse killing the residents of Jimbuku Bay, she realised. It was Ocean Green's ecologically sound refrigerants.

They had to be leaking.

Twenty-five

India hung up on a distraught, almost hysterical Leo, her mind whirling and already planning ahead. She'd ring Mikey first and then the feds. Between them they'd get a team of cops here within minutes and they'd have hard evidence to use in an official investigation, thanks to two crates of P24 on-site. Next up she'd warn Ellie not to return home, then she'd call Scotto. Jesus, what a story! Trembling with excitement, India reached for her phone, and then decided she'd better get the hell out of here first. She could call everyone once she was under way.

Her fingers were on the ignition keys when she became aware of a vehicle pulling up alongside. For a second she thought it wanted her parking space, but as she looked over to ask it to let her out, her heartbeat froze with shock.

It was a cop car.

The muscles in her stomach contracted as the sour taste of fear rose to her mouth.

Two uniformed cops stepped out. One she didn't recognise, but she did the other.

Bryce Zhuganov was smiling as he came over.

Fingers trembling she quickly pressed the central-locking button and was about to start the car, then realised she had nowhere to go. They'd boxed her in. Bryce came to her window. The other cop took up position by her passenger door.

Bryce tapped on her window, indicated she open it.

India wound it down a couple of centimetres.

'G'day, Miz Kane,' he said.

'Hi.' Her voice was scratchy with fear. Bryce heard it too, because the smile broadened.

'Would you step out of your car, please?'

'Why?'

'Please, step out of your car.'

'Not until you give me a reason.'

To her horror he unholstered his gun and she was lunging to close the window but it was too late. He had slid the barrel through. Tilted it so that it pointed at her lap.

'This reason enough?'

Desperately she glanced across at the other cop. He was standing back from the car, both hands on his pistol, stance low-slung and ready for action.

Sweat streaming, India reached for her mobile.

'Don't. Or I might have to shoot you for reaching for a weapon.'

She dropped her hand.

'Out of the car. *Now.*'

A dozen crazy possibilities raced through India's mind. Could she ram the car in front? Ram the car behind, then the cop car and charge away? Would it be possible? No, but it would create a lot of noise. People would notice. She mustn't get out of the car.

She leaned forward, pretending to be reaching for the central-locking button and, hoping her body was blocking his vision inside the car, she made one last attempt for her mobile.

'I'll shoot!' he yelled. 'Don't think I won't!'

The other cop was now standing well back and she knew he was taking Bryce seriously.

Frantically she scanned the street for help. A couple of cars drove past slowly, and there were two people at the far end of the street, staring, but they were too far away.

'You've five seconds,' he warned. 'Five. Four . . .'

India made a lunge for the ignition then thought better of it.

‘Three. Two . . .’

‘Okay, okay.’ Her voice was trembling. ‘I’ll come out.’

The second India unlocked the car Bryce pulled open her door and hauled her outside, spinning her around and ramming her face-down against the bonnet of her ute. Quickly, he patted her down.

She heard a truck driving down the street and made to turn her head but Bryce pushed his pistol hard against her neck.

‘I want you in the back of my vehicle,’ he told India.

‘Where are you taking me?’

He didn’t reply, simply yanked her backwards and, with his gun still jammed against her neck, marched her to his car and forced her inside. A Plexiglass partition with heavy-gauge metal mesh separated her from the front two seats. Her doors had no handles on the inside. The windows were tinted. No point in waving or gesticulating madly to pedestrians who couldn’t see her.

She saw the other cop hop into Stewie’s ute, buckle up and start the engine. Dread drenched her. What was he going to do with it? Burn it to a husk so there wouldn’t be any lead for Mikey or the feds to follow? Oh, God, this was looking really bad. She should never have got out of the thing, but Bryce would have shot her, she had no doubt.

They drove for over half an hour back through the city. India studied her mobile prison for any weapon – even a piece of broken plastic or a dropped match might help – but found nothing. She wondered how Bryce had found her, whether Leo had dobbed her in. Or if someone had spotted her with her binos outside KES. Perhaps someone in Cape Cray had mentioned her to someone who was related to the Zhuganovs and they’d known all along that she was around.

Ginny’s voice. *They’re all related to bloody everybody. Can’t move for the buggers.*

The miles slipped away as they headed north, and then

she saw a green and white road sign: *Shoalhaven* 84. Bulimba 145. India stared at the sign, unable to believe what was happening. They were headed for Jack's place. What would happen when they got there? Would Jack kill her? And where was Jimmy?

Struggling to be calm, she turned her mind to Ellie. If she didn't escape, Ellie would return to her smartie-coloured house and she and her baby might die. *P24 . . . It attacks your lungs.*

Jesus, and what about Western Australia's health minister? Hadn't he promised every hospital clinic new refrigerants from Ocean Green?

She wondered how Ocean Green could get away with using a poison and her mind jumped back to when she'd first trawled the Internet, the Zhuganov-owned industrial cleaning service, the Zhuganov at the top of the pile in governmental safety checks on manufactured products. Always one of the family in just the right position with the right power to help another relative.

As she'd predicted, Bryce turned right at the sign: *Goondari Stud.* The road was now following the sea, and she remembered slowing down all those days ago to watch the surf.

When he came to the first gate and got out, India immediately leaned back on the seat and punched at the rear window with both feet. She was panting as she pounded at the glass, but it was too strong, no doubt reinforced, because nothing happened.

She glanced up front to see Bryce was returning to the car. Hurriedly, she took up her seat again. She didn't want him to know how determined she was to escape. She wanted him to think she was too scared to move, so she could catch him off guard.

He drove through the gate, but he didn't stop and close it behind him. Did this mean he'd be returning shortly?

They entered the valley and approached the second gate.

This time when he got out to open it, India dived for the mesh and hooked her fingers around the cold metal and pulled and yanked, hard as she could, in the desperate hope another prisoner might have loosened it, that a hinge might break ... but it was solid and unforgiving, so she abandoned the grille and lashed her boots at the side windows.

Quick glance ahead. Bryce was returning. She put every effort in the next kick, but the glass held.

She wanted to scream with fright and frustration as he hopped inside and continued along the track, but she kept quiet. The only way she could maintain her strength was to keep her fear bottled up and out of sight. She heard a rattle as they passed over the cattle grid. Saw horses in paddocks on either side, grazing peacefully. Then the huge white monstrosity of a mansion, and the rubbish tip.

A grey Nissan was parked in front of the mansion and she felt a whimper flutter in her throat.

Jimmy was here.

Twenty-six

Bryce parked next to the Nissan, hopped out. The second he slammed his door, the five dogs rocketed down the ceremonial stairway and tore straight for him, barking madly.

Tear his throat out! she willed the dogs, but Bryce was calling to them, and she saw them slow, start to wag their tails. The cop bent over and petted one of the German shepherds, then the spaniel.

As he straightened up he waved a greeting at someone, and Jimmy came into view. Jeans, blue denim shirt, big leather boots, carrying what looked like a baseball bat. He came to Bryce and clapped him on the shoulder. Bryce clapped him back. Classic Aussie male greeting. They started to talk. They weren't looking at the car.

India started kicking at the side window. Thud-thud-thud. There! It had cracked! There was a crack in the corner. All she needed was one more almighty kick . . .

Her boots were about to smash through the glass, she was sure, when a figure appeared and the door suddenly opened. India's feet hit nothing but air and she sprawled backwards for a second, but then she was rolling on to her side and charging outside, uncaring about Bryce's gun. She'd rather be shot trying to escape than have Jimmy slash her throat.

But he'd been ready for her. As she exploded from the car, something hit her very hard on her shoulders and she went sprawling to the ground. Another whack and pain blasted through her. It felt as though her shoulder blades had shattered. Her lungs were rasping and groaning.

'You really don't know when to give up.' His voice was admonishing.

He was going to kill her. She had nothing to lose. So she lay there and tried to get her breath back, not thinking about the pain, but thinking how to hurt him.

'Get up, cunt.'

She moaned and pretended to try and get to her feet and slumped back on to the ground as though it was too painful. In that brief effort, she'd seen Bryce was behind Jimmy, pistol in hand. Jimmy was tapping his baseball bat against the ankle of his boots.

'Get up,' he repeated.

She put out a hand as though she needed help and moaned some more. Waited for him to come closer. But she'd read him wrong. He raised his bat and whacked it against her shoulders again and this time she screamed.

'I'm not stupid,' he said.

She was shuddering and shaking, her shoulders pulsing red-hot. She couldn't stop the groans jerking from her throat.

'Now get up before I hit you again.'

India put her palms on the ground and forced herself to her knees. Made it to her feet. Stood there, swaying. She heard a horse whinny and she could smell dried grasses and manure.

'Walk to the stables.'

Almost crippled with pain, she walked unsteadily ahead of him, towards the stable block. The dogs, she saw, had gone. Terrified of getting a whack themselves, no doubt. As she stumbled forward she scanned the area around her, looking for a piece of wood, a nail, but the ground was clear, just shreds of straw and pebbles . . .

There. A small rock just ahead that would fit in her hand.

She stumbled and was going to fall to her knees, grab the rock, but he said, 'You fall over, you get another whack.'

If he hit her again, he might break something and she'd be unable to move, to fight back. She had to wait for another opportunity.

As she passed the horse box, she thought she heard the sound of an engine in the distance. Jimmy had heard it too, because he said, 'Go see who it is. Get rid of them.'

Jimmy jabbed her between her shoulder blades with the bat and a stab of pain shot into her neck.

'Move, bitch.'

He prodded her past a couple of stables and as they approached the third there was a clatter of hooves, and a big, black head snaked out and snapped at them with yellow teeth. Through her blur of pain she recognised Jack's pride and joy, Grafton Statesman. Aka BB. Bloody Bastard.

She was looking at the horse and wondering if she could let him out, create a diversion, when the next second an iron railing thudded against her skull.

She folded slowly to the ground. Her head was buzzing like a swarm of bees and then everything went quiet and dark. She could feel the tickle of straw against her cheek but nothing else. Gradually, even that tiny sensation bled away, and although she tried to fight against it, she lost consciousness.

When she came round, she was lying on her side, her head aching so hard she wondered whether Jimmy had cracked her skull. Her shoulders and back were throbbing mercilessly, and she wasn't sure if she was glad to be alive or not she hurt so much.

After a while, a sharp, pungent smell of ammonia seeped slowly into her senses and she opened her eyes. She was lying on dirty straw in a stable. It was dark, and for a moment she thought it might be night, but then she took in the light leaking through the cracks in the door. Jimmy had merely shut her inside.

She had no saliva and as she tried to swallow, she became aware her mouth was stuffed with cloth, and that more cloth was wrapped around the lower half of her face, keeping the gag in place. Her feet were bound with rope, her hands tied behind her back.

Up shit creek without a paddle, she thought.

She pictured Polly helping Mikey make bread, her skinny arms coated in white flour up to her elbows. Polly had nicknamed her after Damala the eagle hawk because she thought India was so brave. She'd be horrified if she could see her now, lying on dirty straw, waiting to die.

A trickle of energy returned. She had a family to return to.

Bracing herself against the pain, she started to roll on to her front but stopped at a violent clatter to her right. Slowly, she turned her head to see a huge black form against the wall of the stable, head collar strung tight and tied to a ring in the wall.

Oh, shit. It was BB, Jack's psychopathic stallion. At least he was tied up. So long as she kept clear of his hooves, she should be okay.

Hauling herself to her knees, she dragged her hands over her hips. Then she fell back and despite the crashing pain in her shoulders, eased her bound hands past her thighs and feet, until they were in front of her, but she couldn't stop the grunts and groans of agony exploding from her throat at the effort.

BB started throwing his head violently against his head collar, his eyes rolling white in the gloom.

India concentrated on untying the ropes binding her feet. They were tight, but she persevered until they were free. Shuffling through the straw and away from the increasingly restless stallion, she used the wall to get to her feet. Feeling sick and dizzy, she willed herself not to pass out.

She started to wonder where Jimmy was, but forced her mind away from him and began to pick at the knot at the back of her head which held her gag. He'd tied it so tightly she wasn't sure if she could undo it, and hurriedly tried to get her woozy mind into gear.

Hands free first or gag?

Hands.

She looked around for something to cut the ropes with but all she saw was a black horse jerking his head and rolling his body against the waist-high manger running along the wall adjacent to him. Turning her concentration back to her gag, she paused when she heard a man's voice outside.

'Hey,' Jimmy said. 'How's it going?'

'Pissed off, since you ask,' another man said. 'I've meetings back to back in Melbourne and Sydney, but no, I can't live my own life. I have to be here when he asks.'

It sounded like William. But what would William be doing here? Was she hallucinating?

'Ever think there might be a reason for it?' Jimmy responded.

'Oh, there's always a reason. But I'm sick of it. I want out.'

It *was* William. She was shouting, *William, William, William*, but she made no sound apart from a faint gargling noise behind her gag, so she lunged for the door and battered her wrists against it.

'What the hell's that?' William said.

'BB. He's been a pain in the backside so I shut his door.'

India was making so much noise she couldn't hear what they were saying, but no way did she sound like a horse. William would have to investigate, he *had to*. She began kicking the door. Then she hit it some more with her fists.

She heard BB's enraged squeal behind her but she was riveted to the sound of a bolt snapping open. The next instant the top half of the door swung wide.

William stared at her, expression appalled. 'India? What the hell . . . ?' He started to fumble with the second bolt but Jimmy appeared and put a hand on William's arm.

'Don't even think of it, Bobby-boy,' he said.

'But she's *tied up*!'

India's fingers were fiddling with the knot at the back of her head, digging and seeking a purchase. She was willing William to look at her, so she could communicate with her eyes and form a plan. Like he would punch Jimmy and she'd bust out of here. Anything to give her a chance, but he was focused on Jimmy.

'That's the least I'm going to do to her, believe me.'

'You can't!'

She took in the way BB's hooves were thrashing as he plunged against his rope, and then she felt her forefinger sink through the knot. Yes! She yanked and tugged at the bond, desperate to free her gag.

'It's called damage limitation.'

'No, Jimmy. We talked about this. We agreed. You scared her off . . . she went *home*!'

'I lied.'

India was fighting to loosen the cloth, only half taking in what they were saying.

'Let her go.'

'NO.'

The deep gravelly voice smashed between the two men like a block of concrete dropping from a great height. She saw the solid breadth of chest, the sloping fighter's shoulders. Her stomach and entrails went cold. Oh, Jesus. Jack was here.

Small silence, then William's voice, sounding fierce. 'Her boyfriend's a *cop*. For Christ's sakes, will you just *think*. If she disappears, we'll have half the Australian police force on our doorstep.'

'Shut it,' Jack said.

William went quiet.

'It's all sorted,' said Jimmy. 'I swear.'

Another silence. Then, 'Tell me.'

'Tony flew in yesterday and Pete and Anne are sorting it as we speak. The offices are being cleared. Trucks, paperwork. We can't help the ship being where she is at the moment, but it's her last pick-up. Hammond says she'll be gone in twenty-four hours. There'll be nothing for them to find. *Nothing*, so long as this interfering bitch is out of the way.'

'No,' William said again, voice hard.

Jack moved to William and put an arm around his shoulder. Spoke quietly. 'Bobby. You want to know where we picked her up?'

'I don't care. I've already told you I don't want her hurt. I want you to *let her go*.'

Eyes fixed on the men, she increased her efforts to rid herself of the gag. Life and death. *She had to talk to William.*

'We found her outside Ocean Green.' Jack's voice was gentle, almost as though breaking the news of the death of a loved one. 'She followed a certain delivery there. You know the one.'

William swayed so violently she thought he was going to pass out.

'She . . . she knows about the P24?' His voice was faint.

'Why else was she there?' Jimmy interjected harshly. 'Picking up a brochure so she could order a new fridge?'

'I *told* you it was a mistake to use it.' William bleated, his face ashen. 'Cutting costs like that . . . but you wouldn't *listen*.'

'The second it gets out, you know you'll be finished,' Jimmy sneered. 'No one will want to buy your precious eco-rubbish any more.'

William looked as though he was going to be sick.

Suddenly the knot gave way and she spat out the wad. 'William,' she croaked. Desperately she rubbed her lips with the back of her hands, working her tongue against her gums until she felt the relief of saliva flood her mouth. 'They're going to kill me. Please, you've got to *help me*!'

'I don't want her hurt,' said William, but his voice had lost its protesting edge and she could see he was trembling.

'So you've said a thousand times,' Jimmy snapped. 'Now for Christ's sake piss off and let me get on with it.'

'Don't let him kill me!' she shouted. 'Please, William, I'm your *friend*!'

'Oh, Jesus.' His voice wobbled.

'William!' India yelled. 'I saved Katy, *remember*? What about your oath?'

Her words seemed to have an effect. William shrugged Jack's arm off his shoulder and reached determinedly for the stable door bolt, but Jack stopped him with a hand on his arm.

'Bobby,' his voice was soft, 'what will happen when Katy finds out?'

William stilled.

'You really think Katy will still want you?'

William looked desperately at India, and it was then that she saw the worm of fear writhing at the back of his eyes.

'William, my cop friends know everything,' she spoke fast. 'I told them this morning. And when Katy discovers you stood back and let this man *kill* me—'

'They know fuck all,' Jimmy interrupted. 'She's just bullshitting to save her ass.'

He abruptly swung the upper half of the stable door shut with a bang, and bolted it shut.

She heard William say chokingly, 'I don't want this.'

'Then you'd better leave us, little brother. Since your fragile sensibilities can't take it.'

Twenty-seven

India stumbled back. William was Jimmy's *brother*?

Oh my God. She almost flinched when more thoughts crashed through. Jimmy had called William Bobby-boy. Was he Bobynin Zhuganov, owner of the blue truck, Get Active, and Ocean Green? William was Jack's nephew. She had a flashback to Ellie's front yard, Jimmy kicking her, Kuteli protesting.

It was meant to be a warning . . . Bobby told us not to.

William had been trying to protect her. But what about his surname? Oh God, of course.

That mob have changed their names all over the place. Lot of 'em don't like being thought of as foreign. You've Reillys, Grants and Marsdons. They're all related though.

Add Hughes to that, she thought.

Trembling, her vision swimming, she tuned her senses to the stable door and realised she couldn't hear any voices outside. Had William gone?

She thumped the door and yelled for help, and when she realised she could be wasting valuable time, she stopped.

BB was lashing his hind feet furiously at the manger behind him, squealing with rage, his skin twitching as though he was being bitten by a swarm of biting insects.

Christ, she thought. I hope his head collar holds. Frantically she scrabbled at the knot holding her wrists and looked around the stable but knew there'd be nothing sharp in here. Not with a valuable stallion inside. Could she use BB to her advantage? How could she use a half-maddened horse? He wouldn't let her near him, and if she let him free, he'd probably kill her.

Her mind raced through various scenarios, and as it raced, her teeth were working at the rope. She took a step towards the horse and he reared up as far as his head collar would allow. His nostrils were dilated and his ears flat against his jerking head, his massive neck muscles straining.

No way could she approach him, she decided, and at the same time she pulled a tongue of rope through a loop, and felt the rope around her wrists loosen. Heart banging away in a strange combination of fright and hope, it didn't take her long to untie herself, maybe three minutes or so, and she quickly massaged her wrists, grateful that Jimmy had done such a sloppy job in his obvious rush to avoid William seeing her. Would William go against his brother's wishes and come to her rescue?

She pressed her head against the rough wood of the stable door and listened. Nothing. What the hell, she thought, and pounded it again with her fists.

BB gave an enraged bellow and swung his hindquarters towards her. And then she heard the clunk of a bolt being shot back on the other side of the stable door.

'William!' she yelled.

A dry laugh. 'Sorry,' said Jimmy. 'It's just me.'

India didn't even think. In eight paces she was crouched in the manger and alongside the surging, maddened form of BB. His hindquarters were pumping as he continued to kick and she knew if she misjudged it, one blow from his hooves could kill her.

BB jerked his head as the top part of the stable door opened, and as he did so, his body swung next to her, and stilled. His gleaming black skin was inches from her face.

Another clunk as Jimmy shot the bolt to the lower door.

Crooning softly to the horse, she put a hand on his withers, but he didn't flinch or seem to feel her. He was trembling, his attention seemingly riveted to the stable door.

India raised herself on the manger's lip, hand still on the horse's neck. BB was snorting, but he wasn't kicking or thrashing. She ran her hand firmly from his neck and along his back, where a saddle would sit, and felt him shift not away, but *towards her.*

'Okay, boy,' she whispered. 'Be nice, now.'

Murmuring under her breath as Aunt Sarah had taught her, she told him how beautiful he was, how lovely and kind and sweet, and as she raised her leg over his back she expected him to rear or buck or squeal when he felt the weight of it, but he didn't and she pushed off from the manger with her other foot and slithered into position.

She could feel BB's tension, his muscles quivering, and she kept crooning gently to him as she leaned past his neck and felt along the rope for the knot tying him to the metal ring in the wall.

Light flooded the stable as both doors swung wide, but she didn't look round. She was concentrating on the rope and she saw it was a slip knot, and she was practically halfway along BB's sweating and twitching neck as her fingers reached for the free end.

'What the . . . ?'

India gripped the end of the rope and pulled. The knot unravelled and the rope spilled free. Grabbing it in both hands, she hung on to a handful of mane and dug her boots into BB's ribs.

'Go, boy, go!' she yelled.

It was as though the racehorse had seen the ticker-tape lift in front of his eyes. She felt him stiffen beneath her, and then his hindquarters bunched and he surged for the stable door.

Ducking low against the horse's neck, India saw the silhouette of Jimmy with a pistol in his hand and she put another desperate boot into the horse's ribs. She didn't want BB to balk or shy away, she wanted to *run him down.*

But BB didn't hesitate. He charged for the door as though Jimmy didn't exist and Jimmy was trying to move out of the way but he wasn't quick enough. BB hit him like an out-of-control truck and India closed her eyes, hearing Jimmy yell as the horse crashed into him and then she felt her mount slip, start to lose his balance and BB was skidding, clattering wildly and trying to right himself and she could feel his hooves lashing madly, and Jimmy was entangled, and he was screaming, *screaming* . . .

And India was urging BB not to fall, for Chrissakes, and he was twisting, desperately kicking his hind legs, trying to find a purchase when Jimmy suddenly went quiet. BB heaved himself upright, India still astride, arms practically around the horse's neck, and in the second before BB bolted, she glanced down.

Jimmy's arms were unnaturally splayed, his shirt torn, pieces of bone jutting through. Blood. Lots of blood. His hair was thick with it, along with a greyish ooze.

And then they were off, India clinging to BB's neck. They were careering past the mansion when she heard the shots.

Quick glance over her shoulder to see Jack's sturdy shape with a shotgun, firing from the hip, but they were too far away, and the horse hadn't been hit, she hadn't been hit, and BB was swinging right down the main track, away from the homestead and the rubbish tip, and the sound of the shots diminished with every second.

It had to be the most incredible, most terrifying experience of her life. Astride a racehorse, bareback, with her hands wound into his mane, he had to be doing at least forty Ks and she prayed he wouldn't stumble: if she hit the ground at such a rate she'd snap all the bones in her body.

To one side she caught a glimpse of horses in the paddock galloping alongside, their tails flying, heads down and rumps pumping.

She prayed BB would begin to slow down but he seemed to think he was at the races and was galloping hard and fast. Rucking the rope from his head collar until it was taut, she increased the pressure.

'Hey, boy,' she tried. 'Ease up now. Easy.'

He tossed his head to one side against the rope and, amazingly, increased his pace. India immediately eased the pressure on the rope but BB didn't slow down.

Glancing aside she saw the horses in the paddock had reached the fence and were skidding aside, heads high, tails in the air.

'Hey,' she said. 'You've won, okay? You can slow down now.'

BB was galloping full speed, blowing easily, his head and neck bobbing in a steady rhythm. Sand and dust sprayed beneath his hooves.

A handful of mane in each hand, she glanced ahead and her heart just about stopped. They were heading straight for the cattle grid. It would snap his legs like matchsticks and she would be thrown to the ground and break her neck.

India let go of his mane, leaned back and hauled on the rope. She was digging her backside into his spine, legs clamped hard with her heels well clear of his ribs, giving him all the signals she could that it was time to check his pace, make him realise something was up and respond, but he wasn't taking any notice.

With all her strength she heaved the rope to the right, wanting to bring his head round, but he was too strong and it barely budged a millimetre.

The grid was a handful of paces away and she was willing him to *stop,* when the horse saw it, but it was too late. He was going so fast nothing would pull him up. BB was like an express train with its brake cables cut.

The horse's rump was down, his front legs thrust out in front, but it was too late, they were going to crash.

At the last second BB flung his head high and he began to

rear, his forelegs reaching, and although the huge body beneath her was bunching, he was off-balance and uncoordinated and she thought, No, please don't try and jump . . .

But BB was already hurling himself into the biggest kangaroo hop a horse had ever attempted and India had no choice but go with him.

Suddenly weightless, she found herself hovering above his back, legs akimbo. All that connected her to the horse were her hands, gripping his mane. The power from his hindquarters had shot her into the air. She was yelling as they descended. Waiting for the cattle grid to break his legs, shatter every bone in her body . . .

BB crashed to the ground with horrifying force. India slammed on to his spine and felt him start to go down. She was still clutching his mane as he fell, trying to work out which way to go to avoid being crushed, but then BB skewed and rose, took a couple of staggering steps.

And suddenly, with a lurch, he broke into an unsteady trot, India still clinging on. He was blowing hard and distressed, his ribs pumping in and out, but he wasn't limping.

India reached down and hugged his neck. 'You star,' she told him, tears of relief and gratitude on her cheeks. 'You jumped the grid. I don't believe it. You star.'

He gave a snort and although she wanted to think he was responding to her, she knew it was nothing but his body reacting from stress and relief. That he'd be clearing his airways and settling his finely tuned body into recovery mode.

'Snort all you like,' she said. 'I think you're brilliant.'

She let him trot gently at his own pace for a while, and after half a K or so, he dropped into a walk. Her breathing had settled, and so had BB's.

The horse was walking as quietly and politely as a family gelding, and India wondered if the stallion didn't need a little excitement in his life to keep his temper calm.

Listening to his hooves thudding gently on the dusty track, she tried to work out what Jack would do next. Should she ride BB to the coast road, where she could flag down a car and get help? The horse seemed to be moving fairly freely, and his ears had pricked up, so she reckoned that was the best plan. Especially since she couldn't think of another, aside from walking, which would take four times as long.

Besides, she didn't fancy riding BB through the night without headlights. Not only would she not be able to see but, thanks to his black coat, nobody would see *him*. They might get hit by a car if they walked along the road.

India was wondering if she should tie BB up before it got dark and hide until daylight, when she thought she heard an engine. She swivelled round to see two plumes of dust along the track. Two Toyota traybacks were going flat out and headed straight for her.

Twenty-eight

India barely had to touch her boots to BB's flanks and he broke into a canter. Neck-reining him off the track she headed into the low scrub. She chose to head for the thicket of trees and rocks stretching across the hills to her near left. It would slow her down, but even the best ute on the market wouldn't be able to follow her in a forest.

For the first couple of hundred metres the ground was pretty clear but then she spotted a rabbit hole. Hell, if BB stuck his foot in one of those it would have the same effect as hitting the cattle grid. She risked a look behind her to see one ute headed straight down the track, the other bouncing and bounding at an angle towards them. When she saw it was gaining, she forgot all about the rabbit holes and kicked BB up a gear.

She tried to calculate how long she'd have to ride before she hit the forest. Probably about five minutes. Too long. She gave BB another boot and he accelerated fast. Wow, it didn't take much to get this guy going.

Leaning close to his neck all she could hear was the thudding of hooves and BB's hot breathing, and then she took in the sound of an engine roaring. A quick glance over her shoulder and she saw the ute was catching up.

'Come on, boy,' she said. 'Boulder Cup time.' And she kicked his ribs, hard as she could.

She wasn't sure what she expected, but it wasn't this sudden surge of power. It was like pushing the gas of a Ferrari. India was crouched low, head down, holding on for dear life, threads of black mane stinging her eyes. She didn't dare risk a look to see where the ute was, in case she unbalanced the horse, or herself. She had to go for it, no holds barred.

She could hear the engine above BB's thundering hooves and knew the car was closing in, but the trees were coming up fast and she was trying to work out when to pull the horse up but then remembered he didn't use his brakes until it was too late.

It was dark ahead, lots of shadows and tree trunks and bush. She felt as though she was astride a rocket headed straight for a wall.

She pulled hard on the rope and, to her astonishment, felt BB slacken his pace. She yanked harder, but he'd done all the slowing he felt was necessary and she was hoping he knew something she didn't when suddenly they plunged into the forest.

Flattening herself along his neck, she heard crashing and smashing of foliage around them. A low branch whipped over her head, just missing her. Slowing into a canter, BB swerved wildly to the right and she nearly came off, but when she saw he'd jigged around a large rock she forgave him.

Then they were in a clearing. She gave him a kick and he surged into a gallop. She saw the mess of trees coming at them and couldn't see a gap that would take her and the horse, so she heaved on the rope but BB had other ideas. He wasn't going to stop for anything. She buried her head in his mane and waited for the smash.

At the last second he dropped his hindquarters and at the same time she felt his shoulders rise a little and she knew he was, at last, learning to use his brakes. He was sliding into fourth gear, then third, and the next instant he was cantering between two gum trees, dropping quickly into a brisk trot before snaking around a clump of enormous rocks. Without being asked, he broke into a canter when the ground cleared, and dropped to a trot at the next thicket of trees. He was threading his way through the forest as fast as he could, and she was amazed that he'd cottoned on so quickly. Maybe he thought he was on a cross-country race, but whatever was going through his brain, she welcomed it. She could hear him blowing, and the snapping of twigs beneath his hooves, leaves and light branches brushing past, but her senses were fixed on the faint sound of two engines. One appeared to be behind them, the other on her right. India booted BB left.

A little later the trees thinned and she quickly hauled on BB's rope when she saw they were nearing the edge of the forest. The horse abruptly slowed, and when she pressured further, came to a full stop, ribs heaving. BB turned his head to the left, ears pricked, and she could see his round, deep-brown eye had fixed on something. India followed his gaze, but it took her a few seconds to look past the trees and at the tan block of colour that was the flank of a parked ute. She heard the faint crackle of a radio and a man's voice, but she was too far away to hear what he said.

India swung BB back into the forest and headed for the other side. Easing the horse to the edge of the forest, she had a quick look, and immediately reined him back, gasping in dismay. Jack had called in the troops. There were two more utes and a couple of dirt bikes.

Praying she hadn't been seen, she waited for the shouts, the engines to start up, but all remained silent.

Only one direction to go in now. She barely brushed BB's flanks with her boots and he broke into a brisk canter, obviously glad to be on the move again. They weaved their way east. The ground rose into a steep hill but BB didn't slacken his pace. They climbed steadily, India gripping his mane as he wound his way around boulders and bushes, almost always trotting, sometimes breaking into a canter when it was clear.

Half an hour later they broke free of the forest. It took her a second to take in the fact she wasn't being flogged by branches or leaves any more, and that the air was cool and still.

BB took three paces forward then stopped, head flung high, long ears flicked forward like twin arrows.

They were on top of an escarpment with the sun sinking behind a band of hills to the west. She could see the shadow of a valley below, and what looked like a dry river bed, shining silver with sand.

She looked down at the near-vertical slope of loose shale and knew she'd fallen into a trap. Jack had positioned men and vehicles around the forest to force her to this point. No person with any sense would walk down there, let alone attempt to ride a horse down the slippery scree. In the distance she heard the clatter of bike engines and men's shouts. They were beating the forest, heading her way. There was no way she could go back.

Heart in her mouth, she gently tapped BB's flanks, asking him to ease his massive form over the lip of the mountain. She expected him to balk, shy his head and back away, but it was as though he'd been waiting for her request all along. He gave a snort that she felt right through his body. He shuffled his hooves as though readying himself for something, then he gave a little rear. And plunged over the edge.

They were sliding and scrambling down the scree of rocks, India leaning so far back her shoulders almost brushed his rump. Occasionally she thought she heard the buzz of a bike's engine, but it was hard to tell with the stones and pebbles avalanching around the horse's hooves.

He wasn't trotting or cantering, but he was setting one hell of a pace downhill. A kind of high-speed shuffle that had her knees around his withers and her calves practically gripping his neck. Jesus. It was nearly dark. What if he fell into a crevasse?

She was pulling on the rope, asking him to slow down, when BB gave an angry toss of his head and suddenly put on a surge of speed that flung her hard against his spine. At the same time, she saw a flash of headlights at the far end of the dry river bed. They had to be half a K away, and she knew they were trying to block off the final exit, keep her contained in the forest. She had to cross the river bed without being seen, let them think she was skirting the escarpment.

The horse was lunging downhill at such a rate she was gasping with fear that he'd break a fetlock, a leg, but he kept going and she was hanging on and praying . . .

And then they hit the bottom of the scree and although she knew he must be tiring, she gave BB a whack with her boots, for encouragement, and they rocketed down the valley.

BB slowed at the end of the valley and swung right, for a steep, rocky slope. She glanced up. At the top all she could see was a star winking. It wasn't a slope as much as a never-ending climb to the heavens, and she wondered if the horse would make it. Don't think about it, she told herself. Help him by distributing your weight over his shoulders. Think light, and don't drag him down. You are a feather. You are nothing but a breath of air on this horse's back.

BB was blowing hard as he climbed. No galloping or trotting now. Just a hard, determined walk. Head down, shoulders working, his hindquarters pushed and forced them higher, and higher.

Suddenly, the ground levelled. BB paused, his flanks heaving and soaked with sweat. India looked down to see the ute had switched off its headlights and was parked. Two shadows stood on either side of the car, facing the scree and the forest behind her. Both had their hands to their faces. Binoculars, she thought, but they were looking the wrong way.

She'd done it. She'd slipped through their net.

Twenty-nine

India let BB pick his way carefully down the other side of the mountain and when they reached the bottom, she brought him to a halt and slid from his back. Her legs trembled like filaments in a light bulb when they touched the ground. Clutching BB's head collar she used his solid form to prop herself upright until she felt some strength return. She felt as though she'd been squeezed through an old-fashioned laundry mangle her shoulders ached so much, but she forced herself to move round the horse and run her hands over his legs. He had a gouge in his near foreleg which was bleeding, and several more deep scratches across his chest, but otherwise he looked okay.

When she went to pick up his rope, BB swung his head towards her and nickered, brushing her fingers with his velvet-soft nose as though checking on her too.

'Oh, but you're a beautiful beastie,' she murmured, 'not a bastard at all. How could they have called you that all this time?'

He nosed her hand very gently while she brushed her other hand up along his long, arrogant head and smoothed the skin behind his ears, and then, without her asking him to, he walked on.

The moon was high in the sky, a sliver of mercury the size and shape of a nail clipping that lit everything pale grey. The night was still and silent aside from the soft shambling of BB's hooves and the occasional thud-thud of a startled kangaroo. India hugged her arms around herself, trying to keep warm. She could see their shadows stumbling like exhausted companions alongside, and she put a hand on BB's shoulder, telling him that she'd look after him when they got to wherever he was taking her. The rope was slung across his withers and he was free to do what he wanted. But whenever he turned left or right, she didn't argue or think about it. She just followed.

BB led India through the bush, occasionally stopping to sniff the air, and then he'd nose India's hand gently and start walking again. It was just after ten p.m. when they came to a fence. The chill night air held the hay scent of the outback and the distinct odour of fresh manure. A horse gave a whinny nearby and then there was the sound of snorting and a small grey mare trotted into view. India saw a huddle of sheep beneath a tree, and at the far end of the paddock, a darkened homestead. No mansion, no rubbish tip outside. No stable block adjacent.

She led BB around the fence, the grey mare following, until she came to a gate, and popped him inside. He touched noses with the mare who gave a little squeal, which India took to be delight since she was touching noses back, ears pricked. In return BB gave a long, groaning sigh that sounded like satisfaction. Horse romance, she thought. Without it, BB wouldn't have led her here. He'd have returned her straight to Goondari.

With a final grateful pat, India left BB and cautiously approached the homestead. Set in front of the verandah was the biggest dog kennel she'd ever seen but, luckily, no dog. Just two vehicles. A white Toyota ute and a tractor. The ute was unlocked, and she glanced inside. No keys. She wondered if the house was unlocked too, and whether the keys might be on the hall table.

'Strange sort of swap you be making,' a voice said behind her.

India swung round.

'Jack's horse is worth ten times my ute.'

Slowly India put up her hands, her gaze travelling from

the shotgun levelled at her chest to the tiny old woman behind it. Stick-thin shins stuck out below a T-shirt five sizes too large. Long grey hair floated around her head like seaweed in the shallows of the sea. Next to her was an enormous dog. A dark brindled Great Dane with a chest Mike Tyson would have been proud of and a head the size of an armchair. Jesus, she thought. He must weigh over two hundred pounds.

'I don't mean any harm,' said India.

'What you be doing with Jack's horse, then?'

'I, er . . . borrowed him.'

Long silence and then the woman chuckled. The chuckle increased until she was laughing so hard India thought she might drop the gun.

'Would you mind putting the gun down?' India asked, not wanting to get shot when the gun hit the ground and went off.

'Oh, oh,' the woman gasped, 'sorry.' A satisfying *clunk* followed as she broke the shotgun and hooked it with years of obvious practice over her elbow. '*Borrowing* Jack's horse.' She was still laughing. 'They didn't say anything about that. Just that if I saw you, to ring them straight up.'

India stood quite still. 'And are you going to ring them?'

'Don't be so bloody stupid.' She stepped close to India and looked at her with enormous interest. 'I wouldn't piss on Jack if he was on fire.'

Nor would India, but she didn't say anything.

'Let's go in. It's brass monkeys out here.' The woman gave a shiver.

India looked at the dog.

'Don't mind Ricky. He may be big, but he's got no brains to bite anyone. All he does is eat and sleep.'

The old woman walked towards her house, her pace surprisingly fast, and India followed. Perhaps she could persuade the woman to loan her ute to her. And if not, grab the keys and just steal the thing. She had no intention of walking for the highway when she could drive. Inside, lights were snapped on and India saw a neat home with green-patterned carpet and crocheted doilies on tables. Faded prints of Australian landscapes, silk flower arrangements and the smell of dried lavender. No car keys on a hallside table. No keys hanging on the back of the front door.

'Now,' the woman said, striding into the kitchen, 'let's have a beer while you tell me the story. We've got a bit of time. Would you like something to eat? I've a pot roast I can warm up if you like.'

India declined, knowing she had to keep moving, keep lengthening the distance between herself and Jack. 'Just some water, thanks.'

The woman went to the fridge and popped herself a beer, then filled a glass from the tap and handed it to India who gulped it down. 'I'm Maggie, by the way.'

'India.'

'And you're in trouble with them.'

'I guess I am. A bit.'

'You should know that Jack and I are neighbours.'

'What does that mean?'

'That you're not the first to run here.' Maggie looked away, suddenly uncomfortable. 'There was another, three years back.'

But India was only half listening. She was moving around the kitchen, eyes flicking, searching for the ute's keys.

'Still gives me nightmares, you know. Wake up blubbering like a goddamned baby.'

Toaster, bread bin, a pot filled with pens and old stamps. No keys.

'I've never told nobody. Nobody to tell. But now you're here, trying to get away from them too.'

'Yes.'

'Maybe if I tell it, I won't dream about it no more.'

'Maybe.'

India had just spotted a massive plastic bowl by the

phone, filled with newspaper clippings, old envelopes, mail and an address book. It looked like Maggie's day-to-day filing cabinet and she walked over, hoping Maggie chucked her keys in there as well.

'I saw this bloke running for my house, see. Right up my front drive. Big bugger he was, an aborigine, going like hell. But he didn't stand a chance. They had dirt bikes and utes. Jimmy shot him in the back.'

India forgot all about car keys and swung round. 'Jesus.'

'I couldn't report it,' Maggie added sadly, 'or I'd have ended up in the same grave. Typical of them to bury the poor sod on my property. I planted a tree on it, you know.'

'Jesus,' India said again, unable to think of anything else to say.

'Yeah, well, Jesus wasn't around when he was needed, was he?' and Maggie was cursing religion and Jimmy, Jack and every Zhuganov and taking determined swigs of beer in between, but India's memory was spiralling backwards and she was in the Internet café listening to the old man talking about Albert.

Last time I saw him, it was at the Nelson . . . Wearing one of his godawful floral shirts. He left when Jimmy turned up.

'Maggie,' she interrupted, 'what was he wearing? The guy Jimmy shot?'

Maggie stared at her. 'Fuck if I can remember. I wasn't looking at his clothes.'

'It wasn't a Hawaiian shirt?'

Long silence. Then Maggie came close, her expression horrified. 'You knew him?'

But India didn't have time to talk it through and she turned her attention back to the bowl and saw she'd been right. Three sets of keys, one lot with a Toyota tag. She began to reach for it but Maggie was quicker.

'No,' she said firmly. 'They'll have all the tracks covered. The highway too. You'd be better off hiding here, with me.'

She glanced at the yellow plastic clock on the kitchen wall. 'They'll be here in a bit, anyhow. They said they would.'

India's heartbeat instantly picked up. Going to the windows she had a peek. No cars, no headlights that she could see.

'I've got the perfect hiding place,' Maggie told India.

Muscles aching, wishing she could just get in a car and *drive*, India started to make for the door. 'I think I'll take my chances on foot.'

'The state you're in? You'd last three seconds.' Maggie's eyes started to twinkle. 'I've a much better plan.'

Tucked up at the rear of the massive dog kennel, India nestled on Ricky's vet bed that smelled of old dog and rotten meat and waited to see what happened next. She hadn't wanted to hide so close to the house, but Maggie had insisted.

'Safest place in the whole world. You think they'll be looking for you on my doorstep? Anyhow, with Ricky there, who'd have the guts to put his head inside?'

India reached out a hand and patted Ricky. He hadn't appreciated being dragged outside and chained inside his kennel and he ignored her. She tried to peer around his huge bulk and look through his doggy door but he filled the space like a marshmallow squeezed into a test tube and she couldn't see a thing. Which, she supposed, was the point.

It had taken Maggie a good ten minutes to persuade India not to run. Not that she didn't trust the old woman, but if Bryce and, God forbid, Jack came out, she wasn't sure if Maggie could hold her own against them.

'Ha!' Maggie roared with laughter. 'I've known Jack since he was in bloody shorts and ankle socks. Little brute. Even had him over my knee for bullying Becky one time. My daughter. Little sod. Wouldn't mind giving him the strap today if he wasn't so big. He could do with a damn good hiding, that man.'

India shuffled down, pushing what she took to be a soft toy aside, along with a . . . she recoiled. It was spongy and wet, with a long shaft of smooth, light stone. She exhaled. A bone, that's all it was. A fresh bone for Ricky.

Curled on her side, she lay her head on her arm and tried to ignore the pain still groaning through her shoulders. Thankfully, Ricky's vet bed was surprisingly soft and comfortable. About an inch thick, it had a layer of foam topped with a synthetic spongy material not unlike sheepskin.

She thought over what Maggie had said about Jimmy chasing that man down and shooting him in the back. An aborigine. A big bugger going like hell. Had it been Albert? Well, if she got out of here alive, she'd have the cops dig up the grave beneath Maggie's tree and find out. God, their arrogance was breathtaking. To bury a man they'd murdered on a witness's property. It showed they had no fear. It showed their ultimate power. Which is why, she thought, they'd done it. They *revelled* in their power.

India awoke with a start when Ricky lifted his head with a slap of chops. Barely two minutes later she heard engines roaring, then there was a flash of white, another and another, and tyres were crunching on stones, doors opening and slamming shut, and her skin bristled at the next sound. Metallic clicks of guns being loaded.

Thumping on the front door.

'Maggie! Maggie, open up! It's the police!'

Long silence.

'Maggie!'

A slight squeak as the door opened.

'Jesus, Maggie, put that down, will you?'

'Sorry, Ray. Just a precaution.'

'Is it loaded? Is the safety catch on?'

'Oh, it's loaded all right, but I'm not sure about the . . . Oh, thank you, Ray. You're always such a help.'

'Maggie, Jack's horse is in your paddock.'

'Is he? Well, blow me down if all my dreams haven't come true. I've always wanted a nice foal by him.'

'Jesus Christ, are you saying you haven't seen that woman round here?'

'The one you rang up about? Nah. Haven't seen a thing. Been tucked up tight. Had a long day you know, old hut paddock needed fencing and you know how that always takes it out of me, bloody hard work and—'

'Where's Nick's ute?'

Sound of footsteps on the verandah.

'Oh, bugger,' Maggie said. 'Nick's going to kill me. He's always nagging at me not to leave the keys in it.'

Nick was, Maggie told her earlier, her grandson, and he'd driven his ute to Port Headland two days ago.

'What's the rego?'

'Oh dear, Ray. I am sorry. I can't remember.'

Ray gave instructions to someone to radio everyone with a description of Nick's ute.

'She's a car thief?' asked Maggie. 'Is that why you want her?'

'No. Because she killed Jimmy.'

India felt goosebumps rise all over her skin.

'She killed Jimmy?' Maggie repeated, sounding more disbelieving than shocked.

'Yeah. She ran him down with that goddamn horse. Broke both his arms and then the horse kicked him in the head. Cracked open his skull. He was dead before he hit the fucking ground. Jack's doing his nut. He wants the Kane woman on a plate . . .'

India stopped listening to Ray when Ricky gave a growl. It came from low and deep inside him, like distant thunder, but she didn't think anybody who wasn't inches from the dog could have heard it. Cautiously she peered round his bulk then realised that wasn't such a good idea and wriggled to the back of the kennel, and shut her eyes in case someone shone a torch inside.

'Steve, you go round the back,' a man said quietly. 'Phil, you scout the perimeter. Check every chook house, every shed. I'll do the inner circle.'

Tiny sound of boots scrunching on grit. Then silence, but Ricky's rumbling picked up.

'Hey, big boy,' the man said in a gentle undertone. 'You got anyone hiding in there with you?'

Ricky's growl grew to a subdued roar.

'You threatening me? I don't think so. I heard you were a real pussy cat.'

India could feel Ricky's growl start to vibrate his body. Jesus, she thought, I hope he doesn't turn on me.

'Ricky, you're a layabout.' The man chuckled. 'You won't do nothing unless it involves a ham sandwich. You're not even showing your goddamn teeth, and I'm thinking maybe—'

'Dennis,' Maggie called out. 'I wouldn't if I was you.'

'It's okay, Mags, we all know your dog may be big, but he's nothing but hot air. I just want to check—'

To India's horror, Ricky launched himself outside. The kennel gave a creaking, tearing sound and then there was a metallic *snap* and the dog stopped short, quivering and snarling and frustrated at the end of his chain.

'Fuck,' the man said, gasping. 'He nearly got me. Fuck.'

'For goodness' sake, Dennis.' Maggie's voice came near. 'Don't you know not to mess with a dog when they're on their own turf? He's got his stuff in there. You know, his special toys. Couple of bones.'

Ricky was still lunging against his chain, barking furiously, and the kennel was shaking and trembling and India prayed it wouldn't break apart under the pressure.

'Leave the poor bugger alone,' Maggie said. 'He hasn't done anything to deserve you trying to stick your head in his home. Why don't you come inside and have a drink? I haven't seen you for ages anyways. How are Judy and the kids?'

'Okay, thanks. Jeez, Maggie, that bloody dog—'

'I've some of Nick's Scotch inside,' Maggie suggested brightly. 'He says it's real good.'

It was only after Dennis left that India realised she was covered in sweat. Shivering and shaking all over again, she knew she was near the point of collapse. Please God, make them go away. I can't stand any more of this.

Ricky had stopped growling and was standing there, sniffing the air. India counted the minutes passing. Five. Ten. Fifteen.

Then a lot of boots on gravel. The sounds of leather and metal. Men murmuring.

'Listen up, guys,' a man said. She recognised Dennis's voice. 'It looks like she's gone down the Narooma track. Steve's found fresh tyre marks and reckons we're barely forty minutes behind. Phil, I want you to cover the coast road. Tony, there's another track that leads off Narooma, you can get to it by cutting across the bush . . .' He paused when a mobile chirruped. 'Yeah,' said Dennis, and then, 'Christ, boss . . . Oh, Jesus Christ . . . I'm sorry. Yeah, yeah. We'll bring her to you. Alive, I swear it. Guaranteed.'

Small silence.

'That was Jack.' His tone was hoarse. 'He just found Bobby. He's hanged himself in one of the stables. Dead as a fucking doornail.'

India felt a wave of dizziness. She could hear a lot of subdued curses but they suddenly seemed terribly far away, as though they were on the other side of a mountain.

'. . . Kuteli's team are covering the highway,' Dennis said. 'Jack's already put a chopper in the sky. He'll give us what we need. The rest of you, let's go.'

Car doors slammed, engines roared and gravel spun. White lights flashed inside the kennel, and then they were gone. Ricky sniffed the air some more and gave a huge shake from his shoulders to the tip of his tail, rattling his chain and making the kennel shudder. Then he came inside and did two circles before flopping sideways and landing his head on her lap.

She ran her fingers over his broad forehead and down his long, soft ears. She could see William the first time she'd met him, wearing his beautifully tailored suit, his quick grin as he tucked her arm in his to escort her to his picnic. And then Ned was in her mind, and Emma, Vince and Marie, Danny and Halim and *The Pride*'s bosun; and William took up his place behind them, tilting his head in that elegant way of his, as if in acknowledgement.

Thirty

'Rest up for a while,' Maggie told her. 'You're safe here.'

They were eating a reheated lamb pot roast at the kitchen table accompanied by bottles of cold beer. India's hair was still wet from her shower, and since her clothes were in the wash, she was wearing a pair of Maggie's grandson's shorts and an oversized fleece that came to her knees. She had bruises all over her shoulders and back, scratches along her arms and face from charging through the forest with BB, and although she felt like hell, at least she had nothing broken, nothing sprained. No muscles pulled.

'And when you're feeling up to it,' Maggie continued brightly, 'you can stick Jack behind bars, where he belongs. You've got to do it, you know. He won't stop, not now you've killed Jimmy. He'll blame you for Bobby's death too. And he'll spend the rest of his days tracking you down. And anyone you care for. You've got to get him first.'

India knew Maggie was right, but she felt so inadequate, so *small* against the prodigious Zhuganov family. Like an ant attempting to fight off a dozen cockroaches.

'I'd be better off leaving the country,' said India, and then remembered that the Zhuganovs had offices in America. Where else in the world did their tentacles stretch? Russia, obviously. Probably the whole of Eastern Europe. What about Brazil? Japan? Could she start a new life in those places? Christ, she didn't even have her passport with her. And even if she did leave the country, she couldn't abandon Mikey and Polly. She buried her head in her hands. She should never have started this. There was no way she was going to survive.

Which was why, after a four-hour sleep, she was dressed in her trusty and battered old jeans again and driving Maggie's ute to Perth. She may be an ant, but even an ant could deliver a nasty bite before it died.

Come nine a.m. India was ready to face Perth's rush hour. She hadn't taken the highway but driven tortuously across country and now she was on the outskirts of the city, using the back streets and keeping her eyes out for any cars behind her.

She tried to keep her thoughts focused, so she wouldn't allow herself to think about Mikey and the abyss that stretched between them. The abyss she'd created by stepping to the other side of the chasm and refusing to allow him to follow. Cracking open her window, India lit a cigarette. Bless Maggie, she thought. Not only had she given her two packs of Nick's Silk Cut, but a flask of coffee and a stack of lamb sandwiches that would keep her going for a week.

She passed the Dingo Flour building on the Stirling Highway with a big red dingo painted on its side, then the Matilda Bay Brewery, and then she was crossing the Swan River which was whipped into an angry grey froth and nothing like the smooth, blue lake-like expanse she'd seen when she'd returned from Jakarta. Swinging south-west on Queen Victoria Street, she took Phillimore to Cliff Street, bounced over the railway tracks and pulled into the car park on the left. Her heart squeezed when she saw the familiar No Fishing signs ahead. She was here again. Fremantle Port.

'Say that again?'

The chief stared at her in amazement.

'The ship's here,' she repeated. 'Jimmy mentioned

someone called Hammond who said she'll be gone in twenty-four hours. Which means some time today.'

'Hammond?' he repeated.

'You know him?'

The chief turned to his computer and tapped on his keyboard. India stood by his shoulder, watching a screen listing ship's agents and representatives spring up. He scrolled down a page and pointed out a name. Geoff Hammond, Minang and Company, ship's representatives.

'You said he told Jimmy the ship would be gone soon?'

'Yes.'

He grinned. 'You've cracked it, sweetheart. You've found someone who knows who owns the goddamn ship. Now all we have to do is get him to admit it in court, and we've got the bastards by the balls.'

'But what if he scarpers before we can grab him? We've got to get the ship. Then we've *evidence* to nail them with properly. Stick the guys who sank *Sundancer* behind bars.'

He started to tap on his computer keyboard again. India went and stood by the window and looked out at the wind-chopped harbour, the distant coat hanger shapes of cranes and two fat cylindrical towers marked CALTEX.

'Take a look,' the chief said, swinging his screen round. 'There's no *Pride* listed. But if she used a false name . . . She might have used a similar prefix. You know, like the rest of them. *Glory*, *Prince*, *Regent*.'

'Plus she may have come from Jakarta,' said India. 'Anything fit the bill?'

More taps as the chief checked. 'Nope.'

India ran her eyes down the list. Nothing jumped out at her, and she shook her head. The chief scrolled on, and halfway down the third page she saw it.

'The *Prize*?' she said.

He checked it out. 'Not your ship. She's from Singapore. *Prize Oldendorff*. Got her Lloyd's rego and all.'

India studied the list again and saw three ships that might

fit the bill, and asked if she could see them. She also wanted to see the *Prize*, to satisfy her curiosity.

The chief looked hesitant.

'Please, Chief.'

He rolled his eyes. 'God, I'm a sucker for a pretty face.'

They drove down Victoria Quay, past a passenger terminal, then ducked beneath a railway bridge and swung left over the Swan River, then left again, to North Quay. The land was flat as a table top with silos, cranes and stacks of containers. They overtook a groaning 44-wheeled truck towing two containers, then came to a gate with three guys in high-visibility vests. The chief gave them a wave, and the boom was raised.

Deep in the heart of the docks, the chief swung round various fork-lift trucks, accelerating hard when it was clear, sounding his horn regularly, doing more waving as he drove. India ducked as low as she could in her seat, a yellow hard hat hiding her face. If Jack came after the chief she'd never forgive herself. After five minutes or so, she felt the ute slow, then he said, 'Here's one of them.'

India shuffled upright to see a gleaming new ship the size of the Empire State Building toppled on its side and painted a glorious shade of blue. The *Source of Taupo. Auckland.* Nothing about her was familiar.

'Nope,' she said.

The chief showed her two more ships, one from Fiji, the other from Cape Town, and she shook her head at both.

'This one's the last on your list. Any good?'

The breath stopped in her throat. The ship was around 100 metres long and had four winches and derricks, one big hold. Rust bled down its flanks and it had a four-storey block at the back, painted white. Heavily laden, the ship sat low in the water and had fresh paint on the port side of her bow. Fresh paint where the damage sustained from ramming *Sundancer* had been repaired. It was the ship she'd been on in Jakarta.

'Chief,' her voice was trembling with excitement. 'This is it.'

She climbed out of the ute. The wind snatched at her clothes and made the oil-skimmed puddles shiver into rainbows. The ship's hatch was open and a crane was lowering a container inside. Another truck carrying a container was waiting its turn. India walked quickly to the stern. A dent like a footprint sat squarely on her transom, as though she'd been kicked in the backside by a boot.

She could barely believe it. The ship that had sunk the Greenpeace boat sat almost opposite the jetty where *Sundancer* had been prepped all those months ago.

'What the hell . . . ?' The chief was staring at the ship's name, *Prize Oldendorff*.

Like all ship's names it stood proud of the metal, but if you were looking for it you could see the D through the Z, and that the rest of the name had been altered.

'It's not possible.' His mouth hung open. 'She shouldn't be here. I mean, we've security arrangements, checks . . . We're tight as goddam *ticks*.'

India recalled *The Pride* which the chief had checked out when she'd first met him. That particular *Pride* operated out of Hong Kong and had been Lloyd's registered and classified, 100 per cent legitimate. Jimmy and William had taken the ship's identity and used it, just as they'd used another identity today.

'The schedule says she's from *Singapore*,' the chief said, tone protesting and obviously still in denial.

'I'll bet someone in your office has been altering your records,' said India. 'Someone related to the Zhuganovs. Someone in debt to them, or open to bribes.'

The chief paled. 'It would take more than one person to pull this off.'

'It's a big family.'

'Christ.'

She watched the second truck move forward and the crane lock on. The driver walked round and uncoupled the container, and the crane bore it up and across and down into the hold.

Pushing her hard hat back India looked up to see a figure standing on the port wing of the bridge, watching the proceedings. Something about the man looked familiar and she stared hard at him, but he was too far away for her to make out his features. All she could see was that he had black hair and brown skin, but when he moved she thought she saw a flash of white. She didn't know what it was, but it jarred at her and she hurriedly moved into the lee of the chief's ute, in case he saw her and recognised her too.

The chief came to stand beside her.

'Those containers are full of illegal waste,' she told him. 'They're taking it from all over Australia and shipping it off to Chennai.'

'What sort of waste?'

'Industrial, chemical, stuff you have to wear protective clothing and gas masks for.'

The chief looked at her. 'And she never even lodged a form thirteen, telling me she was transporting dangerous cargo. Fancy that.'

'We've got to get her cargo inspected.' She quickly checked the figure on the bridge but he had gone. Her tone turned urgent, excited. 'How about Customs? When they find all that crap on board, we'll have them!'

'Forget Customs, I'm calling the cops. Christ, I'd better alert the FESA guys—'

'FESA?'

'Fire and emergency services. What if the stuff's leaking?' He began to head for his ute. 'I'd better place an exclusion zone round her before we check her out, maybe move her to a safe location.'

He'd just put a hand on the door handle when he

paused. 'Shit,' he said. He was looking at a ute driving towards them. 'Best if you get out of sight. Most guys stop to have a chat if they see me. I don't want anyone pegging you. Soon as I get rid of them, we'll hit the emergency buttons, okay?'

More than okay, she thought, hopping into his ute. Not only did they have a ship's representative who could testify, God willing, that the Zhuganovs owned the ship, but they also *had the ship*!

Pulling off her hard hat, she crouched in the passenger footwell. She heard the sound of an engine slowing alongside, then it was switched off. A car door slammed and a man spoke, but she didn't hear the chief's reply. Go away, she willed the man. The chief's busy, he's got emergency buttons to punch.

The chief said something, maybe three or four words, but his tone sent a flurry of cockroaches over her skin. He sounded angry, but it was tinged with fear. Christ, what was going on?

Cautiously she crept out of her hiding place and peeked through the window.

The chief was standing between the two utes, his face white as bleached bone. India felt her own face tighten when she took in the pistol jammed in the chief's stomach, then the man holding the gun.

He had a thick black moustache and a stripe of grey hair running from his forehead to the crown. His skin shone as though it had been layered with grease.

It was the man who'd shot the bosun.

The man who had tried to kill her.

Rajiv.

Thirty-one

What the hell was Rajiv doing here? No time to ponder it, she had to do something, and *fast*. Heart pumping, she twisted her head and saw the chief had left his keys in the ignition. Then she checked to see if he'd left the handbrake on. She had to do this fluidly, with no mistakes. She took a deep breath. Counted, one, two, three . . . and sprang onto the passenger seat then leaped across into the driver's, throwing her legs well clear of the handbrake. She didn't dare look at Rajiv or the chief for fear she might falter. Cowering and sweating, dreading a bullet smashing into her, she released the handbrake and turned the ignition.

The engine roared into life and she jammed the stick into drive and stuck her foot hard down on the gas.

Bang!

The passenger window exploded into a spray of glass, but she didn't slow down. She was charging along the quay and she wasn't hurt, she hadn't been shot, thank God, thank God . . .

Barrelling past lines of ships and trucks, she was panting hard and gripping the steering wheel so tightly she almost expected it to buckle. Jesus, how to rescue the chief? Chuck a U-turn and run Rajiv down? The idea held quite a lot of appeal since she couldn't think of anything else as immediate. Shit, shit, shit. India glanced into her rear-view mirror.

A hollow opened up inside her.

She had to have been 200 metres away, but she could have been standing within two feet the picture was so clear.

There were three guys. And one was on the ground, sprawled and unmoving between the other two. The chief was down. Had they shot him?

Jamming her foot on the brake she waited until the speed dropped and then she spun the wheel hard to the left. With a howl of tyres, the ute swung full circle and India gunned the engine.

So help me God, she thought, charging back down the quay for the men leaning over the still form of the chief, I'll take one of you, to the left or the right, but come what may I'll have one of you smacked on to my bonnet in the next few seconds.

Christ, she thought. I'd better buckle up . . . One hand on the wheel she fumbled for her seatbelt, managed to click it in place. She was bearing down on the men, and swearing under her breath. Shit, shit, shit.

At the last minute, they looked up. One of the men rushed aside but the other man stuck his hand in the air, three fingers raised. She didn't know what it meant, didn't care. Only one man to run down now, and as she tore towards him she saw it was Rajiv.

She was belting past the truck that had been waiting in line to deliver its container, just metres away from Rajiv, when he took two steps, and stopped. He was astride the chief's body. If she hit Rajiv, she'd pulverise the chief as well.

India hauled the steering wheel to the right. There was a hideous screech of rubber as the weight of the ute shifted wildly to the left and then she swung past Rajiv and the chief – both men could have touched the car they were so close – and then there was a brief, eerie silence. The ute's right tyres had lost their grip and were slipping.

She'd hit a patch of oil.

She didn't panic and go for the brakes but lifted her foot off the accelerator and pressured the steering wheel into the skid. The ute's rear was already sliding left and she wasn't breathing, she was waiting for the ute to respond but it was like asking BB to stop when he was charging for the cattle grid and the ute was spinning one-eighty degrees far too fast and she was wailing, 'Nooo!' and praying not to be tipped into the harbour when she felt the ute react and begin to reduce speed. She was feeding the steering wheel further into the skid when a forklift truck suddenly appeared in front of her and she couldn't help it, she pulled the steering wheel to the right.

She promptly lost all control.

'Oh, fuck,' she said, and her voice wasn't loud or filled with alarm. It was simply resigned. She knew she'd lost the battle and she braced herself as the side of the ute swung straight for the forklift.

India awoke with a vibration beneath her cheek, a cold metal shuddering that reminded her of something. She lay there, mind numb, trying to think what it was, but then the pain in her body took over. Her shoulders and neck felt as though they had red-hot knives sawing their tendons. Her arms didn't want to move but when she insisted, they came up to her face and traced her mouth, her nose and her eyelids.

She blinked a couple of times, feeling her eyelashes brush against her fingertips, but why couldn't she see?

Trying to ignore the agony riding her muscles, she rolled onto her side and pushed herself up on one elbow. Blinked some more. Nothing. It was black as night, black as the oil that had made the chief's ute skid into the forklift truck. She concentrated past her pain for any clues where she might be. She could smell traces of some sort of chemical and vomit. Had she been sick? It wouldn't surprise her. She felt like throwing up from the pain pounding through her body more than the confused rolling beneath the metal floor.

A blast of realisation hit her. She was on a ship. A big

ship, given the motion against the waves. Bigger than *Sundancer*. She had no doubt she was on *The Pride*.

Climbing painfully to her feet she felt as though she'd been beaten with a telegraph pole, but at least she hadn't broken anything. Her bruises would heal, if she lived long enough to let them. Knees bent to absorb the rolling of the ship, she shuffled forward, hands outstretched. Her eyes were open wide, but she could see nothing, not even a pinprick of light.

Okay, she thought, I'll pretend I'm in my cabin on *Sundancer* and they've blindfolded me for a joke. I'll try and find a wall of some sort, and then maybe a door. And it might be open, you never know your luck. They may have left me for dead and not bothered to lock the thing.

She slid her feet over the metal floor, feeling the judder of the engines beneath her and, what felt like an hour later, her fingertips connected with what she thought was a wall, a rough metal wall that was ribbed every metre or so. Walking carefully she followed the ribbed wall, and when it fell away, she realised it turned left. She followed its flank another six metres or so, and then it fell away and she turned left again.

Hell, she thought. It wasn't a wall, but a container. She was in one of the holds along with the general cargo. She swallowed hard, trying to keep her panic under control but it was spiralling and growing every second. So, she yelled, 'Shit, *shit*!' and immediately she felt better, so she cursed again.

'India?' a man's voice called. 'You okay?'

Shocked into immobility, she peered in the direction of the voice.

'India?' His voice was filled with anxiety. 'Where are you?'

'Chief?'

'Christ, you just about gave me a heart attack. I went to get you some water. Hey, hang on a tick.'

A tiny white light flicked on, like the glow from a firefly, and although it didn't light anything around her because it was so small, she felt her hopes leap. *She wasn't alone!*

India immediately started for the white firefly of light.

'Steady as you come, now. Take it slow, 'cos there's crap all over the place, ropes and stuff, so be careful.'

She didn't really hear what he said she was so desperate to get to him, but when she tripped over something and nearly fell headlong to the floor, she slowed down. Took it step by step.

The light didn't seem to increase as she edged her way towards him, but then she realised she could see walls of scarred metal, edged with patches of red. They were in a hold the size of a lecture theatre with a hatch cover for a ceiling, steel floors and rows of containers. It was a giant, cold room, slamming with echoes from the sea beneath the hull.

'Hey, how's my favourite reporter?'

'Alive. I think.'

The chief was grinning, but she could see a runnel of blood darkening his shirt collar and he was standing slightly off balance, as though he'd wounded one side of him, like his hip or leg.

'Are you all right?' she asked.

'All the better for seeing you, believe me.' He came over and gently tucked her into an embrace. 'You're a real trouper, you know? I saw you bugger off in my ute, going flat out, and I thought: That's the last I'll see of her, then the next second, you're back, aiming straight for that bastard.'

She felt his chest rise and fall.

'You mind if I turn off the torch? Got to save batteries.'

'God, no. Where did you find it?'

'It's attached to my car keys. They didn't do a very good job of searching me. I've a screwdriver too.'

She heard the small click as he switched off the torch and

the instant darkness made her sway, but the chief's arm was around her shoulders and holding her close, so she didn't stumble.

'You okay?' he said, and the way he held her against his big, solid girth, his thighs bending with hers against the sliding of the ship, along with the tone of his voice, anxious but not crazed with worry, reminded her of Mikey so much, she gave a choked sob.

The chief held her a little tighter and said, 'It's okay, India, I'm here,' and she closed her eyes, and it wasn't the chief who was holding her with his quiet reassurance, but Mikey.

Mikey, who had taken Polly and vanished into the outback so she could bring Jimmy down.

Mikey, who ran rego plates when she asked, and worried himself sick about her.

Mikey, who made love to her until she cried out his name.

She had wanted a neon-bright sign to crash on top of her to tell her whether she ought to marry him or not, but it was in the reeking darkness of a steel-hulled ship in the middle of God-knew-where, that it came to her.

She was scared of dying, but she was more scared of living without Mikey.

Why she hadn't seen it before, she couldn't think. She had been like one of Katy's wombats, turning its back on a plentiful supply of free food and a comfortable life and instinctively digging for freedom without rationally thinking what it was doing until it ended up in a wasteland of desert without food or water.

She pulled the chief close, wishing he was Mikey, and although she knew he wasn't – he didn't smell the same, no wood smoke, just oil and the sweat of fear – she hugged him just the same. He embraced her back, gently, like Mikey would, aware of her bruised body. 'You thirsty?' he asked.

'Very,' she said.

'There's a tap over here. Took me a while to find, but it's not far. Here, take my hand. I'd use the torch, but—'

'Let's save the batteries,' she agreed.

It took a while for them to get there, but it was worth it. Fresh water ran over her mouth and down her neck, into her shirt. It tasted sweet as syrup against the chemical smell hanging in the air.

The chief took her hand and led her away from the puddle of water. She joined him on the floor and leaned against a pallet.

'I've done a tour of the place,' he said. 'I've some rope and a bucket.'

'Great. You tie them up and I'll drown them.'

He chuckled. 'It's a deal.'

The ship's motion began to change as the sea picked up. There was a lift to the bow and then a giant *bang* as it came down hard.

'We're well into open water,' said the chief.

India shivered at the thought of what was going to happen to them. Rajiv no doubt planned to chuck them overboard once they were well clear of the coast. Would he shoot them first, or simply let them drown? Then she realised they hadn't been tied up and reckoned on the latter. He wouldn't want to leave any evidence of foul play for a forensics team should their bodies wash up on shore.

She wondered why Rajiv hadn't killed her while she'd been unconscious, and guessed he'd held back because Jack had wanted her brought to him alive. The orders had obviously adapted to the circumstances. India Kane was now to be fish food.

'How are you feeling?' the chief asked.

'Sore as hell,' she sighed, 'but all my limbs are in reasonable working order, if that's what you're asking.'

'You up for an escape attempt?'

'God, yes.' India carefully pushed herself to her feet, trying to muffle her groan. 'What's the plan?'

'It's a bit risky, but I'm going to light a fire and bank on someone coming down to investigate.'

India thought of *The Pride*'s broken generators and autopilot. 'I bet their fire alarms don't work.'

'If not, they'll smell the smoke pretty quick. Seamen are always paranoid about fires on board.'

'You've got some matches?'

'Yeah. One of those little booklets I picked up somewhere. Didn't realise I carried so much shit in my pockets till now.'

India followed him to the far end of the hold, where he'd already made a surprisingly substantial pile of rags, rope, sandwich wrappers and pieces of oily newspaper, and watched him put the bucket close by before lighting it. Within two minutes, it was blazing away and the hold and its containers and hatch cover was bathed in an eerie, flickering orange light.

'This way.' The chief led her towards a metal door at the opposite end of the hold to the fire. 'You hide behind there . . .' He indicated a red container and suddenly the ship gave a corkscrew roll and she nearly lost her footing, but the chief had hold of her. 'Quick, mind.'

'What about you?'

He brought out his screwdriver. 'Come out only when I say so, okay?'

She swallowed. 'Shouldn't I be there with you? In case a whole lot of them come down?'

'Let's keep it simple. I don't want to stab you by mistake.'

India did as he said and hid behind the container. The smell of spilt diesel blanketed the chemical odour, and she breathed shallowly, praying the fire the chief had lit wouldn't take over the hold and burn them to death. Barely five minutes had passed when she heard an almighty great *clang.* Her heartbeat doubled.

The door was opening.

Thirty-two

India desperately wanted to have a look but didn't dare in case a crew member spotted her. Listening hard, all she could hear was the rumble of the engines, but then there was a man's exclamation, and then two voices rose into a panicky language she didn't understand. She heard footsteps running away from her.

'India, *quick*.'

She bolted from behind the container to see the chief beckoning urgently. A brief glance to her right showed her two guys in overalls. One was racing for the bucket, the other the tap. They were shouting.

Then she was through the door and the chief followed her, banging it shut behind them and slamming the bolts into place.

'That was brilliant,' she panted.

'Worked better than I thought.' He gave her a grin. 'Two down, maybe six or so to go.'

They were in a long, evil-smelling corridor, lined on either side by rusting walls. The light was a dull yellow from two bulbs nestled behind a protective metal lattice. She put a hand on the steel wall when the boat heaved starboard and followed the chief down the alley. He halted in front of an iron ladder, the screwdriver glinting dully in his hand.

'I'll go first. If anything happens scoot out of sight and hide.'

To her relief nobody was waiting for them at the top, and she continued to follow the chief along what felt like miles of badly lit alleyways. She tried not to groan as she walked.

Her body was aching and throbbing but she concentrated on thinking positively.

When they approached a porthole she was surprised to see daylight. She'd thought it was night. She had a quick glance outside and saw it was raining. Acres of grey sea churned under a darkening sky and she reckoned they had maybe an hour before night fell.

They came to an ancient, rasping metal door, and the chief had to put his shoulder to it and shove, and almost fell through. India was right behind him and smacked into his back when he stopped dead.

A squat brown man stood facing them. He wore oil-stained trousers and held a pistol. It was pointed at the chief's chest. He jerked the pistol at the screwdriver and the chief obediently dropped it to the floor with a clatter. Another jerk of his pistol indicated they move ahead of him.

'G'day mate,' said the chief, sounding amazingly calm. 'How's it going?'

The man barked something, but she didn't understand what he said.

'Distract him,' the chief murmured to India.

When the chief walked forward, the man screamed incomprehensibly but the chief just shrugged and spread his hands wide. 'Don't understand you, mate. Sorry.'

The chief was closing in on the man when he yelled again and pulled back the hammer of his pistol, priming the gun.

'Hey, you!' India shouted at him and lunged to her right, still shouting.

Crack!

There was a clank as a bullet hit metal and India dived to the ground. Another shot blasted through the air. Her ears were ringing, her right knee screaming with pain, but she wriggled around to see the chief had his hands around the man's throat and was slamming his head against the wall. The man went limp. India scrambled across and grabbed the pistol. Hands trembling, she checked the chamber. Four bullets left.

The chief was breathing hard and sweat ran from his hair and down his face.

'Well done,' she told him, gasping.

He didn't answer, he was concentrating on rummaging through the man's pockets. He withdrew a bunch of keys, then hefted the man up and half-carried, half-dragged him to a series of huge lockers below the accommodation block. Unlocking the first one he came to, the chief peered inside. India saw boxes of canned food, some sacks of rice. The chief heaved the man inside and re-locked the door behind him.

'I've a plan,' he panted.

'Tell me.'

He outlined his idea and India gave a nod. 'Let's go for it.'

'You mind if I have the gun?'

India handed it over. He passed her his screwdriver. Not the greatest swap in the world, she was thinking, when he suddenly ducked his head and planted a kiss on her lips. It happened so fast she didn't have time to react, just stare at him.

'I've wanted to do that ever since we met,' he grinned. 'For good luck, eh?'

'Good luck, Chief.' She smiled back.

Inside the accommodation block the air was hot and heavy with the smell of frying onions and cigarette smoke. She could hear the blare of a TV, gunshots, explosions, then the distinctive accent of Arnold Schwarzenegger: they were watching a video. The crew's mess-room door was open when they approached. With his back against the wall, the chief raised the pistol and whispered, 'If we're quick enough . . .'

She gave him a nod and prayed the crew would be absorbed in watching the film. Holding her breath, she watched the chief scoot past the door. Nobody yelled or came charging outside. Now it was her turn.

Her heart was thundering and she took a breath. She turned her face away from the doorway as though if she couldn't see the crew, they couldn't see her either, and in three quick steps she was past. The video continued to play, and she heard a crew member speaking over the blare, loud but conversational. They hadn't been seen.

Treading carefully, she followed the chief along another corridor and up an iron staircase, using both hands to steady herself against the increasing roll. From time to time the ship met a deep trough and plunged downwards to pause with a dull *boom*, and the whole infrastructure shuddered until it rose on the other side and kept going. They halted outside the bridge door. It was ajar, and she could hear a radio playing inside.

Clutching the screwdriver, she waited behind the chief. He gave her a quick glance and mouthed, 'Okay?' and she nodded back. She saw him take a breath. Steeling himself for what was to come.

He raised a foot, smashed the door open and sprang inside.

'Nobody move!'

'Ayahh!'

'You move, I shoot you!'

Silence.

'What is it you are wanting?' It was Rajiv's voice.

'Get on your knees. Put your hands behind your head. Tell your friend to do the same. And do it *slow*.'

A smatter of Indonesian.

India stood outside, trembling and sweating and gripping her paltry screwdriver.

'That's right, no sudden moves, and keep your hands where I can see them . . . Hey!'

Bang!

India leaped into the air. Who had shot who? Was the chief okay?

Bang, bang!

God, what was going on?

Another gunshot.

The chief only had four bullets, she had to *act.*

India moved to the door and peered around and her breathing jammed. The chief and another guy were on the floor. But Rajiv seemed to be okay, he was standing over the chief with his gun and she heard the wet, metallic *snick* as he primed it.

She went straight for him. She didn't know if she had the guts to stab a man and simply rushed at him, wanting to stop him from killing the chief. He started to spin round but she was faster and she rammed him with her shoulder and then they were falling on top of the chief and she was beneath Rajiv, and she was yelling, trying to bring the screwdriver up, but it was immovable against the weight of his body. She lashed out with her feet, heaving her torso, but it was like trying to shift a sack of wet sand. She felt something warm seep through her shirt but she couldn't think what it was in her fight to free herself. His breath reeked of nicotine and garlic and she was scrabbling, trying to free her legs, pushing against his shoulders. With a final, huge effort, she shoved him aside.

India was on her feet, gasping.

Neither Rajiv nor the chief moved. The guy in the corner had half his head blown away. He wouldn't be going anywhere.

In the distance she heard a man's shout, which galvanised her. She raced to lock all the bridge doors. Rain was rattling against the windows. A man crooned on the radio. It sounded like Frank Sinatra. Surreal.

India grabbed Rajiv's gun which had fallen to the floor, and that was when she saw where the screwdriver had gone.

She couldn't see any steel. Just the yellow plastic hilt

sticking out of his upper stomach, about four inches above where his belly button would be. She could see his chest moving slightly and realised he was alive. Hurriedly she checked his gun, three bullets left, and stuck it in her waistband. She put the chief's on the bridge.

'Oh, God,' she said aloud. The chief was covered in blood. She bent over him and pressed her fingers against the underside of his wrist, desperately searching for a pulse. Her face was close to his and she was looking at her fingers on his wrist, trying to discern if she could feel his breath against her cheek when he said, 'I'm in heaven already?'

Still holding his wrist, she peered into his face. 'I'm not sure about that.'

'You lock the doors?'

'Yes.'

'We've a chance then. Help me up, would you?'

He was pale and sweating and breathing hard.

'I'm not sure if that's a good idea.'

'Just do it, woman.'

The chief put an arm around her shoulders and she helped him drag himself to his knees.

'So far, so good,' he panted. 'Get me in the chair. I'll be fine once I'm there.'

The chair was padded and, like *Sundancer*'s, stood starboardside of the wheelhouse. Positioned at the centre of the helm was a wheel that came to her waist, the size of a dustbin lid. A big dustbin lid.

They manoeuvred themselves awkwardly past Rajiv and managed to reach the chair before the chief fell.

'Good stuff,' he gasped.

'Where are you shot? Can I—'

'Hand me the radio.'

He then turned his wrist, looked at his watch. Said, 'Fuckin' A.'

'What?' she demanded. 'What is it?'

But the chief had already set the frequency and was speaking into the handset. 2182 kHz.

'Mayday, mayday, mayday. This is Hank Gregory, harbour master of Fremantle Port. I am with India Kane and we are being held captive on board *The Pride of Tangkuban*, sailing under the name *Prize Oldendorff*.' He rattled off their position, his voice remarkably clear and strong. 'Our lives are in danger, please send help.'

He listened for a bit, but nothing was forthcoming, so he repeated the message several times. Then some more. Glanced at his watch, and did some more listening before sending the same message. The radio remained silent but the chief didn't look too down about it. Just showed her his watch. Four minutes past ten.

'We caught it.' Despite the white sheen on his face, he looked pleased. 'All shipping stops radio communications from the hour to three minutes past the hour, and the half hour to three minutes past the half hour. The time is set aside for emergency or distress calls. Someone will have heard us, I'm sure of it.'

India frowned. 'What about the crew? Wouldn't they have heard you too?'

'Well, yes.'

'What if they call back and pretend it was a hoax?'

'The call will be forwarded to the Marine Emergency Response Centre in Canberra. They'll look into it.'

'But if they think it's a hoax—'

'Don't, India.' The chief slumped, his breathing hoarse. India was reaching to put the radio back in its cradle when she heard several fists banging against the starboard door of the bridge, along with a lot of yelling. Then the lights went out. One second the bridge had been aglow with red and green dots, the next it was completely dark.

'Shit,' the chief gasped. 'They've blown the fuses. Radio's gone now.'

There was an almighty *thud* against the port door of the

bridge. It sounded like a wrecking ball. Her heartbeat picked up into a gallop. The door was steel, and she assumed the windows were reinforced glass, but they wouldn't hold up for long against a prolonged assault like that.

'India,' the chief managed, pointing at the gun tucked in the small of her back, 'open the door and shoot them, would you?'

Thirty-three

'Shoot them,' the chief panted, 'we get control. I don't want them stopping the engines. We act tough, they won't mess . . . with us.'

Another metallic *bang*, and then another, near the lock. Her mouth felt as though it was packed with chalk. Hands slick with sweat, she pulled out the pistol from her waistband and primed it.

'Are you sure?' Her voice trembled.

'If you don't . . . they'll kill us. But if we show who's boss . . . they don't want to die . . . any more than we do.'

Rain was hammering against the bridge windows like dollar coins being fired from a cannon. The noise was incredible, but all her senses were riveted to the regular *bang* against the port-side door.

'Do it, India. For God's sake . . .'

Don't think. Just do it.

She spun round, shot back the bolts and yanked open the door.

The man outside froze. Overalls, brown skin, flat black hair, a mole at the corner of his mouth, a sledgehammer at his side. She had the gun in both hands and her legs were planted firmly, her knees soft to absorb the rolling of the boat, and she was bringing up the gun and aiming for his chest when she saw the faint gleam of white of his teeth as he opened his mouth to yell and she hesitated.

Do it, India.

The man seemed to sense her hesitation and he brought

back his sledgehammer and then he was moving towards her, swinging the hammer to strike . . .

She pulled the trigger.

He paused, his body motionless. The sledgehammer dropped to the ground with a clank.

India re-primed the gun.

Then he staggered and slumped against the railing, and she was lowering the pistol, wanting to pull the door shut against the man she'd shot, but out of the corner of her eye she saw another man rushing for her.

This time she didn't hesitate. She simply pointed the gun at him and squeezed the trigger.

He dropped like a stone and she didn't wait to see if he was alive, she slammed the door shut and backed away from it, pistol in both hands, ready for them both in case they suddenly blasted through the door and came for her.

'India.'

She was shaking, her teeth chattering like road drills. Jesus, God. She'd shot two men.

'Come here.'

She walked to the chief, feeling as though her legs were on stilts and she wasn't fully in control of them. Her fingers felt numb, her skin cold. He reached out and took the pistol from her, and chambered a round. Put it on the bridge. Then he hooked an arm around her waist and pulled her close. She had tears on her cheeks, but she wasn't crying.

'You did good, okay?'

She stood there a long time, listening to the hammer of rain on the windows and the slamming of the ship, the chief's arm a band of warmth against the chill inside her. After a while the chief leaned his head against her ribs and she absent-mindedly stroked his hair. It was rough and springy, like mountain heather might feel. Nothing like Mikey's hair, which was thick and soft as . . .

She pulled free of the chief's embrace. What the hell was she doing, thinking of Mikey? Where he was safely tucked away in a desert-bound town, she was . . . well, she was on the bridge of a stonking great container ship in the middle of the ocean, without lights or a radio.

'Chief?' she asked. 'What's next?'

The chief didn't answer. She felt a jet of alarm and looked down to see his eyes were shut, and his head lolled to one side.

'Chief?' India patted his cheek and called to him, but he didn't respond. *'Chief!'*

She strained to see past the water crashing against the windows and was glad she couldn't see much outside because she reckoned if she did, she might panic. They were in the middle of a storm, she knew, but the ship, rearing and plunging like a demented sea-horse, seemed to be doing okay.

She was shivering against the sweat cooling on her skin. If she left the bridge, they would kill her. Her only chance was to stay where she was, and get the ship safely to a harbour. She could do that, surely. The engines were still going, obviously on autopilot.

Out of nowhere, she saw the bosun waving a pair of binoculars at her, grinning. *I am autopilot!*

Not any more, thank God, she thought. It's been fixed, and although I haven't a clue how to switch it off and turn the ship around, I'm sure something will come to me. I'd rather die trying than give up to the men outside. What I need is a map and some light.

She felt the chief's trouser pockets, searching for his booklet of matches. 'Come on,' she muttered aloud, 'I can't believe you ditched them.'

Running her hands over the chief's shirt, she immediately felt the small, flat square in his breast pocket. Sliding it free, she lit a match, raising it high as she moved around the bridge. She quickly checked Rajiv was still unconscious before taking up position at the ship's wheel. The match sputtered out, so she lit another and kept her attention on keeping her balance and searching for anything that might help her. Holding the trembling thread of matchlight over the chart table, she saw a pair of clips holding a flashlight just beneath it.

Her heart lifted.

Grabbing the flashlight she turned it on and swung its pool of white light to the chief. His shirt was drenched with blood. Hurriedly India started to search the bridge for a first-aid kit. Loose gear was sliding back and forth as the ship continued to roll. She found a bunch of papers and peered at them. Lading bills. She pushed them aside. In the third cabinet she found a small torch and just behind a toolbox, a cheerful red box with a white cross on its lid.

Torch between her teeth, India used the scissors from the kit and cut the chief's shirt away. The bullet had smashed through his left breast and she could see splinters of white bone through the mouth of the wound, but the first thing she had to do was stem the bleeding.

She packed the lacerated flesh with sterile pads and taped them firmly into place. It wasn't much, but she hoped it would be better than nothing. Praying he'd be okay, she turned her attention to the chart. She wasn't sure what she expected, but it wasn't this blank of nothing with contours spreading across it. Where was any indication of land? Scrabbling at the corner of the map she swung it aside to the one below. This one she recognised. She could see the outline of Western Australia shaped like the muzzle of a lion, and then she flipped the other chart back.

She recognised nothing.

For goodness' sake, you're at sea, she told herself. Of course there's nothing. Use the compass. Use your *brain.*

A gust hit the ship and she staggered to the wheel, hung on. *The Pride* heeled starboard, bow digging down low, then she rose and settled again.

I have no sodding idea what the hell I'm doing, she

thought. I could be trying to land Concorde from 50,000 feet for all the effect I'm having. Okay, keep calm. Take your time. She took a couple of deep breaths and lined the ship on the compass, due east.

'No, you've got it all wrong.'

'Chief?' She almost chucked the charts in his face. 'Well you do something about it!'

'Keep . . . hair on.'

'Jesus, I'm sorry.' She could feel the tears on her face but they weren't anything to do with grief or sorrow. They were tears of anger, borne from fright.

'Pass me . . .'

India pulled over the chart and shone the flashlight down.

'You want to go . . . to Antarctica?'

'No.'

'Okay. Disengage the autopilot.'

'How?'

The chief talked her through it, then told her to spin the wheel.

'We've got to risk it,' he said, 'try and pick a lull between the waves and hope she doesn't broach.'

The muscles in her cheeks were aching from gritting her teeth for so long, but she did as he said.

The Pride gradually turned and as she did, her keel dug in and waves were crashing over her decks, and then they were broadside to the waves and a blast of wind slammed into them and she heeled sharply to starboard, yawing.

'Hold it,' the chief said.

India held it.

Another wave came, but *The Pride* let it crash over her foredeck and although she slewed further starboard, rolling steeply, the hull lifted, and she was still sailing, powering forward.

The chief shifted up to check their progress.

'Port,' he told her.

They were slanting across a trough, almost diagonal, and the next wave didn't break and the ship was rising when he repeated the command, but much louder.

India did as he said.

'More.' His tone turned urgent.

She spun the wheel and brought the ship straight. Amidships, Cuan would have said, but Cuan was miles away, and it was just the chief and her . . .

'Port, dammit!'

She wound furiously and the chief yelled, 'Enough!' And the ship settled herself to take the next wave straight, and the one following.

Then the chief was plotting and drawing vectors, measuring angles. Without any electronics, he told her, he had to estimate their position by what, in the old days, was called dead reckoning; basing their position on the compass card, forward speed and wind conditions. His breathing was loud and rasping as he ran through what she should do if he lost consciousness again, where to keep the compass to maintain their course, how to stop the ship and drop the anchor, and when.

She had no intention of sailing a giant metal shoebox through a storm on her own. Surely, there had to be another radio somewhere? Then they could talk her in. Glancing at Rajiv, her skin prickled when she saw he'd moved. Shit. She'd better find some rope and tie him up. Torch in hand, she rummaged through the bridge again, then she moved into the master's cabin, a shambolic mess reeking of dirty clothes and bedding, and pulled cupboards open and swept their contents aside. To her delight, she unearthed a sturdy roll of duct tape, and then, in a drawer beneath the bunk, she found a handheld VHF radio.

Thirty-four

Clutching the radio, India shot back to the bridge, hope bubbling through her veins like champagne.

'Chief, look!'

His face split into a lopsided grin. 'Well, bugger me if you aren't my ray of sunshine. Get us within twenty Ks of the coast, and we'll have the troops on board, no worries.'

India checked the compass and corrected their course a fraction. Then she took the roll of duct tape to Rajiv. She didn't want to touch him, but she knew she had to. She wanted to bind his hands behind his back but doubted she could move him so she settled on taping not just his hands together, but also his feet.

Returning to stand by the chief, she pulled out a bandage from the first-aid kit. She saw the chief had plotted their course on the map with surprisingly bold strokes. God, good job she hadn't been left in charge for too long, she'd have had *The Pride* sailing for New Zealand.

'Chief, I want to bandage you, put some pressure on that wound. Okay?'

He leaned forward and let her slide her arms around him along with the crêpe, until she'd used up all the bandage and he resembled an untidy mummy.

'Nurse India,' he murmured.

She gave a snort.

He smiled into her eyes. 'Marry me.'

She touched his cheek. 'I'm already hitched.'

'Lucky bugger.'

He closed his eyes and, after downing a couple of

painkillers from the first-aid kit, India went back to the wheel. Ahead, a big wave was looming for the bow. *The Pride* rose for it. Up and up, and then she plunged into the crest, hesitated, and launched out the far side, spray streaming off her deck before she fell into the following gulley with an almighty *bang* that had the whole infrastructure shuddering.

Christ, India thought. I hope she hangs together for the ride.

India spent the night at the wheel, checking their course and trying to keep alert, exhaustion and pain racking her body. The waves increased until she reckoned they were three storeys high, with spray howling from their tops. She prayed they wouldn't encounter any rogue waves that might turn them side-to, because the next wave could hit them at a different angle and the entire boat would roll over and submerge.

'C'mon, *Pride*, stay with it,' she said.

Occasionally the chief would come to and blearily check she was doing okay before slumping back into his stupor. She thought a lot about Mikey as the ship churned through the wild darkness of sky and ocean. How much she loved him. How stupid she'd been. Whether he'd still marry her. God, she hoped so. And if not? Well, she'd face that when the time came.

It was around two a.m. when a larger wave crested before the ship and wrenched her out of her musings. *The Pride* met it more sideways than head on, and she hung on to the wheel as the wave avalanched over their port side and the ship lurched wildly to starboard. She could hear things crashing and breaking up below, but gradually the ship settled herself, meeting the waves head on like she was supposed to and lunging forward.

India wiped her face of sweat. Jesus. This trip was taking ten years off her life. What she wouldn't do to be sitting on the verandah of a small house on the edge of the desert, with a view of low-slung hills glowing tangerine in the sunset, and Polly and Mikey barbecuing supper.

A little while later, a wave slammed into the bow and India jerked upright. She'd almost been asleep on her feet. Hurriedly she flicked on the flashlight and checked the compass. Altered their direction to align their course.

Concentrate, you silly cow. Keep awake . . . She searched for something to occupy her, and her gaze alighted on the charts. She studied the chief's mathematics but it didn't make any sense to her, so she flipped back a page. Saw *The Pride*'s route. A bell was ringing in her head and then she remembered what the chief had said.

You want to go . . . to Antarctica?

She gave a groan out loud at the confirmation she'd been dreading. The Zhuganovs weren't shipping the waste to Chennai and South East Asia, they were dumping it. That was why they'd been so far south, where there where no witnesses, except a million or so macaroni penguins, to see tens of dozens of containers floating in the ocean before they finally sank.

The skin all over her body contracted as she remembered the fleet of ships operating out of the United States. This was an international operation. They weren't just confined to dumping Australia's waste, but America's too. No wonder they wanted her dead. If she pulled one block from the bottom of the stack, the whole lot would come tumbling down, and they knew it.

A sudden vision of Ned sitting at the kitchen table, expression earnest, and behind him the poster of a whale cruising through blue water with her calf alongside. As if the whales weren't in enough trouble already, she thought. Caught in fishermen's nets, trying to avoid noise pollution, oil explorers, a steadily depleting food supply, now the poor buggers had a toxic tide to cope with as well.

*

The conditions had gone from bad to horrendous. Instead of abating, the storm kept getting worse. The seas grew into ten-metre swells and the winds were moaning around the ship, sounding like the deep bass of an organ playing.

The chief had roused enough to make India take the ship off autopilot and she was now pointing her into the sea, wanting to follow the chief's advice to hang on and take the pounding until the storm blew out. The most *The Pride* was making was three or four knots, which wasn't much, India knew. It was a walking pace. Which was fine by her, since they weren't headed for Fremantle any more.

Occasionally she'd lose power, and she'd panic, thinking the engines had gone, but after a while she realised they were churning through nothing but mountains of froth and foam, and the instant they grabbed the sea, they'd bite and the power would return.

All she could see through the bridge windows were great patches of foam breaking over the bow, and suddenly the white foam wasn't there any more, and she couldn't see anything except a huge dark wall, that she thought was the sky, but then *The Pride* started to rise. Oh please God, no. We'll never get over that. India held the wheel in hands that she couldn't feel any more as *The Pride* continued to climb, her bow rising steeply, reaching for the crest, angling now at forty-five degrees, and India was yelling at the ship not to slide back down the face of the gigantic wave or she'd bury herself in the trough and the wave would catch her bow and flip her over, pitchpole her and drive her beneath the sea.

Despite her instincts screaming at her to stop, *stop*, India kept the speed up as the chief had instructed, facing the wave dead on and keeping her rudder control. Still *The Pride* reared, and the wave wasn't breaking, it wasn't breaking, which she knew was good news because the chief had told her that, not that she could remember why, but *The Pride* was going for it, clawing her way to the top and trying to get over the top before the wave broke . . .

The Pride plunged through the crest of the wave, and for a second 3000 tons of ship hung in space, water and foam spraying from her decks, and then she fell into the trough.

A sudden weightlessness, a swoop in her stomach, and India was clutching the wheel, holding her breath as the ship plunged down the back of the giant wave.

As the ship hit the bottom of the trough, there was a *boom* and the port-side window of the bridge blew out with the sound of a cannon going off. Water gushed inside. Wind screamed through the blown-out window. Pieces of metal, screws and bolts, things that shouldn't move on a boat, were flying everywhere.

Eyes squinting, head ducked against the flying debris, she fought to keep *The Pride* steady into the wind. The chief had been flung to the floor but she had no time to go to him. Better to keep the ship afloat than be bent over him and caught unawares by the next wave.

Soaked to the skin, ankle deep in water, she shook her face free of salt water and kept the pumps and engine running, and prayed the crew were doing their stuff, making sure the filters weren't clogged, that the props were free, working to keep the ship functioning and her steerage intact.

A wave broke on the starboard side and more water poured through the window. How long do storms last? she wondered, wet and huddled, shivering against the wind shrieking through the window. A day? Two days? God, she'd never last that long.

A couple of minutes later, to her astonishment, the lights came on. Red and green dots sprang up on the bridge and the overhead bulbs gave a couple of flickers, then steadied. 'No, no,' she wailed. *Turn them off, godammit, turn them off.* If any more windows had blown out and enough water had got in, then it could have worked its way into the engine room, soaked the wiring, and then the entire boat would be electrified. All the circuits would go. The ship would be crippled. The VHF, the radar, everything would be inoperable. But more frightening was the fact that anyone standing in water could get electrocuted. Oh, holy fucking shit.

India desperately looked around, wondering what she could climb onto to avoid getting zapped. She wasn't sure if it worked like that anyway, but she still looked, and found nothing that wasn't well and truly soaked in water. Including the chief. She saw the blood on his shirt had watered down, turned to pink, but the crêpe on his breast was a sodden, deep, dark red.

She wanted to go to him, check his wound, but she didn't dare leave the helm.

Bracing herself against the wheel, she felt her initial panic subside. She hadn't been electrocuted. Not yet, anyway. As another wave shoved them over on one side, she checked her watch to see she was right in the middle of the emergency radio communication on the half hour. Hitching the radio out of its cradle, she sent another mayday. 2182 kHz. It wasn't quite as coherent as the chief's, and involved a lot of urgent pleading, but she thought she'd got her message across. She continued to mayday, hoping for someone to respond, but nobody did. Not a cough, not even a crackle of static in return.

She was concentrating so hard on the radio that it took her a couple of minutes to realise something had changed. The ship wasn't heading straight into the waves any more, but slamming from side to side, lurching forward, then rolling backwards. The sea had turned into a confused mass of energy, and the waves were coming from different directions. They were, she realised with dread, right in the eye of the storm.

The Pride was taking huge waves broadside, and India was struggling to turn her round, face them head on, but as soon as she'd got the ship straight, the wind would shift along with the waves, and they'd be coming at her from the stern, forcing the ship nose-down in troughs, then slamming into her broadside again. At some point, no matter how much she tried, she knew a wave could come that would flip the boat over on to her side, and then the water would gush in through the shattered windows, and drown the ship from inside.

India didn't know how to combat such an eventuality. In desperation she dived for the chief and slapped his face, shook him by his shoulders and yelled at him until he came round.

'What do I *do*!' she yelled.

He swung his eyes blearily around. Worked his mouth. 'Head . . .' he said. India bent close to catch every word. 'Into the storm . . . hope you don't meet any . . . king waves.'

He slumped back and India stood there, working hard at the helm, wishing she hadn't asked. Fuck, fuck, fuck. Head into the storm, indeed. What the hell had he thought she'd been doing all this time?

Another succession of waves came at her, slamming into them from starboard, trying to somersault the ship over and onto her back.

India gritted her teeth and held on.

Head into the storm.

The Pride was shuddering and rolling, and India knew she could pitchpole at any second given the wrong wave, or get driven down to the point of no return. There were no life vests, no survival suits. If the ship went down, she'd go down with it.

Thirty-five

India was sweating in the calm of a trough and fighting to keep the ship straight, wrestling against the wind blasting through the blown-out window, when she heard an engine's howl and her whole body tensed, not knowing what it was, wondering if the ship wasn't about to blow up, when the sound increased, and then abruptly vanished.

What the hell . . . ? Her whole body was trembling, trying to take stock. Foam was washing in great patches across *The Pride*'s bow, and the sea was heavy and shock-like. But she hadn't met a giant wave recently, and they were, amazingly, still afloat. Still chugging at a walking pace – three knots – and with full steerage.

But what the hell had made that noise, a noise like a . . . ?

Before she could think any further, it came at her again. A shriek through the storm. Blasting past and then away.

Holy mother of God, please, let it be what I think it is.

India lunged frantically for the bridge windows, but she couldn't see anything except black and the occasional flash of white as a wave crashed across the bow.

The radio crackled. A man's voice broke through.

'*Pride*, do you read?'

The next second the unmistakable roar of a plane shot past.

India grabbed the radio. 'Yes, oh yes. I'm here.'

Short pause while static crackled.

'I take it you're India Kane?'

'Yes, it's me. I mean, I'm India.'

'Hi, India.'

'Hi.'

'India, we're from the Customs Service of the civil maritime surveillance, Broome. We hear you've a problem.'

'Just a bit.'

'Maritime Emergency Response C called us at one hundred hours. Had a bit of trouble locating you. Sorry for the delay; the conditions aren't exactly nice.'

'No,' she said, thinking how understated the conversation was. 'They're not that great.'

'We heard you're having a little trouble with the crew.'

'They want to kill us.'

Long static pause.

'Is Hank Gregory there? Can we talk with him?'

'He's here but he's wounded. Unconscious.'

'Right.'

The pilot went on to tell her that normally military resources were never used for maritime search-and-rescue operations, usually they'd have chucked an AP-3C Orion from Adelaide in the air, but for her and the chief, they'd pulled out all the stops. She didn't know what it meant. An aircraft was an aircraft, thousands of feet up in the bloody sky and of no use to her whatsoever. Brusquely, she said as much to the pilot.

'It's a military op, okay? Not a rescue mission. We'll be covering you until dawn breaks. Then a couple of helicopters will be here with the cops. They'll sort you out.'

'Cops?' she repeated. Her mind emptied itself of a ship being torn apart by the sea and became a blur of panicked memories. Constable Bryce pointing his gun at her as she sat in her car. Dennis, who'd stuck his head into Ricky's kennel. And then there was Sergeant Kuteli and Detective Inspector Zhuganov. She wasn't sure she wanted the cops to sort her out and said so.

'Sorry, I should have been more specific. They're from the TRG, the Australian Tactical Response Group. They'll look after you, no worries. They know what they're doing.'

That was more like it, she thought. The Zhuganov family wouldn't stand a chance against that lot.

As he circled *The Pride*, the pilot reassured India that she was doing fine, and despite the fact she knew the airplane couldn't do much except watch the ship battle through the storm, its presence was enormously comforting. She wondered what the crew were doing, then considered their restoring the electrics to the bridge.

They don't want to die any more than we do.

By four a.m. India felt brave enough to re-set *The Pride*'s autopilot for the coast of Western Australia. The ship had picked up speed and the wind had changed its deep organ groan to a high-pitched wail. Waves eased from tower blocks into neater, more well-behaved semi-detached houses. Before she could change her mind, she put on the autopilot and scrambled for Rajiv's cabin and his overhead cabinets and grabbed what she could. Raced back to the bridge and heaved two blankets over the chief. Put a pillow under his head. Then she pulled off her sodden clothes and put on some of Rajiv's. Two pairs of tracksuit pants, thick socks, two T-shirts and a fleece. They reeked of his sour, bitter sweat, but she didn't care. They were warm, and they were *dry*.

She struggled to keep awake, feeling the stiffness in her neck and shoulders. Her legs felt as though they were about to give up and her throat and mouth were parched, her head thick and achy. What she wouldn't do for a coffee. She yawned, blinking back the tears of fatigue. Not long to go, she promised herself.

A couple of hours later, the rain started to ease. To the east she could see a pale strip of grey on the horizon and realised they were leaving the storm behind, or the storm was blowing itself out. Either way, she didn't care, Fremantle was getting closer every minute.

As the light grew, she finally saw the airplane. A red and white striped Dash 8–200 with *Customs* emblazoned on its flank. It was part of the maritime fleet that reported on illegal immigration, fishing, imports and exports and environmental hassles, and currently keeping an eye on *The Pride.*

The radio crackled into life as the pilot wished her good morning.

'The choppers are here, India. Time for us to say goodbye.'

She thanked the Coastwatch crew and watched the helicopters take up position on each side of the ship. The plane banked steeply to its right and quickly vanished from sight.

'We docking yet?' The chief's voice was faint and his skin was pale and waxy looking. Getting more and more worried, she pleaded with one of the choppers to airlift him to hospital. Sorry, they said, but they had to secure the ship first.

Two minutes later a rope snaked out from one of the helicopter's loading ramps and soldiers abseiled down, like drops of oil speeding down a dipstick.

India didn't unlock the bridge doors until she heard several almighty great bangs on the metal and a man's voice yelling, 'Open up!'

Cautiously she opened the door, Rajiv's gun in her hand.

A soldier was in a crouch, aiming a gun at her chest. 'Drop it!' he screamed.

India let it fall to the ground with a clank. 'Sorry.'

He ducked down and retrieved the gun and quickly stepped inside. More soldiers pushed in from behind. He surveyed Rajiv and the screwdriver sticking out of his belly, the duct tape, and raised his eyebrows.

'He tried to kill me.'

'And that guy?' He was pointing at the chief.

'I'm . . . one of the good guys,' the chief managed.

India went and held the chief's hand. God, it was cold,

too cold. 'Please, we've got to get him to a hospital,' she was gasping. 'He's wounded really badly.'

Things happened fast after that. The second chopper came low to hover above the deck, sending down a basket. The chief was strapped inside and sent aloft. Then Rajiv. Next, it was India's turn. Swinging wildly in the wind, she clutched the sides of the basket and looked down. Saw a bunch of crew members huddled miserably at the bottom of the accommodation block, wrists handcuffed behind their backs. Four soldiers stood watch over them, assault rifles cradled.

Last on board was the guy who'd screamed at her to drop her gun when she'd opened the bridge door. Drew. No surname, no rank. Just Drew. He looked as hard as a marine could, all six foot six of him. Shoulders like a block of wood and an expression that matched; she was glad to have him on her side. The instant Drew was inside and buckled up, face impassive, the chopper dipped its nose, the turbine whining to a high pitch, then it accelerated.

India watched the paramedics work. One on Rajiv, the other on the chief. The chief's face was already in a plastic mask as the medic took off her untidy blood-soaked bandages and replaced them with smart new ones, lots of pressure on his wound. Then he pushed needles into veins in the chief's arms, hooked up various bags to various monitors. His movements were practised and assured, but his face was tense and worried.

'Will he be okay?' she called over the rotors.

The medic didn't look up. India looked across at the paramedic working on Rajiv and yelled, 'Can't he pitch in? Two hands better than one? I mean, that guy tried to *kill us*.'

The urge to pull the medic off Rajiv and get him helping the chief started to balloon out of control and she was half out of her seat when a hand heavy as a tree trunk landed at the base of her neck. The shock of it made her pause. Then the hand circled her neck, warm and strong and surprisingly gentle.

'They're doing their best,' Drew said.

She sank back into her seat. Concentrated on gripping the chief's hand and trying to instill it with warmth and life and well-being. Please, God, don't let him die, she pleaded. He says he's a coward but he's not. He's as brave as a lion, strong as a rock, and if he dies I'll never go to church again. So just make him better, will you? I know it'll be a long haul, which he'll hate, lots of physio and stuff he'll have to go through, but he'll come out the other side okay, I know it. He's a lion.

The rotors eased to a roaring clatter as the helicopter settled on the hospital's landing apron. A blur of white coats and cops in uniform rushed to greet them, clothes snatching in the downdraft. The chief was bundled outside first, shifted onto a trolley, and India was tearing alongside his trolley and then they were inside the hospital. Jesus, she thought. It was so *hot*.

They were careering along their second corridor when, amazingly, the chief came round. Probably all the commotion, she thought, and gave him a grin.

'Hey, my hero,' she panted.

She watched his lips move beneath the mask. Heard his voice, muffled and raspy.

'Hey . . . my favourite—'

'Save it, Chief. Save your energy. They'll have you fixed up and playing golf by next week, no worries.'

They burst through a pair of rubber doors and a woman was yelling, 'GUNSHOT WOUND!' and there were people in green gowns and bright lights and someone was pulling her away but she was fighting them and the chief was looking at her and she yelled, 'Don't you bloody die on me!' and he gave a grimace that she knew was meant to be a smile and she saw him muffle, 'Wouldn't . . . dare,' and he was smiling in a face so white it was almost blue and hands were tugging at her and he'd gone so still, she wasn't sure if he was breathing, but then she heard his voice, so faint, rasping, not like his at all through the mask, but it was his and he said, 'Kiss me.'

India pushed the hands off and went to him and bent over and pulled the mask away and pressed her mouth on his. His lips were cold and dry and chapped and she scooped his upper lip infinitely gently into her mouth, then his lower lip, warming them, giving them moisture, tenderly trying to kiss him to life.

'Heav . . .' he murmured against her mouth.

She didn't know what he meant, didn't care, she just wanted to keep him conscious, keep him *alive*, and she shut out the people who were shouting and tugging and wrenching at his body, and it was just her and the chief, his eyes on hers, and she cradled his face between her palms, brushing her thumbs over his thick, curly eyebrows, and kissed his forehead, the stubble on his chin, the corners of his mouth.

'. . . en,' he said.

Heaven.

'Me too,' she said.

And then he died.

Thirty-six

India sat numbly on a padded bench outside the operating theatre, unable to cry. Perhaps she was too tired, too exhausted. Perhaps it was because she'd heard that Rajiv was, according to the hospital staff, *doing well.*

She didn't want Rajiv to do well. She wanted him dead and the chief alive. She wanted Rajiv buried in a coffin fifty feet under and the chief with his feet planted in grass on top, playing golf.

Hey. How's my favourite reporter?

Already missing you, she told him.

The corridor was swaying, rolling from side to side, forward and back, but she didn't fight it. She closed her eyes, sinking in the sensation of being back on *The Pride.* Because that was how it had been when she'd been with the chief, battling that monster of a storm.

A hand on her shoulder. A hand that she knew was the size and weight of a crate of wine but felt like a butterfly.

'India?'

She gave a nod. Didn't open her eyes.

'You know an Ellie Sharpe?'

Her eyes opened. Saw acres of blank white wall. Heard the sound of aluminium trolleys rattling and smelled antiseptic and faintly, the raw stale scent of adrenalin from the soldier at her shoulder.

Drew said, 'She's left messages all over the place. Apparently she's having a baby and wants you there.'

'Ellie?' India repeated, tone blank, as though she'd never heard the name.

'Yeah. She's here. In the other wing.' Drew cleared his throat. 'You want me to take you to her?'

Her mind couldn't seem to engage any sort of gear, but she said, 'Of course.'

Ellie's hair was plastered in sweaty strings against her scalp, and she looked exhausted. She was also beaming from ear to ear and clutching a yelling blob of baby to her chest.

'We did it without you,' Ellie said smugly, glancing at a nurse standing to one side, looking just as smug.

'Well done,' India said, emotions flat as an ocean without wind.

'It's a girl,' Ellie added.

Wrinkled as hell, red-faced and squalling; India didn't think she'd ever seen anything so ugly.

'Do you want to hold her?' Ellie asked, making a little shove of the bawling bundle towards her.

Without thinking, India took a step back.

'Oh, come on, India,' Ellie scolded her. 'You are her Godmother, you know.'

Deeply reluctant, India took the howling creature in her arms, felt the small head flop and hurriedly brought her hand up to support it. Awkward, feeling inept, India scooped the baby close to her chest where she reckoned she wouldn't drop her. Christ, she thought, she was heavy. And warm. Warm as freshly baked bread. Pink and red and wrinkled, with tufts of wildly curly dark brown hair on her head.

India stared at the baby's hair, fixated.

Ellie was laughing. 'No, I didn't play away, if that's what you're wondering. I know Ned and I are blond, both our families, but maybe she'll turn blond later. Or it's a gene that's come through . . .'

But India wasn't listening. She was brushing a curly filament from the baby's forehead and pressing her lips where the curl had been. The baby promptly stopped squalling and stared up at her with milky blue eyes.

'What are you going to call her?' India asked, still looking into the baby's eyes. Her voice was rough and husky and filled with unshed tears.

'Well,' said Ellie, sounding remarkably brisk, 'at least we can't call her Albert. That's a saving grace.'

Albert, who'd cursed Jimbuku Bay and who Ned had wanted to appease.

'So I've called her Rose,' Ellie continued. 'As in India Rose Kane. But her middle name's up for grabs if you've got one.'

'Leone,' said India without hesitation. 'The lion.'

'Rose Leone Sharpe she is then,' Ellie said with satisfaction, and India closed her eyes and pressed another kiss on the baby's forehead. Her skin was softer than BB's velvet nose, softer than anything she'd known before. 'We got them, sweetheart,' she murmured softly as she rocked the baby close. 'Me and the Chief. We got the men who killed your Daddy.'

Baby Rose was lying face down on Ellie's chest, arms and legs akimbo, little face squashed against Ellie's left breast, while Ellie interrogated India about why she was wearing two sets of tracksuit pants and a fleece that was stinking out the entire wing of the hospital, and India was gazing longingly at Rose and wishing she was face down and fast asleep when someone came into the room.

'I was wondering when you'd turn up,' Ellie said.

'Sorry,' a man gasped. 'I tried to get here earlier . . .'

'At least you made the effort,' Ellie was astringent, 'whereas India here only managed to be here by accident, but that's nothing particularly unusual, as both you and I know. But Rose and I coped okay without you guys. Honest.'

India slowly turned her head. Filled her eyes with the

man standing at the foot of Ellie's bed. A man who was tall and broad with a dumper-truck shovel of a jaw and a wary expression.

He didn't have curly dark brown hair, but black, and he had no tattoos. Not a single one.

She felt a wave of love so strong she nearly fell over.

Lucky bugger.

He was looking at her as though she might have contracted leprosy and she was looking at the abyss that had separated them, wondering if he'd dare cross the chasm for her or if he'd turn his back.

She was yelling in her head: *Please still love me, please.*

Tentatively she went to him and touched his face. He didn't move. Her throat was aching as she looked him in the eyes and said quite clearly, 'I do.'

He opened his arms.

Epilogue

Mikey and India were sipping sundowners on the third evening of their honeymoon when Scotto's newspaper clippings arrived. He'd couriered them up with a little card telling them Polly was fine, and so were Ellie and little Rose. His house had never been so noisy, he added ruefully, but he wouldn't have it any other way. Honest. He'd sent two clippings, and she and Mikey read them on their balcony overlooking Hayman Island and the Coral Sea.

The first was from the *West Australian*, page three, and headlined, 'Private zoo opens emergency clinic'. It detailed the story of Penselwood Farm building a state-of-the-art veterinary surgery for bush-fire victims; they were set up to take any kind of animal from cattle and sheep to wombats and emus. There was no mention of William or his suicide. It was a simple, local story, with a picture of Katy holding a baby wallaby wrapped in bandages. India could see she'd lost a lot of weight, but the haunted expression was fading, and the shadows under her eyes had gone. She was smiling.

India turned to the *Sydney Morning Herald*. Front page, headline news.

FAMILY CHARGED WITH TOXIC WASTE DUMPING

By Scotto Kennedy

SIX months after being arrested for dumping toxic waste, including heavy metals and cyanide, into the Southern Ocean, the owners of a recycling and waste management company face twenty years in prison each and a collective fine of $60 million.

Jack Zhuganov, of Kemble Environmental Services, has been held without bail. He was charged with eleven felony counts of hazardous waste being dumped improperly, posing a threat to the environment.

Also arrested were fifteen other members of the family who helped the Australia-wide operation, along with owners of over a hundred companies who knowingly allowed the Zhuganov family to dump their illegal waste for them.

Greenpeace, with the help of the Australian Maritime Safety Authority, has brought the case of the sinking of their ship, *Sundancer*, before the court. Further charges are expected.

Arrests have also been made in Los Angeles. Keith Zhuganov of Green Waste Inc, California, has been fined $23.3 million and will be arraigned next month at the superior court in Santa Ana, according to Bill Reigler, a district attorney in the Orange County enviro protection unit, and faces similar charges to his brother, Jack Zhuganov.

Further investigations are being undertaken in other parts of the world, including Ukraine, Kazakhstan, Turkey and Bulgaria.

'This is an enormous international operation,' said the spokesman for the International Maritime Organisation, Stewart Fernely. 'And we have every intention of shutting it down and severely punishing those involved.'

'Kazakhstan?' she said. 'God, I'm glad I didn't have to go all the way over there to stick them behind bars.'

'Me too.' Mikey took the clippings from her and put them

inside their room. He returned with two pairs of flippers and snorkels.

'Let's go see if that wrasse is still about.'

It was exactly two hours later when it happened, and India thanked God when the news came through that she knew all her friends were safe.

She was sprawled on a beach of soft white sand, her snorkel and flippers beside Mikey's as they studied a sky smudged with the milky way. They'd been snorkelling with underwater torches, and were drying off in the warm, tropical air and trying to spot shooting stars.

At nine p.m. Queensland time, India had stopped looking for shooting stars and was studying the wedding ring on her finger, thinking it felt so weird that she thought she might have to ditch the thing. It was as though she'd been branded. Which, she supposed, was the point. She was Mikey's woman. Hands off. But then he had a wedding ring too, which wasn't such a bad thing. Hands off my man, she thought, and rolled over and pressed a kiss against his sea-salted flank.

India reckoned it was just as she kissed Mikey when the freak king wave hit Jimbuku Bay. She spent days working it out, and she wasn't quite sure why she wanted to know the second it happened, but she did.

Created in the Indian Ocean by an underground tremor, possibly a landslide, the leviathan wave hit the town at eleven p.m. It came from nowhere, and nobody had predicted it. Like an unstoppable ocean liner, cresting at a run-up height of over thirty metres and thundering at over 200 Ks an hour, the towering wall of water had swallowed the smartie-coloured houses in a gigantic blast and the entire estate had been annihilated.

No one died, because nobody was living there any more, but Shoalhaven had been flooded out, and one woman found an aluminium boat bobbing on her lawn, another a salmon the size of a Labrador flapping in her back yard.

Experts from Australia and around the world held intense debates and studied ocean floors and weather patterns and said it was an inexplicable freak of nature, but the locals knew differently. They remembered Albert. And they knew that, finally, Jambuwal had wrought his vengeance.